PRAISE FO

"Fans of Amish fiction will love Amy Clipston's latest, *The Bake Shop*. It's filled with warm and cozy moments as Jeff and Christiana find their way from strangers to friendship to love."

—ROBIN LEE HATCHER, BESTSELLING AUTHOR OF
WHO I AM WITH YOU AND *CROSS MY HEART*

"Clipston closes out this heartrending series with a thoughtful consideration of how Amish rules can tear families apart, as well as a reminder that God's path is not always what one might expect. Readers old and new will find the novel's issues intriguing and its hard-won resolution reassuring."

—*HOPE BY THE BOOK*, BOOKMARKED
REVIEW, ON *A WELCOME AT OUR DOOR*

"*Seasons of an Amish Garden* follows the year through short stories as friends create a memorial garden to celebrate a life. Revealing the underbelly of main characters, a trademark talent of Amy Clipston, makes them relatable and endearing. One story slides into the next, woven together effortlessly with the author's knowledge of the Amish life. Once started, you can't put this book down."

—SUZANNE WOODS FISHER, BESTSELLING
AUTHOR OF *THE DEVOTED*

"[*A Seat by the Hearth*] is a moving portrait of a disgraced woman attempting to reenter her childhood community . . .

This will please Clipston's fans and also win over newcomers to Lancaster County."

—PUBLISHERS WEEKLY

"This story of profound loss and deep friendship will leave readers with the certain knowledge that hope exists and love grows through faith in our God of second chances."

—KELLY IRVIN, AUTHOR OF THE BEEKEEPER'S SON AND UPON A SPRING BREEZE, ON ROOM ON THE PORCH SWING

"This heartbreaking series continues to take a fearlessly honest look at grief, as hopelessness threatens to steal what happiness Allen has treasured within his marriage and recent fatherhood. Clipston takes these feelings seriously without sugarcoating any aspect of the mourning process, allowing her characters to make their painful but ultimately joyous journey back to love and faith. Readers who have made this tough and ongoing pilgrimage themselves will appreciate the author's realistic portrayal of coming to terms with loss in order to continue living with hope and happiness."

—RT BOOK REVIEWS, 4 STARS, ON ROOM ON THE PORCH SWING

"A story of grief as well as new beginnings, this is a lovely Amish tale and the start of a great new series."

—PARKERSBURG NEWS AND SENTINEL ON A PLACE AT OUR TABLE

"Themes of family, forgiveness, love, and strength are woven throughout the story . . . a great choice for all readers of Amish fiction."

—CBA MARKET MAGAZINE ON A PLACE AT OUR TABLE

"This debut title in a new series offers an emotionally charged and engaging read headed by sympathetically drawn and believable protagonists. The meaty issues of trust and faith make this a solid book group choice."

—LIBRARY JOURNAL ON A PLACE AT OUR TABLE

"These sweet, tender novellas from one of the genre's best make the perfect sampler for new readers curious about Amish romances."

—LIBRARY JOURNAL ON AMISH SWEETHEARTS

"Clipston is as reliable as her character, giving Emily a difficult and intense romance worthy of Emily's ability to shine the light of Christ into the hearts of those she loves."

—RT BOOK REVIEWS, 4 ¹/₂ STARS, TOP
PICK! ON THE CHERISHED QUILT

"Clipston's heartfelt writing and engaging characters make her a fan favorite. Her latest Amish tale combines a spiritual message of accepting God's blessings as they are given with a sweet romance."

—LIBRARY JOURNAL ON THE CHERISHED QUILT

"Clipston delivers another enchanting series starter with a tasty premise, family secrets, and sweet-as-pie romance, offering assurance that true love can happen more than once and second chances are worth fighting for."

—RT BOOK REVIEWS, 4 ¹/₂ STARS, TOP
PICK! ON THE FORGOTTEN RECIPE

"In the first book in her Amish Heirloom series, Clipston takes readers on a roller-coaster ride through grief, guilt, and anxiety."

—*BOOKLIST* ON *THE FORGOTTEN RECIPE*

"Clipston is well versed in Amish culture and does a good job creating the world of Lancaster County, Pennsylvania . . . Amish fiction fans will enjoy this story—and want a taste of Veronica's raspberry pie!"

—*PUBLISHERS WEEKLY* ON *THE FORGOTTEN RECIPE*

"[Clipston] does an excellent job of wrapping up her story while setting the stage for the sequel."

—*CBA RETAILERS + RESOURCES* ON *THE FORGOTTEN RECIPE*

"Clipston brings this engaging series to an end with two emotional family reunions, a prodigal son parable, a sweet but hard-won romance and a happy ending for characters readers have grown to love. Once again, she gives us all we could possibly want from a talented storyteller."

—*RT BOOK REVIEWS*, 4 1/2 STARS, TOP PICK! ON *A SIMPLE PRAYER*

". . . will leave readers craving more."

—*RT BOOK REVIEWS*, 4 1/2 STARS, TOP PICK! ON *A MOTHER'S SECRET*

"Clipston's series starter has a compelling drama involving faith, family and romance . . . [an] absorbing series."

—*RT BOOK REVIEWS*, 4 1/2 STARS, TOP PICK! ON *A HOPEFUL HEART*

"Authentic characters, delectable recipes and faith abound in Clipston's second Kauffman Amish Bakery story."

—*RT BOOK REVIEWS*, 4 STARS ON *A PROMISE OF HOPE*

". . . an entertaining story of Amish life, loss, love and family."

—*RT BOOK REVIEWS*, 4 STARS ON *A PLACE OF PEACE*

"This fifth and final installment in the 'Kauffman Amish Bakery' series is sure to please fans who have waited for Katie's story."

—*LIBRARY JOURNAL* ON *A SEASON OF LOVE*

"[The Kauffman Amish Bakery] series' wide popularity is sure to attract readers to this novella, and they won't be disappointed by the excellent writing and the story's wholesome goodness."

—*LIBRARY JOURNAL* ON *A PLAIN AND SIMPLE CHRISTMAS*

"[*A Plain and Simple Christmas*] is inspiring and a perfect fit for the holiday season."

—*RT BOOK REVIEWS*, 4 STARS

THE BELOVED
HOPE CHEST

Other Books by Amy Clipston

NONFICTION

THE BELOVED HOPE CHEST

AN AMISH HEIRLOOM NOVEL

Amy Clipston

ZONDERVAN

The Beloved Hope Chest

Copyright © 2017 by Amy Clipston

This title is also available as a Zondervan e-book. Visit www.zondervan.com.

Requests for information should be addressed to:
Zondervan, *Grand Rapids, Michigan 49546*

ISBN 978-0-310-34197-0 (softcover)
ISBN 978-0-310-00095-2 (epub)
ISBN 978-0-310-35288-4 (repack)
ISBN 978-0-310-35991-3 (mass market)

Library of Congress Cataloging-in-Publication Data

CIP data available upon request.

Printed in the United States of America

19 20 21 22 23 24 25 / QG / 5 4 3 2 1

With love and appreciation to Pastor John ("PJ"), Pastor Naomi, and all my friends at Morning Star Lutheran Church in Matthews, North Carolina

GLOSSARY

ach: oh
aenti: aunt
appeditlich: delicious
Ausbund: Amish hymnal
bedauerlich: sad
boppli: baby
brot: bread
bruder: brother
bruderskind: niece/nephew
bruderskinner: nieces/nephews
bu: boy
buwe: boys
daadi: granddad
daed: dad
danki: thank you
dat: dad
Dietsch: Pennsylvania Dutch, the Amish language (a German dialect)
dochder: daughter
dochdern: daughters
Dummle!: hurry!
Englisher: a non-Amish person
faul: lazy
faulenzer: lazy person

fraa: wife
freind: friend
freinden: friends
froh: happy
gegisch: silly
gern gschehne: you're welcome
grossdaadi: grandfather
grossdochder: granddaughter
grossdochdern: granddaughters
grossmammi: grandmother
Gude mariye: Good morning
gut: good
Gut nacht: Good night
haus: house
Ich liebe dich: I love you
kaffi: coffee
kapp: prayer covering or cap
kichli: cookie
kichlin: cookies
kind: child
kinner: children
kuche: cake
kumm: come
liewe: love, a term of endearment
maed: young women, girls
maedel: young woman
mamm: mom
mammi: grandma
mei: my
mutter: mother
naerfich: nervous

narrisch: crazy

onkel: uncle

Ordnung: The oral tradition of practices required and forbidden in the Amish faith

schee: pretty

schmaert: smart

schtupp: family room

schweschder: sister

schweschdere: sisters

Was iss letz?: What's wrong?

Willkumm: welcome

Wie geht's: How do you do? or Good day!

wunderbaar: wonderful

ya: yes

AMISH HEIRLOOM SERIES FAMILY TREES

Ruth m. Mose Byler

Lizanne m. Alvin ("Al") Zook

Martha ("Mattie") (m. Isaiah Petersheim [deceased]) and then (m. Leroy Fisher)

Esther m. Ivan Fisher (Both deceased)

Leroy (m. Martha)   Joel (m. Dora)

Martha "Mattie" m. Leroy Fisher

Veronica (m. Jason Huyard)   Rachel (m. Michael Lantz)   Emily

Agnes m. Wilmar Hochstetler

Paul (m. Rosanna)   Christopher   Gabriel (deceased)

Rosanna m. Paul Hochstetler

Mamie   Betsy

Vera m. Raymond Lantz (both deceased)

Michael ("Mike") (m. Rachel)   John

Sylvia m. Timothy Lantz

Samuel (m. Mandy)   Marie   Janie

Annie m. Elam Huyard

Jason (m. Veronica)   Stephen

Tillie m. Henry ("Hank") Ebersol

Margaret m. Abner (deceased) Lapp

Seth (deceased)   Ellie

Fannie Mae m. Titus Dienner (Bishop)

Lindann

Susannah m. Timothy Beiler

David   Irma Rose Beiler Smucker (m. Melvin)

Irma Rose m. Melvin Smucker

Sarah

NOTE TO THE READER

While this novel is set against the real backdrop of Lancaster County, Pennsylvania, the characters are fictional. There is no intended resemblance between the characters in this book and any real members of the Amish and Mennonite communities. As with any work of fiction, I've taken license in some areas of research as a means of creating the necessary circumstances for my characters. My research was thorough; however, it would be impossible to be completely accurate in details and description, since each and every community differs. Therefore, any inaccuracies in the Amish and Mennonite lifestyles portrayed in this book are completely due to fictional license.

PROLOGUE

Mattie Fisher sat at the table in her large kitchen and fingered the tiny onesie her eldest daughter, Veronica, found in Mattie's hope chest last year. A weight settled on her shoulders as her mind swirled with thoughts of her past, a past her three daughters had no idea existed until one by one they'd found the secret items Mattie had hidden away.

Her fingers moved to the stack of letters her middle daughter, Rachel, found. Raw emotion tightened Mattie's belly as memories from twenty-eight years ago washed over her. Then she touched the birth and death certificates, handprints, footprints, and zipper baggie with a lock of blond hair. When Emily, her youngest, found those precious items, Mattie knew it was time she told her girls about her past. They had questions, and Mattie had a responsibility to answer them.

Closing her eyes, she silently prayed for the right words.

"*Mamm*, are you all right?" Veronica asked as she entered the kitchen, followed by Rachel and Emily. They all turned their eyes to the items Mattie had placed on the table.

"*Ya.*" Mattie gestured toward the empty chairs. "Pour yourselves some tea and have a seat."

Emily brought three cups of tea to the table before sitting down beside Veronica.

"*Was iss letz?*" Rachel's face clouded with concern as she sat down across from Mattie. "Emily invited Veronica and me over for sisters' day, and she said you had something important to tell us. Does it have to do with these things we found in your hope chest?"

"*Ya*, I do have something to tell you, and these things are part of it." Mattie cleared her throat and cradled the warm mug in her hands. Then she forced a smile as her daughters watched her with furrowed brows. "I've told you I've known your father since I was a little girl, but I haven't told you the whole story about how we became more than *freinden*."

Emily lifted her hand, stopping Mattie from continuing. "*Mamm*, I'm confused. I thought you and *Dat* were *gut freinden* and one day he asked you to be his girlfriend and then you got married."

"It was more complicated than that." Mattie ran her finger over the edge of her mug. "I was married to a man named Isaiah before I married your *dat*." She paused. "And shortly after I married your *dat*, I almost ended our marriage."

Her daughters gasped in unison and then, all at the same time, started firing off questions.

"Slow down now. I'll answer all your questions, but you have to give me a chance to explain first." She cleared her throat again, this time past a swelling lump. She paused for a beat as her daughters stared at her, their eyes wide.

"It all started so many years ago."

Mattie closed her eyes for a moment and was transported to the small farmhouse Isaiah rented when he moved from Indiana after coming to visit a friend. He decided to stay after he met Mattie and they fell in love.

She could almost smell the sweet aroma of apple pie as she began to share the story.

CHAPTER 1

Mattie sat at her table across from her mother and sister as the sweet aroma of apple pie wafted through the small kitchen.

"I can't believe you're three months along already," Lizanne, Mattie's older sister, said as she filled Mattie's mug. "Have you and Isaiah discussed names?"

"*Ya*, we've discussed them briefly." Mattie suppressed a smile and held her warm mug in her hands.

She and Isaiah had talked about names last night while listening to the rain beat a steady cadence on the roof above them in the small farmhouse they rented. Isaiah's gorgeous blue eyes had shimmered in the low light of the lantern flickering on the bedside table as he ran his hand over her flat abdomen and shared the names he preferred.

Mattie sipped her tea and then set her mug on the table.

"And . . . ?" Lizanne leaned forward.

"Isaiah would like to name the baby Jacob if it's a *bu*." Mattie folded her hands. "He said it would be after his *daadi*. As you know, his parents are both deceased and he has no siblings."

"What about if it's a *maedel*?" Lizanne grinned. "Do you still like the name Veronica?"

"*Ya*, and he likes it too." This time Mattie smiled. She had fallen head over heels for Isaiah the moment she met him at a combined youth group event four years ago. After dating for two years, they married, and now they were expecting their first child. She couldn't be any happier than she was at that very moment.

"My first grandchild." *Mamm* wiped a tear from her eyes. "I can't wait, but the time will go quickly."

"*Ya*, August will be here before we know it." Excitement sent flutters swirling through Mattie's stomach.

"It seems like only yesterday I was expecting Lizanne." *Mamm* chuckled. "Your *dat* was so worried." She touched Lizanne's arm.

"He was?" Lizanne's eyes rounded. "I've never seen him *naerfich* about anything."

"Men are usually *naerfich* with babies. At least, they are with the first one." *Mamm* placed her mug on the table. "Is Isaiah nervous?"

Mattie touched her chin as their conversation from last night filtered through her thoughts once again. Isaiah's worried expression had nearly broken her heart.

"I don't think he's worried about the *boppli*, but he is concerned about building a *haus*, one that's bigger than this one." Mattie absently folded a paper napkin as she spoke.

"What do you mean?" *Mamm*'s eyebrows rose.

"Isaiah is eager to buy some farmland and build on it, but I'm not. I'm *froh* here in our little *haus*. We'll be fine with one child. We can build a bigger *haus* before more *kinner* arrive. As long as Isaiah and I have each other and our family, we'll be fine."

"You'll have your own farm soon enough." Mattie's mother glanced up at the clock above the sink and frowned. "Where did you say Isaiah went this morning?"

"He had to run to the bank, but he should be back soon."

"It's been quite awhile, hasn't it?" Lizanne chimed in. "Didn't you say his driver picked him up at nine?"

"That's right."

"Well, it's almost noon." Lizanne leveled her gaze at Mattie. "Don't you think he should've been back by now?" Mattie saw concern in her sister's blue eyes as Lizanne tucked a stray strand of golden hair under her prayer covering. At twenty-seven, Lizanne was only three years older than Mattie, and especially since they had inherited the same coloring from *Mamm*, Mattie wondered if she looked the same way when she was wondering if all was well.

"Maybe his driver had to stop somewhere while they were out. Sometimes Teddy has a few stops to make, and Isaiah doesn't mind." A shiver of worry slithered up Mattie's back. After all, just as Isaiah was leaving . . .

No. He told her not to worry.

"He could already be back from the bank and walked out to the barn without coming in to say hello. He mentioned having to repair one of the barn doors. One of the hinges broke during the storm last night."

"Or maybe he ran into a *freind* at the bank," *Mamm* offered. "You know how Isaiah likes to talk. He meets a *freind* no matter where he goes."

"*Ya.* Maybe." But Mattie wasn't convinced. Something was wrong. Maybe it was her hormones getting the best of her. She was so emotional lately that she burst into tears when her mother told her a neighbor's dog had been hit by a car. Mattie had only seen the dog once, but the idea that it had been killed had just devastated her.

"I'm sure he'll be home soon." *Mamm* patted Mattie's hand as though she knew what Mattie had been thinking. "Let's check on that apple pie."

"All right." Mattie followed her mother to the oven. She rested her hand on the counter as *Mamm* opened the oven door and pulled out the pie. Its warm, delicious aroma permeated the kitchen.

"I think it's done," *Mamm* said. "Doesn't it smell *appeditlich*? I just love this reci—"

A knock on the front door interrupted their conversation.

"I wonder who that is," Lizanne said.

Mattie followed her sister to the front door. Lizanne pulled it open, and crisp February air flooded the warm house as two police officers stood on the front porch.

"Is either of you Mrs. Petersheim?" the older officer asked.

"Yes, I am," Mattie said.

Both the officers looked concerned. Suddenly lightheaded, Mattie felt her mouth go dry.

"I'm sorry, ma'am, but we have some bad news." The

younger officer's lips formed a thin line. "There was a . . . situation at the bank."

"A situation? What do you mean?" Mattie's stomach roiled, and bile rose in her throat. She was going to be sick.

"What's going on?" *Mamm* appeared and rested her hand on Mattie's shoulder.

"Ma'am, I don't know how to say this." The first officer glanced at the younger one, whose look fell to the floor of the porch before looking back to Mattie. He took a deep breath.

"A man walked into the bank where Mr. Petersheim was and threatened a woman. It seems to have been a domestic problem between a man and his estranged wife."

"I don't understand," Mattie said, her voice shaking. "Where is Isaiah?"

"The man had a gun, and he pointed it at the woman. Mr. Petersheim tried to intervene."

"Where is Isaiah?" Mattie demanded, her words louder and her voice foreign to her own ears. Her whole body trembled.

"Calm down, Mattie." *Mamm* squeezed her shoulder.

The younger officer cleared his throat. "Mr. Petersheim moved the woman out of the way just as the gun went off. He was shot in the chest at point-blank range."

"He passed away at the scene," the older officer added.

"What?" Lizanne asked from somewhere behind Mattie.

"He's . . . gone?" *Mamm*'s hand dropped from Mattie's shoulder.

Mattie's world tilted and a gasp escaped her mouth. Her heart felt as though it were lodged in her throat, making it difficult to breathe. She reached for the doorframe as the room spun. She gasped again and stepped backward, her leg colliding with a small bench.

Isaiah! No!

"Mattie!" *Mamm* reached for her.

"Mattie!" Lizanne echoed as she grabbed Mattie's hand.

"Ma'am?" The first officer stepped into the foyer and grabbed Mattie's arm just before her knees buckled and the room went black.

• • •

Mattie folded her hands in an attempt to stop them from shaking as she sat at the front of her father's largest barn. Four months had passed since Isaiah's death, and the stale air from the late-June day was nearly unbearable, causing beads of sweat to collect on her temples.

She wiped away the moisture with one hand and then rested it on her protruding belly. She glanced across to where Leroy Fisher, her best friend since childhood, sat next to his attendants—his younger brother, Joel, and Leroy's best male friend, Hank Ebersol.

Leroy wore his Sunday best—a crisp white shirt, black vest, black trousers, and black suspenders—as he and Mattie sat in front of the small congregation that included their families and close friends. They'd sung a hymn, and then the minister launched into a thirty-minute sermon based on Old Testament stories of marriages. Leroy's deep brown eyes were fixed on the minister as though he were hanging on to his every word.

Mattie, however, couldn't focus. It was as though she were stuck in some surreal dream. Today her formal name would change from Martha Jane Petersheim to Martha Jane Fisher. Her eyes stung with bereavement. Not too long ago, she'd hoped and prayed to become Mattie Petersheim, Isaiah's wife, but now she would lose that connection with Isaiah forever. She wasn't ready to let go of Isaiah and the warmth and comfort that came with being his wife.

She smoothed her trembling hand over the skirt of her royal blue dress as her thoughts turned to the day she married Isaiah. She'd worn a purple dress on that cold November day, and she'd been completely elated. She'd been even more ecstatic when she told Isaiah she was pregnant with their first child. Mattie had been looking forward to raising a large family with him.

But four months ago, her happiness had been ripped to shreds only a few miles from their home. The local news had hailed Isaiah as a hero for saving the woman from her abusive husband. For nearly a month, reporters stopped by her parents' house and asked questions about Isaiah. Mattie was grateful her father acted as the family spokesman, blocking the reporters from talking to her. Mattie read the stories in the paper, which lauded Isaiah's sacrifice and honor, but the words left her hollow and cold. Although she was proud of her husband's bravery, she was left alone with nothing but her memories and Isaiah's baby growing inside her.

At least she could be grateful for the Amish belief that they should avoid legal matters, excusing her from making any statements at the shooter's trial.

Mattie shifted in her seat and was overwhelmed by the awareness of someone studying her. Glancing to the side, her gaze collided with Leroy's. His lips turned up in a warm smile and she tried to mirror the gesture, but she knew her attempt probably looked more like a grimace.

As she stared into his eyes, her mind took her back to the afternoon before Isaiah died. Leroy, Hank Ebersol, and Hank's wife, Tillie, had come to visit Isaiah and Mattie on that cold Sunday in February. The memory of the aroma of moist earth and wood burning in fireplaces filled her nostrils as if she were still sitting on the small back porch with them. Although the weather was chilly, they had enjoyed gathering outside.

Mattie hugged her sweater over her chest and laughed as she rocked on a glider. Beside her, Isaiah chuckled along with her as Hank shared a story about one of his bumbling hunting trips with his father.

"Hank," Isaiah began through another chuckle, "tell me. How did you manage to fall out of a tree stand?"

"Well, that squirrel was pretty violent," Hank explained as he sat in the neighboring glider beside Tillie. "He was irate when he found me in his tree."

Leroy threw back his head and laughed as he leaned against the porch railing across from Mattie. She grinned up at him, and he met her gaze, shaking his head.

"Was that the only time you fell out of a tree?" Isaiah looped his arm around Mattie's shoulder and she leaned against him, thankful for the shield from the brisk breeze.

"Hmm." Hank lifted a dark eyebrow over one of his brown eyes. "I don't seem to remember falling out of any other trees. At least, I haven't fallen out of any other tree stands." He turned toward Tillie. "I'm not really all that clumsy."

Tillie laughed, shaking loose a wisp of her brown hair that fluttered from beneath her prayer covering. "I didn't marry you for your grace."

"You have a selective memory," Mattie quipped. "I seem to remember Hank falling out of trees fairly often when we were little. Isn't that right, Leroy?"

"Oh, *ya*." Leroy smirked at Mattie. "Do you remember when we were in school and a few of the boys decided to climb the trees next to the swing set?"

Mattie sat up straighter. "*Ya*, I do. You all got in trouble and had to stay after and clean the classroom."

Leroy gave her a knowing look. "And you stayed with us and helped."

"I didn't mind. You were *mei freinden* and would've done the same for me. I felt bad you got caught."

"We only got caught because someone fell out of the tree and scraped his leg." Leroy gave Hank a pointed look. "If you hadn't gotten hurt, we probably would have gotten away with it."

Hank shrugged. "I never said I was born to be a tree trimmer."

"We sure gave Teacher Marilyn a hard time, didn't we?" Leroy asked Hank with a chuckle.

"Do you remember that time you fell in the mud

puddle during recess?" A laugh bubbled up from Mattie's throat.

"*Ya!*" Hank slapped his knee. "And you fell in trying to help us up, Mattie."

Leroy laughed, throwing his head back again.

Mattie sniffed, wiping her eyes. "*Mei mamm* was so furious because she had just made me that purple dress. She asked, 'If Hank and Leroy jumped off a bridge, would you jump after them?'"

Leroy wiped his misty eyes. "Did you tell her you probably would?"

"*Ya*, I did." Mattie grinned.

Isaiah rubbed her shoulder. "I had no idea *mei fraa* was such a juvenile delinquent."

"Only when she was with Hank and me," Leroy quipped.

Tillie giggled. "I didn't have that much fun in school. It's a shame I didn't attend with the three of you."

"I didn't either." Isaiah looked down at Mattie, and the affection shining in his ice-blue eyes sent warmth racing through her veins. The bright afternoon sunlight gave his light-brown hair golden highlights, making him look even more handsome than usual.

"How's work at the hardware store going, Isaiah?" Leroy crossed his arms over his wide chest.

"It's going all right." Isaiah blew out a sigh. "I finally got a little raise, but it's still not enough to buy that farmland I've been looking at. I'm certain it will be bought before I can make a bid for it."

Mattie could feel the irritation radiating off her husband. She instinctively placed her hand on his, hoping her touch would calm him before he spoke again. "Everything will be fine. We can make do in this *haus* for a while longer."

"I promised you a *haus* of our own when we were engaged. We've been married more than a year, and we're still living in the same place I was renting when we met."

"Shh." She placed her hand on his cheek, enjoying the feel of his whiskers. "I'm perfectly *froh*," she said softly. "It's okay."

"You think you have problems," Leroy said, joking. "Poor Hank and Tillie are stuck living next to me."

Mattie smiled at Leroy, silently thanking him for lightening the mood. Leroy seemed to understand her expression, and he winked in response.

Isaiah looked up at Leroy. "How are the plans going for your harness shop?"

"We're going to apply for the loan this week. Hopefully we can start building the shop soon." Leroy turned toward Hank. "It will be nice to just walk out my back door and be at work."

"*Ya*, that's the truth." Hank rubbed Tillie's arm. "And *mei fraa* can make our lunch and bring it to us at work, right?"

Tillie slapped Hank's arm playfully. "You can come in the *haus* for lunch. I'll be busy quilting and cleaning."

"What about Leroy?" Hank asked. "He'll starve if you don't bring him lunch."

Leroy rolled his eyes. "Just because I'm a bachelor doesn't mean I can't cook. I can handle my own lunch, but *danki*."

Tillie stood, gathered up Hank's lunch dish, and stacked it on hers. "I'll wash these before we leave. It's getting late."

"I can help you." Mattie stood.

"No, no." Tillie held up one hand. "You rest."

Isaiah rubbed her back. "Are you sure you're feeling all right?"

"I'm fine. I can help you, Tillie." Mattie stacked her dish on top of Isaiah's and then reached for Leroy's, which was balanced on the porch railing.

"Are you sure you're okay?" Leroy asked.

"I'm fine. *Danki* for asking, though."

She followed Tillie through the back door into the mudroom and then the small kitchen. For the hundredth time, she thought about how much she loved this little house that included a family room, bathroom, and two bedrooms. It wasn't much, but it was their refuge away from the world.

Mattie filled one side of her sink with hot, soapy water, then the other side with clear water. "I'll wash, you dry. Okay?"

"*Ya.*" Tillie leaned against the counter and touched a dish towel. "Do you think Leroy will ever get married?"

Mattie dropped the dishes and utensils into the sink and began to wash a plate. "I'm sure he will someday."

"I've been with Hank for five years now, and I don't remember Leroy ever having a girlfriend. Not even when I first met Hank." Tillie turned toward her, resting her hand on her small hip. "Do you remember him ever dating?"

Mattie paused, thinking back to their years in the

youth group. "I know he was dating one *maedel* for a few months, but then they broke up. He said they didn't have much in common." She dropped the plate in the clean water. "He's only twenty-five. He could still meet someone and get married."

"*Ya*, that's true." Tillie picked up the clean plate and started to dry it. "He'd make a *gut* husband. He's such a nice guy."

"*Ya*, he is."

The back door opened, and the three men walked in just as a rumble of thunder sounded in the distance.

"We'd better get on the road soon," Hank said. "The sky is black in the distance, and it just started thundering. A bad storm is coming."

"Let me finish the dishes." Tillie pointed toward the sink.

"Don't be *gegisch*." Mattie waved off the comment. "I can handle them."

"I'll help her," Isaiah said. "You get on the road now. We don't want you to be caught in the storm." He started toward the door to follow Hank out through the mudroom. "So how are your folks doing, Hank?"

Leroy lingered by the doorway leading from the kitchen to the family room. "Tillie, do you want me to help you carry anything?"

"*Ya*, please." Tillie handed him the cake saver she'd used to tote the chocolate cake they shared after lunch.

"Oh, don't leave all of that." Mattie pointed toward the remaining cake on the counter. "Isaiah and I don't need it." She glanced up at Leroy. "You'll finish it, right? Chocolate cake was always your favorite."

Leroy rubbed his flat abdomen. "Are you trying to fatten me up? If you do, then I'll never find a *fraa*."

Mattie and Tillie shared knowing smiles.

Leroy eyed them with suspicion. "What was that look for?"

"Nothing, nothing." Tillie cut the remaining cake in half and slipped one half onto a plate she took from one of Mattie's cupboards. "I'll leave half for you and Isaiah."

"*Danki*." Mattie picked up another dish to wash.

Tillie put the remaining cake into the saver and handed it to Leroy, then hefted her black purse over her shoulder. "I'm sorry to leave all the cleaning on you."

Mattie grinned. "I'll get you next time we visit at your place."

"I bet you will." Tillie hugged her. "Have a *gut* week."

"You too." Mattie looked up at Leroy. "Take care."

"See you soon."

Mattie followed Leroy and Tillie to the back door and waved as they climbed into Hank's buggy and headed down the rock driveway toward the road. Isaiah climbed the porch steps and rested his hand on her shoulder. She smiled up at him.

. . .

Someone in the small congregation coughed, and the sudden sound jolted Mattie back to the present. She never imagined that visit would be the last one she and Isaiah would share with their friends. The following morning Isaiah had been shot and killed at the bank.

She blinked and rubbed her hand across her hot cheeks in an attempt to refocus on the minister's sermon. In her peripheral vision, she could see that Leroy turned his attention toward her, but then looked toward the front of the barn once again.

Mattie had at first resisted when Leroy asked her to marry him a month ago. She loved him as a friend, but she wasn't in love with him. But after much thought, Mattie decided it made sense to marry Leroy. She wanted her child to have a father and a stable home, and Leroy could provide that. He was also starting a new business and needed a wife to help him run his household. She and Leroy were good friends, and they would make a great team. And, by marrying him, she and her child would no longer be a burden to her family.

Yet now that Mattie sat in her father's barn at their wedding, the whole scene was surreal. Reality hit her like a ton of hay bales crashing down from the loft. She wasn't supposed to be a bride twice within three years. When would she stop feeling so off-kilter? She was going to be a *mamm* in less than two months, but she didn't feel ready to take on that role. Were all new mothers this lost and confused? No, of course they weren't. Most Amish women didn't face motherhood without their husbands.

Husbands they loved.

As if on cue, the baby kicked, and her hands flew to her large belly. A smile played at the corners of her lips.

Lizanne touched her arm, and Mattie looked up at her. Her sister lifted an eyebrow as if to ask if the baby had kicked, and Mattie gave her a slightly perceptible nod. Lizanne placed her hand on Mattie's belly as the baby kicked again, and Lizanne had to stifle a laugh. Tillie leaned over and grinned. Thankfully, the minister continued to talk, oblivious to their silent conversation.

Mattie glanced over at Leroy again, and he gave her a small smile before turning back toward the minister. Thoughts of Isaiah and all she'd lost washed over her once again. She had to make this marriage work with Leroy, but she didn't know how to be his wife. She only knew how to be Isaiah's wife, but Isaiah was gone forever. She swallowed back a thick knot of bereavement that seemed to be lodged in her throat.

Once the sermon was over, Mattie bowed her head as the rest of the congregation knelt for silent prayer. When the prayer ended, Bishop Titus Dienner stood and began to preach the main sermon. The bishop's words were only white noise to her recollection of her first wedding—the joyous celebration, the laughter, the food, and the first night she and Isaiah spent in their little house.

Suddenly, the sermon was over, and Mattie's body began to shudder as her throat dried. She glanced up just as the bishop looked at her and then at Leroy. It was time for her to stand with Leroy and declare their desire to be married. She didn't know if she was strong enough to go through with this. Was it too late for her to back out? And if she changed her mind now, would Leroy ever forgive her?

"Now here are two in one faith," the bishop said. "Martha Jane Petersheim and Leroy Jonathan Fisher." The bishop asked the congregation if they knew any scriptural reason for the couple not to be married. After a short pause, he continued. "If it is your desire to be married, you may in the name of the Lord come forth."

Mattie turned toward Leroy, and he held out his hand to her. She took it, and he lifted her to her feet. His hand was warm and strong, and when she swayed, he held her fast. She peeked up at him as he studied the bishop intently. His face was serious as they took their vows.

Mattie's heart pounded as the bishop read "A Prayer for Those About to Be Married" from an Amish prayer book called the *Christenpflict*.

Mattie and Leroy sat down once again for another sermon and another prayer. After the bishop recited the Lord's Prayer, the congregation stood, and the three-hour ceremony ended with another hymn.

As the men began to rearrange furniture, and the women started preparing to serve the wedding dinner, for a moment Mattie wished she cared about food. The chicken with stuffing, mashed potatoes with gravy, pepper cabbage, and cooked cream of celery she knew were on the menu would have been appealing before Isaiah died. And she knew the bountiful desserts—cookies, pie, fruit, and Jell-O salad—would be delicious. But she hadn't been interested in eating for months, except for the baby's sake.

And now this new realization took her appetite completely.

Leroy held out his hand to her once again. "Are you ready?"

Mattie blinked, staring up at him as reality slammed into her once again and stole her breath. Leroy Fisher

was now her husband and partner. *When will I stop
thinking of Leroy as* mei freind *and instead consider him
my husband? And where do my memories of Isaiah fit
into this confusing new reality?*

She stood.

· · ·

Leroy thought he might burst with joy as he studied his
lovely wife.

Mei fraa!

Mattie was stunning in her royal blue dress as she
stood there looking at him with one hand resting on
her protruding belly.

For years he'd dreamt of this day. He'd prayed he'd
have a wife and a child to bring life and purpose into
the big, empty house he'd inherited when his mother
passed away three years ago. Yet he'd never imagined
he'd take sweet, beautiful Mattie as his wife. God had
blessed him abundantly when he'd brought Mattie into
his life when they were children, and he'd loved her from
afar since they attended school together. And now he
could call Mattie his wife.

Leroy mentally kicked himself. He had no right to
find joy in Mattie's loss. She and Isaiah had been deeply
in love, and now she was drowning in grief. Leroy longed
to take away her pain and help her find joy again. Of
course, that would take time, and Leroy was willing to
wait as long as she needed to grieve her loss. Leroy would
take care of Mattie and her baby. He couldn't stand the
thought of Mattie's child growing up without a father.

Leroy was determined to be the kind of father he and his younger brother never had.

As Leroy continued to hold out his hand to Mattie, she hesitated, her sapphire eyes locking onto his. When her pretty pink lips trembled, her sadness chipped away at his euphoria, but he refused to give up on her. Someday she would learn to love him.

"Mattie?" he whispered as if they were the only two people in the large barn. "Would you like to walk with me?"

"*Ya.*" She finally took his hand.

Leroy enjoyed the soft caress of her skin against his. He looped his arm around her, and her shoulders stiffened. He winced as if she'd struck him. What had happened to the woman who sobbed in his arms the day of Isaiah's wake and then leaned her head against his shoulder during one of their recent late-evening visits on her parents' porch?

Be patient. Give her time.

Leroy left his hand on her shoulder and pushed away the worry nipping at him.

Joel and his wife, Dora, approached them. "Welcome to the family, Mattie," Dora said as she pulled her into a hug.

"Congratulations!" Hank joined them with Tillie at his side.

"Congratulations!" Lizanne echoed, flanked by her husband, Al.

"Leroy." Mattie's father, Mose, gave Leroy's shoulder a companionable pat. "Welcome to the family."

"*Danki.*" Leroy smiled as Mose leaned in closer.

"I'm going to tell you a secret." Mose lowered his voice. "Ruth and I were blessed with two *dochdern*. I love *mei dochdern*, but I always dreamt of having a son. I'm grateful Lizzie and Mattie have blessed me with three *wunderbaar* sons now through their marriages. I was close to Isaiah. He was a *gut* man, and we will all miss him. I'm grateful, however, that you are here for Mattie, and I look forward to the company of yet another son at family gatherings."

"I appreciate that very much." Leroy tried in vain to clear his throat against the lump of emotion that suddenly seemed to swell there.

"I know it's not my place to judge, but I never understood why your *dat* walked out on you and Joel." Mose touched his bushy beard. "He missed out on so much with you and your *bruder*. Ruth and I are *froh* to have you as our son. If you ever need anything, don't hesitate to ask."

"*Danki.*" Leroy's voice was hoarse. All these years he had longed for his father to return and now Mose called him a son. It seemed almost too good to be true. Happiness expanded in his soul.

"I'm grateful that you're going to take care of my Mattie. I know you will be *gut* to her." Mose shook Leroy's hand. "Enjoy the rest of the day."

Then Leroy and Mattie were surrounded by more friends and family members who wanted to share their congratulations. As Leroy shook yet another hand, he hoped Mattie would relax and enjoy the party. This was the beginning of their new life together.

CHAPTER 2

Mattie's heart thumped as she and Leroy walked up the porch steps leading to the back door of his two-story, white clapboard house. The events of the day were a blur. After the wedding service, they spent the afternoon and early evening visiting with their family and friends. The fellowship had distracted her, but now the reality of what she'd done burned through her.

Leroy held a lantern in one hand as he slipped the key into the lock. The latch clicked before he wrenched open the back door.

"Home sweet home." He gave her a tentative smile as he held the door open for her. "I tried to clean up a bit, but I ran out of time. Hank and I have been so busy trying to get the harness shop ready for the grand opening."

Mattie glanced across the backyard, which was shrouded in darkness, and her eyes focused on the outline of the small building that straddled the end of the Fisher property and the beginning of the Ebersol property.

"We should be ready to open in about a week or so," Leroy continued, then paused to look into her eyes. "Are you ready to come into your new home?"

"*Ya.*" Mattie's voice croaked. Heat crawled up her cheeks as she walked through the mudroom and into the kitchen.

The kitchen looked the same as she remembered it from when she was a child and attended quilting bees hosted by Leroy's mother. The large, open room had ample counters and a propane-powered refrigerator and stove, as well as a long table surrounded by six chairs. The laundry room, where the wringer washer was kept, was off the kitchen.

Through a wide doorway that separated the kitchen from the spacious family room, she could see a tan sofa, two burgundy wing chairs, and a coffee table. Off the family room, she knew, was the foyer leading to the front door, the bathroom, a spiral staircase leading to the second floor, and the door leading into the downstairs bedroom.

The downstairs bedroom.

They were married now and were expected to live as husband and wife. Mattie's heart pummeled her rib cage. Did Leroy expect her to share his bed *tonight*? But she was seven months pregnant, and she, well, she wasn't ready for *that*. Leroy had always been her friend, but she'd never harbored an attraction or any romantic feelings for him at all. Yet how could she turn him down? Mattie was supposed to be his wife, submissive to his needs. Sweat beaded on her forehead, and her chest seized with worry.

"Are you hungry?" Leroy asked, apparently unaware of her inner turmoil. "Would you like something to drink?" He crossed the kitchen to the refrigerator and opened the door. "I went grocery shopping on Wednesday. I have some milk and orange juice." Then he pointed to the counter. "I also bought tea. I know you like to have tea when you visit with your *mamm* and Lizzie."

"No, *danki*. I'm not hungry or thirsty. I'm just really tired. It's been a long day."

"Of course." Leroy closed the refrigerator door and smiled at her. "I'm tired too."

Her stomach clenched as she followed him through the doorway into the family room and then toward the downstairs bedroom. She had no idea how to handle this awkward situation. Didn't Leroy feel any apprehension about this at all? Why hadn't they talked about their wedding night before it was upon them?

The door to the downstairs bedroom was open, and she peered in at the large bed, neatly made with a colorful log cabin design quilt. A nightstand sat on either side of the bed, each equipped with a propane lamp and a battery-operated alarm clock. Two dressers lined one wall while a closet filled the far wall.

Leroy stepped into the bedroom and set the lantern on one of the dressers, then turned on one of the propane lamps.

"I put your hope chest over there." He pointed to one corner of the room. "And your boxes with clothes and shoes and your suitcase are in the closet. You can unpack tomorrow. Oh." He gestured toward the family room. "I put your bookshelf out there. Your book boxes are in the corner next to it." He paused and rested his hand on the back of his neck. "You can decide if you want to move the shelf. Just tell me. You don't have to keep things where I put them. This is your *haus*, too, now."

"Oh, the shelf is fine there." She hugged her arms to her chest. "Wherever you say is fine."

"I'm open to suggestions." Leroy let his arm fall to his side. "I put your sewing machine in one of the bedrooms upstairs. You can make it your sewing room and arrange it anyway you'd like. Let me know if you need anything, like a chair or even a new sewing machine."

Stunned, Mattie blinked. "You want to buy me a new sewing machine?"

"Why not? I need to get you a wedding gift, right? I had no idea what to get you."

He pushed his suspenders off his shoulders as he stepped toward the second dresser, and a renewed panic gripped Mattie. Was he going to change right in front of her? If so, did he expect her to do the same?

Mattie remained in the doorway and glanced around for an escape route. The bathroom was close by, but how long could she hide in there before he started to get suspicious? She gripped the edge of the doorway as Leroy rifled through the dressers, pulling out a pair of boxers and a plain white T-shirt.

After closing the drawer, he looked at her and raised his eyebrows. "Are you okay?"

Mattie swallowed. "*Ya.* No, actually, I'm not. It's just that, well, I'm seven months along, and I don't think I should . . . well, um . . ." She was sure her cheeks were aflame. She should be able to discuss the issue of intimacy like an adult.

Why was she suddenly so tongue-tied and nervous around Leroy? During their late-night visits on the small porch at her parents' *daadihaus*, Mattie had poured out her heart to him after Isaiah died. Now that she was Leroy's wife, however, she couldn't string together two coherent thoughts when it came to personal issues. Humiliating tears stung her eyes, and she sniffed.

"Just calm down." Leroy crossed the room and gently touched her arm. "Do you want me to sleep upstairs?"

Ya! I do! And please change your clothes up there too.

"Will that be all right?" Her voice resembled a meek child's instead of a grown woman's.

"*Ya*, it's fine. I had a feeling that would be the case at least for a while. There's a spare bedroom up there, but I haven't moved my clothes up there yet."

"*Danki.*" Mattie breathed a sigh of relief as some of the tension in her back uncoiled.

"The sheets are fresh. Make yourself at home, and let me know if you need anything. *Gut nacht.*" He kissed her cheek. After retrieving a pair of trousers and a shirt for the morning, he grabbed the lantern from the dresser and left the room to head up the staircase.

Mattie sat on the edge of the bed, which creaked under her weight, and glanced around. The house was suddenly cold and foreign, despite the humid June air. She squeezed her eyes shut. She had to be strong—for the baby.

I can do this. I can adjust to a new life with Leroy and without Isaiah.

Mattie looked toward the closet and then shoved herself off the bed. She opened the closet door and located her boxes and suitcase. She retrieved her nightgown and Isaiah's T-shirt, which was the last one he'd slept in before he died. She kept the plain white T-shirt in bed beside her at night since it no longer fit over her belly.

After visiting the bathroom, Mattie returned to the bedroom, closed the door, changed into her nightgown, laid her clothes on a dresser, turned off the propane lamp, and climbed into bed.

She hugged Isaiah's shirt close to her body to breathe in its faint scent. Instead, she was overwhelmed by a new aroma—Leroy's. It wafted over her from the quilt. He smelled like leather mixed with earth and soap. The scent was comforting, but it smothered the faint aroma barely clinging to Isaiah's T-shirt.

It was too hot for the quilt anyway. She shoved it off her body.

Would Leroy squelch her feelings and memories of Isaiah? She wasn't ready to let go of Isaiah. She missed him so much her heart ached for him. She missed the sound of his voice, the feel of his arms around her, the taste of his kisses, and the deep richness of his laughter.

Closing her eyes, she relived the day of the accident as if it were only yesterday.

· · ·

Mattie was washing the breakfast dishes when Isaiah burst through the back door. She looked over her shoulder at his handsome face, twisted in a scowl. "*Was iss letz?*"

"I forgot I have to go to the bank to deposit my pay-

her parents' one-bedroom cottage, and she didn't want to be a burden to her sister and brother-in-law. Marrying Leroy was the best option, the only practical option for Mattie and her unborn child.

But if this was the best option, then why did it feel so wrong?

"I miss you, Isaiah," Mattie whispered into the suffocating darkness. "Why did you have to leave me?"

A choked sob escaped Mattie's throat, and soon she was crying into Leroy's pillow as she yearned for Isaiah to come back to her.

. . .

Leroy stared up at the ceiling and blew out a deep sigh. The single open window did little to move the stifling air in the small, second-floor bedroom. On hot nights like this, he found himself wondering what it would be like to have a ceiling fan. If he had the time, he could try to invent a battery-operated ceiling fan, but then he would have to somehow convince the bishop to allow them in homes. Certainly other Amish families would buy into the idea and help persuade the bishop they were necessary and not too worldly.

Rolling to his side, Leroy pushed the silly notion away. He could survive the remainder of the summer sleeping in the spare room if he had to. In fact, he could survive it through the fall too. He hoped Mattie wouldn't push him away for the entire fall season. Of course he would grant her all the time she needed, but he prayed it wouldn't last until winter.

He swallowed a groan. He hadn't expected intimacy so soon, but that's what Mattie must have feared he wanted when he absentmindedly shrugged off his suspenders before finding his clothes. In fact, he wasn't entirely comfortable with the idea of their being in the same bed now either. Not when she was seven months pregnant. Yes, he had entertained the idea of their merely sleeping in the same bed together, but of course that still would be expecting too much intimacy.

There was a chance this marriage would never evolve to anything more than friendship. At best, they might live like roommates for the rest of their lives, and he would have to get used to the idea of sleeping in this bedroom. He bit back another groan at the idea. Well, if that was the case, then he'd clean up this room and make it livable. He'd given most of the furniture to Joel and Dora when they were married, so he'd have to get a couple of nightstands, a propane lamp, and at least one dresser for his clothes.

Leroy peered across the room at the row of boxes with things he had moved out of the room next door to convert it into a sewing room for Mattie. He had to make time to go through all those boxes and decide what to do with everything, but right now his priority was the harness shop. He would worry about the boxes and new furniture after the baby came.

The baby.

Leroy smiled. He couldn't wait to be a father, and he would be a much better parent than his father had been. Leroy wouldn't abandon his child or walk away when his family needed him most. Instead, he would be a pillar of support and love to his family. His child would never doubt Leroy's love or dedication.

Names rolled through his mind. Had Mattie and Isaiah chosen names before Isaiah died? She hadn't shared that information when they talked, and Leroy wasn't comfortable asking.

In fact, Leroy was hesitant to mention Isaiah's name to Mattie. She'd seemed so fragile today. This was the most emotional he'd seen her since the wake. It was as if she was on the verge of tears off and on all day. Leroy was certain he was supposed to take care of her and her baby, but today he seemed to repel her.

Was the prospect of intimacy the entire problem? Or did she realize too late that marrying him was a mistake? He smacked his forehead with the palm of his hand. He had been kidding himself when he thought she would want to live as his wife.

This is just her first night. Give her some time to adjust to this new life.

The voice echoed the same mantra he'd been mentally repeating all week—*Give her time. Give her time. Give her time.* He'd continue to pray for patience. He'd give her all the support she needed as they tried to somehow make a life together.

Leroy scrubbed his hands down his sweat-drenched face and again entertained the idea of a battery-operated ceiling fan. Maybe some cold water would help him until he invented that much-needed fan. Yes, that definitely sounded like it might do the trick.

He pushed himself up from the bed and started down the hallway toward the stairs, passing the sewing room and the remaining two bedrooms, one of which stored Mattie's baby furniture and supplies. The other bedroom held more random boxes that needed to be stowed in the attic.

He shook his head as he started down the stairs. Mamm *accumulated a lot in her lifetime, but how have I accumulated so much on my own?* He had boxes full of his mother's unfinished sewing projects, material, favorite puzzles and games, and books. But he also had a multitude of keepsakes from his childhood, everything from rocks he'd collected to paraphernalia for keeping snakes and turtles as pets.

One of his drivers had told him about a television program about hoarders, who apparently were people living in homes overcome by possessions they didn't even need. Some of the people featured on the program made narrow pathways between all the piles so they could move through the rooms of their houses. Was he becoming the Amish equivalent of a hoarder? Perhaps Mattie could save him before their home consisted of a sea of boxes with only pathways leading them through the rooms.

A grin turned up the corners of Leroy's lips as his bare feet came into contact with the cool linoleum floor of the family room. He took a step and then stopped short when he heard a quiet noise coming from the downstairs bedroom. Leroy held his breath and listened. Had he imagined the sound?

When he heard it again, he moved to the bedroom door and listened. Why was he spying on his wife? Perhaps she was praying and having a private conversation with God. If so, then he should be ashamed of himself for listening in.

He heard the noise again, but this time it sounded loud and clear. Mattie was crying. No, she wasn't crying; she was sobbing.

Leroy cringed and a pang of regret crashed through him. He lifted his hand to knock on the door and then stopped, his arm freezing in midair. He couldn't possibly barge into her room and try to force her to open up to him. If Mattie had wanted to talk to him, then she would've asked him to stay instead of agreeing for him to go upstairs to sleep.

Still, guilt crawled up on his shoulders and sank its claws into his back. Perhaps he never should have proposed to her. Yet he hadn't forced her to marry him. He made the offer to help care for her and the baby, and the only condition he requested was that they would remain friends if she said no. She took her time considering it, and then she had even chosen their wedding date.

He folded his arms over his chest and swallowed a sigh. If only it were that simple. He definitely had to be responsible for her current misery. He had never seen her as cold and distant as she'd been today, both at the wedding and when they arrived home. He'd tried to tell himself everything would be fine, but now he had to admit that anguish and anxiety had been radiating off her as they drove to the house, and it only became worse when they walked inside.

Give her time. Give her time. Give her time.

It was the best advice for him to follow. Leroy had to shove himself away from her door and grant her privacy.

He padded toward the kitchen to get a glass of water. He would be the most patient, understanding, and loving husband he could be. No matter how much Mattie pushed him away, he would continue to shower her with emotional support.

And maybe, just maybe, one morning Mattie would wake up and realize she loved Leroy and wanted to make their marriage real.

CHAPTER 3

Mattie inhaled the delicious aromas of coffee and bacon. Why was she dreaming about breakfast food? And what was that noise? Had her stomach just rumbled or was that part of her dream?

She rolled over and sighed. Maybe she was just hungry. After all, she hadn't eaten much yesterday at the wedding since her stomach was a knot of nerves.

The wedding.

Her eyes flew open and scanned the room. Where was she? The bedroom looked familiar, but she couldn't place it.

Wait a minute.

She was at Leroy's house. She was Leroy's wife.

What time is it?

Mattie sat up and gasped when she looked at the clock on the nightstand. Almost eight thirty! It was her job to get up and cook for her husband so he could get to work on time. She wouldn't blame Leroy if he was furious with her. What a horrible way to start off her new marriage!

She shot out of bed and pulled on her robe before pushing her feet into her slippers. Glancing in the mirror attached to one of the dressers, she saw the hair falling past her waist was a tangled mess of golden waves. She pushed a brush through it and then hurried through the family room toward the kitchen. Her stomach gurgled again as she breathed in the succulent smells of breakfast. Leroy hadn't been exaggerating when he insisted he could cook.

Mattie stopped before she got to the doorway to the kitchen and sucked in a deep breath. She had to pull herself together and try to behave like an eager, hardworking, dutiful wife. If Leroy was upset with her, she would be strong and not cry. Instead, she would tell him he was right, and she would do better tomorrow.

With her spine erect, Mattie walked into the kitchen. Leroy was standing at the stove with his back to her, flipping eggs in a skillet. He was clad in the trousers and short-sleeved, gray button-down shirt he'd taken from his bedroom the night before. She took in the breadth of his shoulders, his strong, muscular back, and his height. When they were children, she and Leroy had briefly been the same height, but when he turned seventeen, he shot up to nearly six two, towering over her by several inches.

She glanced at the table and found platters with bacon, sausage, and toast in the center. The table had been set for two—complete with dishes, utensils, and mugs.

Guilt drenched her. Why hadn't she gotten up on time to make breakfast for him?

Because you cried until after one in the morning!

A grating sound drew her attention back to the stove, where Leroy scraped the eggs onto a platter. He turned and met her gaze, and she sucked in another breath, bracing herself for his displeasure. But to her utter shock, he smiled at her.

"*Gude mariye*, sleepyhead."

"I am so sorry." She walked toward him. "I forgot to set the alarm. I promise you it won't happen again. I'll set the alarm for six tomorrow, and I'll make sure your breakfast is waiting—"

He held up his hand to silence her, and she closed her mouth.

"Just calm down, now. Everything is fine." He frowned, placing the platter on the counter. "I hope I haven't given you the impression I expect things run on a set schedule. You need your rest, so I'm *froh* you slept in." He pointed toward the table. "And I hope you're hungry. I wasn't sure what you like to eat for breakfast, so I just whipped up a few things. Do you like hash browns? I can put them on too."

"I think this is more than enough, but *danki*." She reached for the platter of eggs. "Would you like me to put this on the table?"

"Sure. I'll get the *kaffi*."

She set the platter on the table and took a seat. He poured coffee into the two mugs before sitting down across from her.

After a silent prayer, they began serving themselves. An awkward silence filled the kitchen, hanging between them like a dense fog. For the first time in her life, Mattie had no idea what to say to Leroy. They didn't even have wedding plans to discuss anymore. It was as though they were strangers or merely acquaintances, and marrying him had somehow driven a wedge into their formerly close friendship.

"How did you sleep?" His voice seemed to echo in the otherwise silent house.

"Fine. *Danki*." Although her eyes were focused on her plate, she was aware of the weight of his stare.

"Was the bed comfortable? That mattress is ancient. We can replace it. In fact, we can go shopping for a mattress tomorrow if you want to."

She peeked up at his brown eyes, and they seemed to plead with her to talk to him. His expression was somehow desperate, and it confused her. What was bothering him? Was he upset after all, if not about breakfast, then about sleeping upstairs last night?

"The mattress was fine. *Danki*." She buttered her toast. "How did you sleep?"

The corners of his mouth tipped up. "Do you think the bishop would approve battery-operated ceiling fans for our *haus*?"

She blinked. "What do you mean?"

"Never mind." He scooped egg into his mouth.

"So it's hot upstairs," she said, now surmising what he meant. More guilt weighed heavily on her shoulders.

She had no right to steal the downstairs bedroom. After all, this was his house, and it had been in his father's family for three generations. It was the house where he and Joel had been born and had grown up, even after their father abandoned the family when Leroy was five and Joel was three. Leroy's uncles had paid all the bills for his mother, enabling the family to stay in this house.

After Joel married Dora, they built a house on Dora's father's farm. Since Dora was an only child, Joel was slated to take over the dairy farm when Dora's father retired. Leroy stayed behind to care for their mother. And now this was Leroy's house.

"You can have your room back. I'll sleep on the sofa."

"No. You will not sleep on that lumpy old sofa. I'm fine. I was just teasing you."

"Oh."

She searched her mind for something else to say. "What do you normally eat for breakfast?"

He lifted his mug. "I'm not fussy, really. Eggs and toast are fine. Sometimes I make pancakes or waffles."

"Okay." Mattie made a mental note. "Do you come home for lunch?"

Leroy nodded while chewing.

"What do you eat for lunch?"

He pointed toward the refrigerator. "There's lunch meat in there. I bought plenty of groceries, so if you feel like you want to make something different, just help yourself."

Mattie studied him. How did Leroy manage to run a business and a household alone? "So you've been doing your own grocery shopping, and you cook. But does Dora or Tillie do the cleaning?"

Leroy laughed, covering his mouth with his hand. "I'm sorry. I didn't mean to laugh. No, I don't ask Dora or Tillie to help me. I do it all." He swirled his fork in the air. "That's why the *haus* is never perfect."

She glanced around, not finding any visible dirt. "It looks *gut* to me."

"Well, since I'm the only occupant, I've always cleaned up after myself. I also do laundry once a week. Believe it or not, men can figure out how to use a wringer washer too."

"Oh. Do you need me to do laundry today?"

"Not unless you want to. You can do whatever you'd like today. I thought you might want to unpack and get settled."

"Okay." She bit into her toast. Leroy had spent the past three years as a bachelor in this big, quiet house and managed all the chores by himself. Did Amish women flirt with him at the grocery store, offering to help him with his shopping? Did they offer him recipes and cooking tips?

"What's on your mind?" Leaning forward, he raised his eyebrows.

"I was just wondering where you learned to cook."

He pointed toward a book on the end of the counter near the sink. "That was *mei mamm*'s favorite cookbook. I always helped her cook when I was a kid, and then I took over when she was too frail to manage meals herself. I guess you could say I've learned a lot through trial and error. I can handle most basic recipes, but I don't attempt anything too complicated."

"Oh."

"Did you pack a cookbook?" Leroy buttered a piece of toast.

"*Ya*, I did toss a couple of cookbooks into one of my boxes. I'll have to go through the book boxes and see which ones I brought. I can't remember what I grabbed."

Leroy scooped the remnants of his scrambled egg

onto his spoon. "I was thinking you might want to make your mother's raspberry pie."

"*Ya*, I can do that if you want me to."

"I'd love it. The raspberries come back every year whether I want them to or not. Your *mamm* used to ask for them, and I'd love it if you made a pie."

"I can make you a pie or two. I have her recipe box in one of the cartons I packed. She gave them to me as a wedding gift."

"Great. Like I said earlier, you can redecorate the *haus* any way you want. In fact, I have the baby's furniture up in one of the bedrooms. Feel free to get that ready. Just promise me you won't do any heavy lifting. I can help you move furniture tonight or tomorrow."

"Okay." She needed to take his focus off her and her list of things to do around his house. "How is the harness shop coming along?"

"It's going well. We're almost done painting. Once we finish that, we have to finish building the displays." Leroy's grin was wide. "It seems like just yesterday that Hank and I started working as apprentices for his *onkel*. We've wanted to own a shop since we were teenagers. It's actually going to happen." He filled her in on all the plans as they finished their breakfast. She tried to pay attention to the details surrounding the grand opening, but her thoughts wandered with memories of Isaiah.

When they were finished eating, Mattie pushed her shoulders back and sat up straight. It was time for her to move past her grief and be a responsible Amish woman. She had to make the best of this situation.

"I'll do the dishes." She stood to gather up their plates and utensils. "You can go get ready to go to the shop."

"Danki." He gave her another tender expression before disappearing from the kitchen.

Mattie carried all the dishes and platters to the counter and then filled up one side of the sink with hot, frothy water.

As she washed the dishes and then set them in the drainboard, she looked out the window above the sink. Two birds fluttered around a feeder, taking turns eating the seeds. What would her life be like now, and what kind of parents would she and Leroy be? Would they become a tender, loving couple that set the right example for her child?

Her thoughts continued to swirl as she scrubbed the utensils, rinsed them, and set them in the drainboard. Leroy had been sweet and accommodating since they'd arrived home last night. But how long would his patience last? At some point he might suddenly demand she start acting like a wife, including sharing his bed, no matter what the emotional cost was to her.

As she picked up Leroy's mug, a hand clamped onto her arm. Startled, she threw up her hands and shrieked, tossing the mug into the air. It crashed to the floor, sending an explosion of white ceramic pieces flittering around her slippers like confetti.

Mattie gasped and clutched a hand to her chest as she worked to slow her racing pulse. She looked up at Leroy as the corners of his dark eyes crinkled and his lips pressed into a thin line. His light-brown hair was combed, and stubble sprouted along his strong jaw. She took in his long, thin nose and chiseled cheekbones. He looked somehow different—older and more mature.

"I'm so sorry. I didn't mean to break your mug." Her lips trembled. "I'll clean it up."

"Don't move." He held up his hand to stop her. "You don't have shoes on, and the sharp edges could cut you through those thin slippers. I'll do it." He got a dustpan and broom from the pantry and swept up the mess before depositing it into the trash can.

"I'm so sorry." Her voice was thin and quaky. "I didn't hear you come up behind me."

"Stop apologizing. I'm the one who should be sorry." He grimaced. "I thought you heard me." He started to reach for her arm and then pulled it back. "It's just a mug, Mattie. It's not a big deal. Are you hurt?"

"No, I'm fine." She pushed a long strand of hair behind her shoulder, and his gaze lingered on her hair for a long moment before meeting her eyes again. It must have bothered him that she hadn't covered her head before coming out to the kitchen for breakfast. She should've grabbed a bandana or scarf, but she had rushed out of the bedroom to help with breakfast.

"I'll see you at lunch?" His eyes held hers.

"*Ya*. I'll have your lunch ready at noon, okay?"

"Sounds *gut*." He held her gaze for a moment longer and then headed out through the mudroom, the screen door clicking shut behind him.

Once he was gone, Mattie leaned forward on the sink and closed her eyes. When would she feel normal again, and would this new awkwardness between Leroy and her ever dissipate?

. . .

Leroy adjusted the straw hat on his head as he walked down the rock path toward the harness shop. The morning sun heated his face and birds sang in nearby trees, mocking his bleak mood. He frowned as the scene in the kitchen filled his mind. Mattie's eyes had been so wide when he'd startled her and caused her to break the mug. Then she'd cowered and apologized as if she'd committed an unforgivable sin.

Her reaction made no sense at all. Why on earth would Mattie ever fear him? When they were kids, they walked to and from school together, and some days they'd discuss everything from their schoolwork to their deepest secrets. They were always close, and he'd always been kind and respectful to her.

Surely Mattie believed Leroy would never, ever hurt her—physically or emotionally. He cherished her, which is part of the reason he wanted to take care of her now that Isaiah was gone.

Leroy understood Mattie still struggled with bereavement, and of course she wasn't ready for their relationship to be intimate, but he'd never imagined she'd completely close herself off to him. How was he supposed to maintain a close relationship and a marriage to someone who barely spoke to him and was startled when he touched her?

Give her time.

Leroy fished the key from his pocket and unlocked the harness shop. As he stepped inside, the smell of paint assaulted his senses. He propped open the front door and then opened the windows lining the walls. The harness shop was a large, open store with a work area in the back. Today Hank and Leroy planned to finish the painting while a friend etched "*Bird-in-Hand Harness Shop*" on one of the large front windows.

Leroy pulled on a smock and respirator. After shaking the paint can, he began painting walls in the main store area. He was grateful for the mundane work to keep him busy, and he longed to shut off his tumultuous thoughts.

As he moved the roller up and down the wall, his traitorous thoughts meandered back to his new wife. He'd made breakfast in an effort to give Mattie time to rest, both for her sake and for the baby's. But she had seemed to be on edge when she entered the kitchen. Her posture was rigid and her eyes were unsure as she spoke to him. Still, she was stunningly beautiful with her golden hair cascading in waves past her waist.

Leroy had only seen her hair uncovered once before. It was when they were teenagers and they'd spent the day with friends at a nearby lake. She'd been breathtaking dressed in a modest red-and-white bathing suit with a skirt covering her to mid-thigh.

Leroy and Mattie had laughed and teased each other as they splashed in the lake. Although she'd left her hair up in a tight bun, it had fallen out after her first jump into the water. She'd removed the remaining hairpins and allowed her thick hair to hang to the middle of her back as she jumped off a rock again and then splashed him in the face. He could still recall the sound of her shrieks and giggles as he'd splashed her back. When she swam away, her hair had clung to her back. He'd yearned to reach out and touch her hair, but that would have been much too forward. Instead, he'd chased her, splashing her again, and she'd giggled in response.

Where was that playful girl now? Was she simply drowning in grief, or was there more to it? And more importantly, how could he get her back?

"I thought you might sleep in today."

Leroy glanced over his shoulder to Hank standing in the doorway.

"Nope," Leroy said, his voice muffled by the respirator. "No sleeping in today. We have too much work to do." He dipped the roller into the paint tray and then moved it up and down the wall.

"Is everything all right?"

"Why wouldn't it be?" Leroy kept his back to Hank as he worked.

"It's just a feeling I get when I see you gripping that roller like you want to choke the life out of it," Hank quipped.

Leroy looked down at his hand, and his knuckles were white. He blew out a deep sigh before dipping the roller into the tray again.

Hank pulled on a smock and respirator and then picked up a roller and began painting at the far end of the same wall. They worked in silence for several minutes, and Leroy was grateful Hank didn't press him to explain his murky mood. The only sounds filling the shop were the whispers of the rollers moving up and down the wall.

"Danny should be here around eleven to etch the

window." Hank finally broke the silence. "Tim said he'd drop off the sign for the road either today or tomorrow."

"Great." Leroy set his roller in the pan and wiped the back of his hand across his sweaty brow.

Then he moved the roller through the paint and began painting in swift, choppy strokes. He had to find a way to convince Mattie he would never hurt her, but he had no idea how much more accommodating he could be. He could offer to move into the harness shop. Maybe he should put a bed in the back so she didn't have to even see him for a while.

How ridiculous would that be?

"Leroy," Hank said, his tone measured. "You can discuss whatever issue is eating at you if you think it might help your mood. I'm afraid you might snap that roller in half if you keep your frustrations bottled up. I don't mean to pry into your private business, but I'm not sure we have the budget for more rollers."

Leroy actually guffawed at his friend's lame attempt at a joke, and it loosened some of the tension in his back.

"Now that sounds more like you." Hank lifted his eyebrows.

"*Danki* for the laugh." Leroy set the roller in the pan. "I'm sorry. I didn't mean to bring my worries to work with me."

"It's all right. I've done it plenty of times." Hank hesitated. "Do you want to talk about it?"

"If you want to hear it." Leroy absently rubbed at the knots tightening in his left shoulder.

"Sure." Hank shrugged. "Isn't that what *freinden* are for?"

"Let's just say things aren't going the way I'd hoped." Leroy pulled off his respirator and sank down onto a nearby stepladder. "I didn't expect things to be perfect between Mattie and me, but she's acting like she's afraid of me now."

"Afraid of you?" Hank's dark eyebrows careened toward his hairline once again. "Why would Mattie be afraid of you?"

"She's been cold and distant ever since the wedding, and last night she was anxious and nervous around me. I'm trying my best to show her I'm not going to pressure her about . . . well, anything." Leroy rested his arms on his knees and peered off toward the wall that was half painted bright white. "I told her to stay in the downstairs bedroom, and I slept in one of the spare rooms upstairs last night. I got up to get a glass of water, and when I came downstairs, I heard her sobbing."

Hank removed his own respirator and frowned. "She's still grieving. There's no way of knowing how long she'll grieve for Isaiah, and you can't rush that."

"I know. I never intended on pushing her at all." Leroy paused to gather his thoughts. "I almost knocked on the door and offered to comfort her, but I figured she needed her space. She'll come to me when she's ready to talk.

"This morning I let her sleep in while I got up early. After taking care of the animals, I made breakfast. I guess I woke her because she came out while I was finishing up. She looked worried, and she apologized for not being up to cook for me. I told her it was fine, but breakfast was awkward. It was almost as if we've become strangers who hardly know each other."

Leroy paused for a beat. "You remember how Mattie and I were when we were teenagers. We used to talk about everything. I remember you once saying it was difficult to get a word in when Mattie and I were around because we talked so much."

Leroy pushed his hand through his thick hair and scowled. "Before I left to come out here, she was doing the dishes while I was in the bathroom getting ready for work. Anyway, when I went back into the kitchen to tell her I was leaving, I startled her, and she dropped and broke a mug. She practically cowered from me, as though she thought I was going to hit her or holler at her. I told her it was okay, and I cleaned it up." He threw his hands up in the air. "I don't understand it. Why would she act like I was going to hit her over a stupid mug? Was Isaiah abusive and we never knew it?"

Hank shook his head. "I don't think so. I never saw any signs Isaiah was violent or had a short temper. Besides, Isaiah was killed while protecting a woman from her abusive husband. Why would he hit his own *fraa* if he was determined to help a stranger?"

Leroy rubbed the back of his neck. "That's what I thought. Mattie's behavior doesn't make sense. She's never been nervous or jittery around me before. Why would it start now?"

"I don't really know." Hank pulled a stool over and sat down in front of Leroy. "You knew this was going to take some adjusting. She just lost her husband, and being with you like this is new. Now you're so much more than *freinden*."

Leroy covered his forehead with his hand. "You're not

saying anything I haven't already considered. I just had hoped we could still be *freinden*. I knew intimacy might take a long time to develop, but I didn't imagine I'd have to walk on eggshells around her. Actually, she's walking on eggshells around me. I keep telling her to make herself at home, but I feel like she's more of a guest." He froze after the words leapt from his mouth.

"What's going through your mind, Leroy?"

"I wonder if she's going to leave me like *mei dat* left *mei mamm*."

"I doubt that will happen. You've been close a long time, and she cares deeply for you."

"My parents were childhood *freinden* too. *Mei dat* just decided he didn't love *mei mamm* anymore and he wanted more out of life. He left all three of us and went to Florida with a woman he'd met at a hardware store."

Hank raised an eyebrow. "I don't think Mattie will leave you for a man she meets at a hardware store or even the farmer's market. Just be patient and pray for her. Let her work through all her emotions at her own pace and she'll come to realize you're not all that bad after all."

Leroy snickered. "Gee, thanks, buddy."

"You're welcome." Hank pointed toward the wall. "That wall is not going to paint itself. Let's get this done so we can open the shop next week and start earning back the money we're wasting on this place."

CHAPTER 4

Determination flowed through Mattie's veins. She was going to make Leroy's house feel more like her home today. After finishing the dishes, she moved to the bedroom where she dressed, pinned up her hair and shielded it with her prayer covering, and then started making the bed.

She moved her hand across the beautiful red, blue, and tan log cabin quilt, admiring the craftsmanship. She made a mental note to ask Leroy if his mother had made it. She yearned to quilt after touching the intricate stitching. She had started a quilt for the baby but then stopped working on it after Isaiah died. Her fingers itched to get back to the one task she loved so dearly. Not only did she love to sew and quilt, but it also helped her work through her thoughts and feelings, acting as a balm when she needed an emotional release.

She finished making the bed and then set off to unpack. She pulled her suitcase and box of clothes out of the closet again and began setting items on the bed. Since Leroy had told her she could rearrange whatever she wanted, she peeked in the dresser drawers. The tall dresser was filled with Leroy's clothes, but the drawers in the shorter dresser, which also had shelves and a mirror, were empty. Had he emptied out this dresser for her? The idea warmed something deep inside of her. Leroy was going out of his way for her and her child, and she was grateful.

She put her underwear and stockings in the top drawers of the dresser. She was adding her pajamas to the second drawer when she heard a loud knock.

"Hello? Mattie?" Tillie's voice sang out from the back of the house. "May I come in?"

"Hi, Tillie! I'm in the downstairs bedroom," Mattie called. "Come on back."

Tillie's footfalls echoed through the first floor before she appeared in the doorway holding a pie plate. The aroma of fruit pie filled the bedroom.

"Hi. How are you this morning?"

"I'm fine." Mattie pointed to the pie. "That smells amazing. Is it cherry?"

"*Ya.*" Tillie held up the plate. "I thought I'd make something for you and Leroy to share tonight. I hope you like cherries."

"I love cherries. *Danki.*"

"May I help you unpack?" Tillie offered.

"That would be great, but I assume you have plenty of your own chores to do today."

"Oh, no. I'd love to help you." Tillie pointed toward the kitchen. "Let me just put this away and then I'll be in to help you."

"*Danki.*" When an ache radiated from Mattie's lower back down toward her feet, she sat down on the edge of the bed and waited for Tillie to return. She glanced toward the closet where Leroy's shirts and trousers hung. Could she make room for her dresses and aprons beside his clothes, just in case he decided not to move them upstairs after all?

"What can I do to help?" Tillie appeared in the doorway again and rubbed her hands together.

Mattie pointed toward the closet. "Do you think there's enough room in there for my dresses and aprons?"

"We can make room." Tillie pushed the trousers and shirts over to the right, jamming them together to create an open area. "There's plenty of room now. Would you like me to hang them up for you?"

"That would be *wunderbaar*. I think I need to rest a bit."

Tillie's eyes rounded. "Are you feeling okay?"

Mattie gave Tillie a handful of hangers from the box beside her on the bed. "*Ya*, but my arms, legs, and back are sore. I get winded so easily now. I thought I was supposed to have a burst of energy."

"I've heard that happens at the very end." Tillie hung up the first dress Mattie handed to her. "*Mei aenti* told me she got a burst of energy just before my cousin was born, and she cleaned the entire *haus*. She even washed the windows. Apparently it's called nesting. After you're done nesting, the baby will be born."

"*Ya, mei mamm* said that too."

As she handed Tillie each dress and apron, anxiety bubbled up inside of her again. She had no idea how to move forward with Leroy and this strange new relationship that now existed between them. Mattie yearned to discuss her confusing feelings with a close friend, but since Tillie was married to Leroy's best friend, she didn't want to make Tillie feel uncomfortable. Instead, she tried to think of something mundane to talk about.

"Leroy told me work on the harness shop is progressing well," Mattie finally said.

"Oh, *ya*, it is." Tillie beamed as she took another dress from Mattie's hand. "Someone is coming to etch the name on the glass front today, and another man is going to drop off the sign for the street. We're right on track for the grand opening next Saturday."

"It's next Saturday? That's great."

"Leroy didn't tell you?" Tillie raised her eyebrows.

"Maybe it slipped his mind," Mattie said quickly. She couldn't bring herself to admit she'd been so focused on her own worries and bereavement that she hadn't heard much of what Leroy shared with her at breakfast.

"*Ya*, maybe. It's going to be fantastic. I suggested we have a party after the store closes for the day. Leroy invited his *bruder* to come. You should invite your family too. We'll have a *gut* time."

"That sounds like fun. I can make some pies."

"That's a great idea. It's going to be a wonderful celebration, you know?" Tillie gushed as she hung up the first of Mattie's sweaters. "Hank and Leroy have talked about having their own shop for years, and now it's going to finally happen."

"You're right. It will be a big celebration."

As Mattie opened a box full of her shoes, a conversation she'd witnessed between Hank and Leroy when they were twenty flooded her mind. They were sitting by the volleyball court at a youth gathering discussing their apprenticeship with Leroy's uncle who ran a harness shop in Ronks. Leroy announced he enjoyed working for Hank's uncle but he wanted his own shop. Hank and Leroy talked about saving their money, buying houses next door to each other, and building a shop they would own together. Leroy and Hank's dream had been born on that very day, and Mattie had been there to witness it. Now, six years later, it was coming true. She was grateful she would be a part of the grand opening to celebrate with her friends.

"Would you like me to put those shoes in the closet?" Tillie offered.

"*Ya. Danki.*" Mattie handed her the box and then opened another one.

She gaped at the sight of her favorite knick-knacks, most of which were gifts from Isaiah. She picked up the small wooden box he'd given her for her birthday when they first started dating. Inside the box was a heart-shaped stone he'd given her as a surprise gift on their six-month dating anniversary. She lifted the heart and moved her fingers over the smooth edges.

"Mattie?"

She peeked up at Tillie. "I'm sorry." She placed the rock back into the box and closed the lid. "I just found something Isaiah gave me." She cleared her throat and placed the box on the dresser where she had put her clothes. Like the drawers, the top of the dresser was bare. *Did Leroy clear it off just for me?*

"This has to be so difficult for you. I'm sorry you're going through so much."

"*Danki.*" Mattie pulled out a wooden frame with a

picture of a sunset Isaiah gave her for Christmas last
year, along with two small candles, one apple spice
scented and the other cotton candy scented. She lost
herself in the memories of when Isaiah had surprised
her with the special candles. She loved to burn them at
night when they would sit in their family room and talk.
She took her time arranging the things on the dresser
to avoid Tillie's gaze.

"Mattie?"

She looked over her shoulder to where Tillie stood by
the closet. *"Ya?"*

"Is something wrong?" Tillie's milk chocolate eyes
studied her intently.

"No. Everything is fine." Mattie nodded despite her
surging grief. "I was just thinking about when Isaiah
gave me these things. He loved to buy me little trinkets.
Candles were his favorite. I had a candle that smelled
like hazelnut coffee, but I dropped it and it broke. He
promised to get me another one, but he never had a
chance." Her throat dried, and she tried to clear it against
threatening tears.

"You must miss him a lot."

"All the time." Mattie picked up the apple spice-
scented candle and touched the cool glass lid. "I hope
I can make this work with Leroy." She cringed as she
admitted the words aloud.

"What do you mean?"

"Everything feels so strange now. I feel like I'm going
to let him down."

Tillie moved to her side, but Mattie kept her eyes
focused on the candle.

"Leroy is a patient man." Tillie rested her hand on Mattie's arm. "He knows you both need to let your relationship evolve naturally over time. He doesn't expect you to suddenly forget Isaiah. He understands you have to grieve. Like the Bible says, 'There is a time for everything, and a season for every activity under the heavens . . . a time to mourn and a time to dance.'" She gave her a bleak smile. "Leroy has waited for you all these years, and he will wait as long as he has to."

"What do you mean?" Mattie brushed her hand over her cheeks.

Tillie furrowed her brow as if in disbelief. "You mean you don't know?"

"Don't know what?"

"I've known you and Leroy for only the past five years, but I know Leroy has loved you since long before that."

Mattie blinked. "*Ya*, he loves me as a *freind*."

"No, Mattie. He truly *loves* you. He was so excited to marry you." Tillie's expression was earnest. "I talked to Hank about it the other night. Hank has always had a hunch that Leroy cared about you. I suggested that maybe Leroy's feelings for you were what was preventing him from ever marrying, and Hank agreed. Leroy actually admitted it to Hank when he told Hank he was going to propose to you. He's always loved you, so he didn't have room in his heart for another woman."

Shaking her head, Mattie opened her mouth to protest, but Tillie held up one finger, shushing her.

"Please. Just think about it for a moment. Leroy had never had a long-term girlfriend, but he jumped at the chance to marry you. Why would he be eager to marry you and take care of your child unless he truly cared about you?"

"No, no, no." Mattie took a step backward, bumping her hip into the dresser as confusion wafted over her. "That's not true. Leroy only offered to marry me because as a *freind* he took pity on my *boppli* and me. We had no real home, and he has this big *haus* all to himself. He's also starting a new business, and he needs someone to help him take care of the *haus* and do all the chores and grocery shopping. We're going to help each other. That's all it is."

Tillie clicked her tongue. "You can't honestly believe that. You know what a great man Leroy is. He's kind and thoughtful. He would never use you to run his household. Don't you see the love in his eyes when he looks at you?"

Tillie has to be wrong! Leroy can't love me!

Leroy was Mattie's confidant when she needed to talk to someone outside of her family. Leroy listened to her without judgment when she first met Isaiah and she was certain she was falling in love with him. Then Leroy listened as she confided her deepest feelings and grief about Isaiah. He helped her move her belongings out of the rented house, and then he visited her frequently at her parents' house. He even allowed Mattie to sob on his shoulder more than once. Leroy was the one person Mattie could count on.

But she never thought he loved her as more than a friend.

Air gushed from her lungs in a loud *whoosh* as it all

came into clear focus in Mattie's mind. Tillie had to be right. There was no other reason why a man would devote his life to a widow if he didn't love her. But at the same time, Leroy was never honest about his feelings for her. How could she have been so blind that she hadn't figured this out on her own?

Why oh why was Mattie's world still spinning out of control? The room was closing in on her, and she had to get out of there before she suffocated on her raging emotions.

She walked out into the family room and started unpacking boxes, stacking books randomly on the bookshelf to keep busy. She had to get rid of this nervous energy before she went crazy. She didn't want to hear this truth about Leroy. Her heart couldn't handle it. She couldn't love Leroy the same way he loved her, and she couldn't handle the fact that she was going to hurt him when he understood she could never love him completely.

"Mattie, stop. Please listen to me." Tillie took Mattie's arm. "I don't understand why you're upset about this. You and Leroy are married now. Just take your time and let your marriage grow. You both need a period of adjustment. Everything will be just fine."

Her friend's words settled over her. "I understand what you're saying, but it still feels wrong. Our love is one-sided. I can't give Leroy the love he feels for me."

"Maybe your feelings for Leroy will develop over time. I've heard of that happening, and there's nothing wrong with that."

"No, no." Mattie shook her head and pain began

brewing behind her eyes. "I can't love them both, Isaiah and Leroy. I'm still in mourning. How can I fall in love so quickly? That's disrespectful to Isaiah."

"Isaiah would understand." Tillie sat down on one of the book boxes. "If something had happened to you, wouldn't you have wanted Isaiah to move on with his life?"

"I don't know. I never thought about it."

"Would you have wanted him to live the rest of his life alone?" Tillie rested her elbows on her knees. "We're not even thirty yet. We're still young. Isaiah would understand that you have to go on." She pointed to Mattie's belly. "You have to raise your *kind*, and Isaiah would want your *boppli* to have a *dat* to guide him or her. You're not doing anything disrespectful. You're moving on with your life."

Tillie made it all sound too simple. Mattie rubbed her brow, where her headache throbbed. Could Mattie ever love Leroy the way he loved her? It seemed an impossible task.

Because Isaiah stole my heart the moment I met him.

Reaching toward her, Tillie touched Mattie's hand. "I'm sorry for upsetting you. I just wanted to tell you everything will be okay. Leroy will give you all the time you need to adjust." She stood and opened the box on which she had been sitting. "Let's unpack these boxes before I have to go home and make lunch. You look exhausted. Would you like to just sit and give me instructions?"

"No, *danki*. I'll help." Mattie returned to her unpacking, and Tillie's words echoed through her mind. She could never adjust to being Leroy's wife now, not when she knew how he truly felt about her.

A heavy burden settled over Mattie's shoulders, but she straightened, pushed her shoulders back. She couldn't love Leroy the same way he loved her, but Mattie had to try harder to be the wife he deserved. She'd start by making him a special meal for supper tonight. The plan took shape in her mind. She could make him steak, potatoes, and homemade bread—Isaiah's favorite. Surely Leroy would enjoy it too.

Somehow they would make this marriage work.

CHAPTER 5

A delicious aroma filled Leroy's senses, causing his stomach to gurgle as he walked into the mudroom later that evening. His eyes widened with a mixture of surprise and excitement as he hung his hat on one of the hooks by the door and stepped out of his boots.

He entered the kitchen as Mattie placed a bowl of mashed potatoes in the center of the table. She looked radiant, clad in the same rose-colored dress and black apron he'd seen at lunchtime. For a brief moment, he longed for a camera so he could snap a photo of her and cherish it forever. Instead, he'd do his best to commit the moment to memory.

"Hi." She gave him a shy smile and then gestured at the table. "I thought I'd make you something nice for supper. I hope you're hungry. I have steak and home-made bread too."

"I'm famished. *Danki.*" Leroy walked over to the table and grinned. He could get used to this—coming home to his beautiful wife and a delicious meal. He was abundantly blessed.

Mattie pointed to his chair. "Have a seat. Everything is ready."

He pointed at the empty glasses sitting expectantly

by their dinner plates. "Let me get the pitcher of water." He started for the refrigerator.

"No, I'll get it. You worked all day." She scurried past him toward the refrigerator. Then she returned to the table and filled the glasses.

"Mattie," he said gently. "I don't mind helping you."

"It's okay." She set the pitcher on the table. "Let's pray, *ya*?"

He nodded, and they sat down across from each other. After a silent prayer, they began filling their plates, and the sounds of cutlery scraping the dishes filled the big kitchen.

Leroy peeked up at her moving her mashed potatoes around the plate with her spoon. He longed to get her to open up to him like she had the day of the wake. He gripped his fork as the memories of that day flooded his mind.

. . .

Leroy arrived at the wake and immediately searched the house for Mattie. When Lizanne told him Mattie had gone outside to get some air, he poured two mugs of coffee from the percolator in the kitchen and hustled out the back door. The cool air hit his body like a brick wall, and he pulled it into his lungs as he hurried down the back steps toward the barn.

Soon the barn came into view, and his pulse and his steps sped up as he moved up the path to where Mattie was sitting on a bench. He silently prayed for the right words to comfort her.

When he was grieving the loss of his mother three years ago, he appreciated his friends who would sit quietly beside him and listen. No amount of advice or words of sympathy helped him, but a friend who lent him an ear offered the solace he craved. He prayed he could offer Mattie the same comfort he'd received, even though he imagined her grief was much deeper and more painful than what he'd suffered.

Leroy's hands trembled as he approached the bench. Mattie's head was bent as she studied a crumpled tissue in the lap of her black dress. Her eyes were dull and rimmed with purple shadows, and her angelic face was contorted into a picture of grief.

"Mattie," he said softly, standing beside her.

"Leroy." Her voice was thick and shaky. "I didn't see you." She wiped the tissue over her face.

"May I join you?" How he longed to see her gorgeous smile again.

"That would be nice." She shoved to the far side of the bench and patted the seat beside her. "Sit."

He sat down on the bench and held up a mug. "Thirsty?"

"*Ya. Danki.*"

Leroy handed her one of the mugs. Mattie immediately took a drink, and he was glad he'd brought the coffee with him. When she shivered, he removed his jacket and slipped it over her thin shoulders.

"*Danki.*" She shoved her arms through the sleeves and hugged the jacket to her middle.

"*Gern gschehne.*" Leroy sipped his coffee.

She looked up at him. "How'd you know I was out here?"

"Lizzie told me."

"She's been fussing over me like a mother hen." Her voice held a hard edge of resentment. "Did she send you out here to fetch me?"

"No. I asked her where you were, and she told me you'd gone out for a walk to get some air. I wanted to check on you."

"Oh."

Then she turned her attention back to the barn as if it held some important information. He forced himself to remain quiet and allow her to share her thoughts at her own pace. They sat in silence for several moments. He took another drink from the mug and then ran his fingers over its warmth.

"He was going to the bank," she finally said.

Leroy held his breath as he waited for her to continue.

Mattie kept her eyes focused on the barn as she continued. "He hadn't gotten to the bank before it closed on Saturday, and he had to deposit his paycheck. He said the hinges broke on one of the barn doors during the storm and he was going to fix it when he got back home." A tear streamed down her cheek, and he fought the urge to wipe it away. "He never made it back home to repair the door."

He looked at the barn, and both doors were fine.

"Al and a few of his *freinden* came over yesterday and fixed it." She answered his unspoken question.

"Oh." Leroy turned toward her, and her lower lip trembled.

"I didn't want him to go to the bank. I had this terrible feeling that took hold of me when he said he was going.

I walked out on the porch with him, and he kissed me good-bye. When he started down the steps, I called him back, and he kissed me again. I wanted to pull him into the house and make him stay with me, but I didn't. I didn't tell him how I felt, and I let him go." She looked up at Leroy as tears poured from her eyes. "It's all my fault that he's dead." She placed the mug on the bench beside her.

"No, no. It's not your fault at all."

"That was the last time I saw him. It was the last time I heard his voice. And *mei dat* had to identify Isaiah's body, and he told me Isaiah was . . . well, he wasn't . . ." Her voice trailed off, and she covered her face with her hands as sobs racked her body.

Leroy froze. What should he do? He wanted to pull her into his arms, but he feared it would be too forward if he touched her. The most they'd ever touched was when she'd fallen while playing volleyball at a youth gathering and he helped her up. Then again, she'd hugged him after his mother died. Perhaps touching now would be permissible due to the circumstances.

Leroy touched her arm, and she leaned over, wrapping her arms around his neck. She sobbed into his chest, and he rubbed her back with his free hand.

"It's okay," he whispered into her prayer covering. "It's not your fault." He breathed in her scent, flowery shampoo mixed with soap. He held his breath as he longed to take away her pain.

Her sobs subsided, and she wiped her eyes before resting her cheek on his shoulder. "The policemen said Isaiah saved a woman from her abusive husband. She had a restraining order against him, and he'd followed her to the bank. They say Isaiah is a hero. I'm grateful she's alive, but where does that leave me and our baby?" She sniffed. "I'm a terrible person for saying this, but I want him to still be alive. I'd rather he be with me than be a hero. You think I'm horrible, right?"

"No, no." He rubbed her back again. "You're not terrible. You're grieving. You love Isaiah."

"*Ya*, I do." She continued to rest her cheek on his shoulder. "I can't believe he's gone. I don't know what I'm going to do."

"You don't need to decide that today. No one is rushing you."

"I have to move out. Isaiah's paychecks from the hardware store pay for our rent and food. I can't afford to live here on my own. I'm going to have to move in with my parents and sleep on their sofa. Lizzie said I could stay with her and Al, but they're newlyweds. They don't need an extra person in their *haus*."

She looked up at him and something flickered in her eyes. She suddenly sat up and shifted away from him. "I'm sorry. I didn't mean to be so forward with you."

"It's fine." He flicked an imaginary piece of lint off his dark trousers to avoid her abashed expression. "We're *freinden*, right?"

"Always," she said with confidence.

"Then it's okay." He smiled at her, and her shoulders relaxed slightly.

She fiddled with the hem of his jacket as her gaze moved back to the barn. "Is the *haus* still full of people?"

"*Ya*." He rested his arm on the back of the bench,

stretching it out behind her. "It's stuffy in there. I understand why you needed to come outside."

They were silent again, and she took a drink from
her mug of coffee. Leroy did the same, just to keep himself busy.

"I can't believe he's gone. I feel like I'm stuck in this
horrible nightmare." She blew out a shuddering breath
as her fingers continued to move over the hem of the
jacket. "I supposed I shouldn't be feeling sorry for myself, but *mei kind* won't have a *dat* either."

Leroy sat up straighter. He couldn't stay silent any
longer. He had to try to console her. But what would
help her the most?

Just be honest. Tell her how you feel.

"I know platitudes won't help you right now, but I
am sorry, Mattie." His voice sounded thin and foreign
to him. "I liked Isaiah. He was a *gut* man, and he was
gut to you. If there's anything I can do to help you, just
ask me."

"*Danki,*" she whispered.

"*Gern gschehne.*" He longed to hug her again. He wanted
to wipe away her tears. But instead, he sat cemented in
place. "Do you want me to take you to your parents' *haus*
to get some rest?"

"No, *danki.* I'd rather just sit out here for a while
longer." She hugged Leroy's jacket closer to her body.

"Do you want me to stay with you?"

"*Ya.* Please don't leave, Leroy."

"I'll stay as long as you need me to." Leroy rested his
ankle on his opposite knee and silently prayed, asking
God to heal Mattie's shattered heart.

. . .

The scraping of Mattie's spoon on her plate brought Leroy back to the present. He pondered why she didn't talk to him anymore and what had gone wrong in their formerly close friendship. Didn't she know by now that he was giving her the time she needed? How could he close the chasm expanding between them?

"The lettering is done on the front window of the shop," he said, hoping to open the door to an easy conversation. She hadn't talked much at lunch either, and he would discuss anything to get her to talk to him.

"Oh?" She raised her eyebrows.

"*Ya.*" He lifted his glass of water. "You need to come and see it."

"I will." She forked a piece of steak.

"The sign is at the road too. You can see it out the front windows."

"I saw it earlier. It's nice."

"I covered it up for now since we're not open yet. I'll uncover it next Saturday for the grand opening. I also called to confirm the ads we're running in the local papers."

"*Gut.*" Mattie chewed and swallowed another piece of steak, then scooped potato onto her spoon. "I thought I could make some pies."

"Great." Mattie wanted to participate in the grand opening. This was progress! "Did you finish your unpacking?"

"*Ya.*" She ran her fingers over her glass of water. "Tillie helped me. I finished the bedroom and the books. I didn't get upstairs to the baby's room, but I can do that another day."

"Do you need my help with anything? I can move furniture in the bedroom if you'd like."

"The bedroom is fine."

"Is there enough room in the closet?"

Mattie paused, watching him for a moment.

Talk to me! Please talk to me!

"The closet is fine," she finally said, not even mentioning his clothes were still there.

He released the breath he'd been holding. "I'll move my clothes upstairs tonight."

"There's no rush. I can make do." She ate another scoop of potatoes. "Who made the quilt on your bed?" She cleared her throat. "I mean, our bed."

"Mei mamm."

"I thought so." She looked down at her dinner plate. "I want to get back to sewing soon. I miss it. That quilt is gorgeous."

The sound of Mattie's sewing machine humming on the second floor would be music to his ears. "Do you need a new sewing machine?"

She shook her head. "There's nothing wrong with mine. Don't waste your money."

"Our money. We're in this together, remember?"

Mattie met his gaze and held it for a long moment. "You don't need to spend any money on a new sewing machine. The *boppli* will be here in less than two months, and I'm going to need some supplies. I wouldn't feel right about you spending money on a new sewing machine when I need to ask you for more baby things."

Leroy frowned. "I don't mind buying anything for you or for the *boppli*."

"*Danki*." She smiled. "Tell me more about the grand opening. May I invite my family to come to it?"

"*Ya*, you should invite them," Leroy told her. "That would be great. We're hoping to open at eight on Saturday." He went into a detailed discussion of how he and Hank envisioned the event would go.

Soon their plates were clean, and Mattie brought the cherry pie Tillie made and coffee to the table. They each ate a piece of pie while Leroy continued to talk about his vision for the harness shop.

When their dessert was gone, he helped her take the dishes to the counter. "You can wash, and I'll dry," he offered.

"I can do the dishes. You go do whatever it is you do after supper."

Leroy lingered beside her as the sudsy water filled the sink. He fought the urge to touch her arm and tell her to relax. But after her shriek and the resulting shattered mug this morning, he decided it was best not to risk a broken dish.

"All right. I'm going to go take care of the animals. Call me if you need anything."

He walked toward the mudroom and then stopped and spun, facing her once again. "Mattie," he said, and she looked over her shoulder at him. "*Danki* for an *appeditlich* dinner."

"*Gern gschehne.* I'm *froh* you liked it."

Leroy sighed as he descended the porch steps toward the barn. He silently prayed for guidance to bring back the funny, talkative Mattie who had walked with him to school and played volleyball with him at youth gatherings.

CHAPTER 6

The hot July sun beat down on her prayer covering and warmed her neck as Mattie glanced toward the harness shop, anticipation rushing through her. It was only Wednesday morning, but three parking spaces and the hitching post already waited patiently for customers to visit the store for the grand opening on Saturday.

She hung the last pair of Leroy's trousers on the clothesline that stretched from the back porch to the barn as she imagined a crowd of tourists outside the store, waiting for the doors to open for business for the first time.

Leroy and Hank had worked late Saturday, Monday, and Tuesday as they built the displays to hold all the leather creations they planned to sell. Weeks ago they'd met with vendors to arrange to sell saddles and other supplies for horses and horseback riding. Leroy was giddy each evening as he shared the store's progress, and Mattie hoped the store would be successful and meet all his and Hank's expectations.

Mattie balanced the wicker laundry basket on her hip as she ambled into the house. A dull ache flared at her mid-back before moving down her legs.

After setting the basket on the counter in the large

laundry room, she massaged her lower back with her fingertips and looked around. She'd rearranged a few of the shelves this morning to make the space more functional. Although she'd loved the tiny house she'd shared with Isaiah, she appreciated living in a house large enough that she could organize to her liking.

She and Leroy had settled into an amiable routine over the last week. They had attended church for the first time as a married couple on Sunday, and it felt strange not to wear a black dress in mourning for Isaiah. Every night she cooked Isaiah's favorite meals for Leroy, and he enjoyed them, telling her the food was delicious before offering to help with the dishes.

Mattie continued to sleep alone in the downstairs bedroom while Leroy retreated to his upstairs bedroom, the one where he had no doubt put his clothes. Last night she had almost invited him to stay with her in the bedroom so she wouldn't be alone with her agonizing thoughts, but she didn't want him to assume she was ready for the intimacy he would expect. She didn't know when she'd be ready for that, and she dreaded what would happen after the baby was born. How long could she continue to refuse him?

Heaving a deep sigh, Mattie walked through the kitchen and family room and climbed the spiral staircase to the second floor. She yearned to organize the sewing room so she could lose herself in a productive task. Perhaps sewing would help her sort through her confusing thoughts and worries.

She padded down the hallway, stopping to peek into the first room. The crib, rocking chair, dresser, changing table, and boxes of baby clothes that had been stored in her sister's attic when she moved out of the rented house were all there. Although the room wasn't organized, it resembled a baby's room.

Mattie stepped inside and ran her hand over the furniture as thoughts of Isaiah crashed over her. Isaiah had wanted to spend hours discussing what they hoped to include in the house they planned to build someday. Although she hadn't wanted him to worry about a place they couldn't yet afford to build, she enjoyed focusing on how many bedrooms they would have. Mattie had dreamt of filling the house with love and children, but all those dreams had been dashed that Monday morning in February.

Bereavement seemed to come bubbling up from her toes. She dropped into the rocking chair, hugged her arms to her middle, and sobbed.

. . .

Leroy hung his hat on the peg on the wall in the mudroom and walked into the kitchen. He rubbed at the stubble on his chin when he found the kitchen empty and the table clear. The clock above the stove read twelve thirty, and he expected to find Mattie waiting to eat lunch with him. When he looked into the laundry room and found it empty, too, a prickle of worry started at the base of his neck.

"Mattie?" He walked through the family room to the bedroom. Alarm rushed through him when he found them both empty as well. "Mattie?"

Where was she? Had she gone out to the shanty to make a phone call or was she upstairs working on the baby's or her sewing room? He started up the stairs. When his boots hit the top step, he heard a noise coming from down the hallway.

"Mattie?" He headed toward the first bedroom. He glanced into it, and his stomach dropped. Mattie was sobbing as she moved back and forth in the rocking chair.

"*Ach*, Mattie." This time he whispered her name, dropping to his knees in front of the chair. "Please tell me what's wrong." He touched her arm as she pulled a tissue from her pocket and wiped her eyes and nose.

She blinked and sat up straight, smoothing her hands over her dress. "Is it lunchtime already?"

His heart cracked at the pain and grief in her eyes. "It is, but I'm not worried about food. Lunch can wait. I'm worried about you."

"I'm so sorry. I came in here to start organizing and unpacking the boxes, and I lost track of time." She tried to stand, and he nudged her back into the seat.

"Sit."

"I don't need to sit. I'm fine. I need to make your lunch." She started to get up again, but he shook his head.

"Forget lunch. You're more important to me."

Her eyes widened.

"Talk to me. I can't stand this silence and awkwardness between us."

When she cast her eyes to her lap, her response was clear. She wasn't going to talk to him. His shoulders sagged.

"I can't help you if you don't talk to me." When she remained silent, disappointment and hurt sliced through him. "Fine, then." He pulled a footstool over to her chair and sat on it. "If you won't talk to me, then I'll talk to you."

Mattie looked down at him through her long blonde eyelashes.

"I remember the day you met Isaiah," he began, and she sat up straight, her intelligent eyes focused on him. "We were at a youth gathering over in Ronks, and Isaiah's friend's youth group was there. We were all playing volleyball, and you were on the same team as Hank and me. I remember thinking Isaiah was pretentious wearing those fancy mirrored sunglasses. In fact, I was going to say something to you about him, but you were already staring at him with wonder in your eyes."

To his surprise, Mattie laughed, and her cheeks blushed hot pink. She looked adorable. "I was that obvious, huh?"

Aha! He'd finally gotten her to talk. He grinned. *This is working.*

"*Ya*, your feelings were obvious. But Isaiah had noticed you too. After the game, he immediately walked over to you." Leroy rested his elbows on his thighs. "I really couldn't blame him for talking to you. After all, you were the prettiest *maedel* in our youth group." He held up his finger in warning. "Now, don't tell your *schweschder* I said that. Lizzie might be upset to hear she's not the prettiest."

Mattie chuckled, wiping her eyes. "You always did exaggerate about things."

"I'm not exaggerating. You were the prettiest, and you still are."

"You're sweet."

"I'm just stating the obvious. I knew it was love at first sight when you and Isaiah talked. Don't repeat that to Hank because he'll make fun of me and say I'm not manly enough."

Mattie gave him a small smile, but he sensed the grief still there. When a tear trickled down her cheek, he reached over and brushed it away. She flinched, and he regretted the forwardness. He hoped she wouldn't always flinch from his touch and that someday she would learn to trust him. "I'm sorry you lost him. I know you were both very *froh* together."

She looked down at her belly and moved her hands over it.

"Did you and Isaiah talk about names for the *boppli*?" He tried his best to tread lightly, but he hoped she would respond.

Mattie met his gaze. "*Ya*, he said he wanted Jacob after his *daadi* if it was a *bu*."

"And for a *maedel*?"

Mattie's fingers traced circles on her belly. "I was thinking of Veronica or Elizabeth for a girl."

"Those are great names."

"*Danki.*" She sighed.

He stood and held out his hand. "May I make you lunch?"

Mattie hesitated. When she accepted his hand, he lifted her to her feet. "No, that's my job. I'll make lunch for you."

"No, I will cook for you. You haven't let me cook once since last Wednesday, and I'm afraid I might get rusty."

Mattie gave him a genuine smile and warmth flowed through his veins. They walked to the hallway and then she stopped.

"Could I see the room you want to make into a sewing room?"

"Of course." Leroy steered her toward the room across the hallway. "I was thinking this might make a *gut* sewing room for you. The natural light is *gut* in here."

She walked over to her sewing machine, which Leroy had set by the window. "This was your *mamm*'s sewing room, wasn't it?"

"That's right." He leaned a shoulder against the door-frame.

"*Mei mamm* and I loved coming here for quilting bees." Mattie hugged her arms to her middle. "Your *mamm* was so sweet. I adored her."

"She thought a lot of you too. She once said you were like the *dochder* she never had. She'd be thrilled to know we're married now." When her smile faded, he said quickly, "I didn't mean she would be *froh* with the circumstances around our marriage. She'd be sorry to hear Isaiah died, but she'd be *froh* you and I are together."

"I understand." She touched her sewing machine and then glanced around at her boxes marked "*Sewing Material and Supplies.*" "I'd like to get back to sewing. I want to make quilts. I can also make potholders and other little things, like tissue packet covers and *kaffi* cup covers."

Leroy's shoulders relaxed slightly. "That would be great."

"I'll sell them." She looked over at him. "I can host dinners to help you with bills, too, but I'll have to wait until after the *boppli* is a little older. I can prepare the meals and clean while the *boppli* naps."

"That's *wunderbaar*, but please don't feel any pressure to work right away after the *boppli* is born. I have money in the bank. We're fine right now." The muscles in his back loosened. It was refreshing to hear her making plans. She was finally imagining herself as his partner and his wife.

Mattie scanned the room, then looked over at him again. "Are you hungry?"

"I am, but I can wait. Take your time."

"Let's go eat. I can organize the room later."

"I'll help you." He stood up straight, allowing her to pass through the doorway first.

As Leroy followed Mattie down the stairs, he hoped she would continue to visualize their life together and envision herself as happily growing older by his side.

. . .

"My sandwich was *appeditlich*." Mattie carried their plates to the counter. "*Danki* for making it."

"*Gern gschehne*." Leroy grinned as he placed their empty drinking glasses on the counter. "Grilled ham and cheese is my specialty."

"Really." A smile played at the corner of her mouth as she leaned her hip against the counter and looked up at him. "Maybe you should've opened a restaurant instead of a harness shop. Or a bakery." She snapped her fingers. "I've got it! You could have a small counter in the harness shop for your baked goods and call it Leroy's Famous Creations."

Leroy threw back his head and laughed, and soon she was laughing with him. The release was so good it almost erased the grief holding her soul in a vise grip.

His eyes locked on her as he reached over and touched one of the ribbons hanging down from her prayer covering. "It's so *gut* to hear your laugh again." He moved the ribbon between his fingers as he spoke. "If opening a small bake stand in the harness shop will keep you laughing, then I'll do it."

"I was kidding." She stared into his eyes. *Has he always had flecks of gold reflected in his deep brown pools?* Something in the atmosphere around them shifted, and alarm tingled at the base of her neck.

"What?" He tilted his head as if sensing her worry.

"Nothing." She cleared her throat and took a step back toward the sink. His fingers released the ribbon, and it bounced onto her shoulder. "I'll do the dishes. You can get back to work."

"All right. If you need me, just call out. We have the windows open." He lingered for a moment, his eyes intent on her face. "You suddenly seem uneasy."

"I'm fine." She pushed the ribbons from her covering behind her shoulders. "I'll have supper ready at five thirty."

"Sounds perfect." Leroy crossed the kitchen to the mudroom.

Mattie turned toward the kitchen sink and began filling one side with soapy water.

"Mattie."

She looked over her shoulder to where Leroy stood in the doorway, fiddling with his straw hat in his hands. "*Ya?*"

"Do you remember when we were *kinner* and we walked to and from school together?" He spun the straw hat in his hands.

"Of course I do." She turned off the faucet and then faced him, leaning against the counter. "How could I forget?"

"Back then we used to talk all the time, and we told each other everything." He took a step toward her with the hat still twirling in his hands. "I shared things with you that I never told anyone else, like how I heard *mei mamm* crying in her room at night."

"I remember that," she whispered, her voice wobbling.

"I only talked to you about *mei dat* and how much it hurt when he left us. I told you how much I missed him. Even though *mei onkels* provided for us financially, they never acted like fathers to Joel and me." Leroy's eyes shimmered with emotion. "I told you I used to pray *mei dat* would wake up one morning and realize he loved our family and would come home."

Mattie's throat dried and she swallowed. "You always trusted me, and I trusted you too."

"I know, and you can still trust me. I'm the same person I was back when we were *kinner.*" He paused. "You can tell me anything, and you don't need to worry about hurting my feelings. If you need to talk about

Isaiah, I'll listen. I know he was your first love, and I'll never try to take his place. I just want you to trust me."

"*Danki.*"

He stood still for a moment as if waiting for her to speak. As much as she longed to pour out all her emotions to him, her lips refused to form the words.

Leroy frowned, and her heart squeezed with renewed guilt.

"I'll see you later," he finally said after a beat. He pushed the hat onto his head and then disappeared into the mudroom. His footsteps sounded before the screen door clicked shut.

A pang of anxiety shot through Mattie. She couldn't let him walk away upset. He deserved better than she was giving him.

"Leroy, wait!" She rushed out the back door after him. "Leroy!"

He stopped at the bottom porch step and faced her, his lips pressed into a thin line.

"Would you help me work on the nursery tonight?" She fingered her apron as she spoke. "Maybe we could work on it after supper if you're not too tired."

His expression softened. "You want me to help you with the nursery?"

"*Ya.* I don't want to work on it without you. It will be more fun if we work together."

"I'd love to help you." The corners of his lips tipped up, and her heartbeat quickened.

"Great." She took a step backward. "It's a date, then."

"A date. That sounds *gut.*" He turned and headed toward the harness shop.

Mattie went back into the kitchen. Tonight she and Leroy would prepare the nursery. She would make an effort to let him into her heart and try to open the communication between them.

. . .

"Do you want me to paint this room?" Leroy asked as he stood in the doorway of the nursery.

"No, I think the walls are fine the way they are." Mattie sat down in the rocking chair and began folding baby clothes before setting them in the dresser drawers. "Besides, you have so much to do at the harness shop."

"I don't mind." He walked over to the pieces of the crib leaning against the wall in the corner of the room. "I can make time to do it if you want the walls freshened up."

"As I said, you have enough to do." Mattie smiled as he pulled a screwdriver out of his back pocket to begin putting the crib together. "I remember when this was your room."

He lifted an eyebrow. "You remember that?"

"I was here for a quilting bee once when I was about eleven, and I snuck up here and peeked into your room." Mattie pointed to the corner where he stood. "Your bed was over there, and you had a shelf over there with all your books, puzzles, and games on it." She gestured to the other side of the room. "And you had a dresser over there, and you also had hooks for your hats and your jackets." She turned back toward him. "I walked through the room and looked at everything, but I didn't touch anything."

A grin overtook his lips, and his brown eyes sparkled in the light of the lantern. "You were spying on me?"

She shrugged. "I had an older *schweschder*. I'd never been in a *bu*'s room. I wanted to see what one looked like."

"Were you impressed?"

"No, not really. It was pretty boring. Just an ordinary room."

They both laughed.

"It's so *gut* to hear you laugh."

"*Danki*." Heat blanketed her cheeks as she returned to her task.

They worked in silence, and once all the clothes were stowed, she stood and rested her hands on her lower back as she stretched.

Then she walked over to the crib and rested her hand on it. "You've put this together fast. *Danki*. It would've been too much bending for me."

"I don't mind helping." Leroy pointed to the wall. "Do you want the crib here or in the other corner?"

Mattie rested her finger on her chin and glanced to the other side of the room. "I think I like it here since there's more light by the window."

"I agree."

"Do you remember where your crib was when you were little?"

Leroy set the screwdriver on the window ledge and then gestured toward the wall. "I think it was right there. I have one memory of *mei mamm* coming in and saying *gude mariye* to me when I was about three. She stood in the doorway and smiled at me. She looked so *froh*."

Mattie sniffed as emotion constricted her chest. "That's so sweet."

"Do you have any memories of when you were that little?"

She paused, thinking back to her childhood, and she laughed. "I remember taking a bath with *mei schweschder* when I was about three or four." She could feel her cheeks flaming again. "We were splashing and laughing. We had a very *gut* time."

Leroy's eyes warmed as he touched her cheek. "I hope we can create *froh* memories like that for our *kinner*."

"I'm sure we will." Her pulse galloped as she looked up into his kind eyes.

He leaned down, and her breath paused as confusion wafted over her. *Is he going to kiss me? Do I want him to kiss me?*

His lips brushed her cheek, and she blew out the gust of air she'd been holding.

"It's late." He rested his hands on her shoulders. "We can work on this some more tomorrow."

"Okay. *Danki* again for helping."

Leroy ran a finger down her cheek and pushed the ribbon from her prayer covering over her shoulder before resting his hands on her shoulders. "*Danki* for letting me help you." He released her shoulders, picked up the two lanterns, and handed her one. "I'm going to head to bed. See you in the morning."

"*Gut nacht,*" she said before heading down the stairs to the master bedroom.

Warmth unfurled inside of her, spreading to her arms and legs as she changed into her nightgown. She was thankful she'd asked Leroy to help her with the nursery.

For the first time since the wedding, she had a feeling they really could make this marriage work. Perhaps the close friendship she'd always had with Leroy could grow into something more.

CHAPTER 7

"Are your parents and sister coming for the grand opening tomorrow?" Tillie asked Mattie as they hung key chains on a display in the middle of the harness shop showroom floor on Friday afternoon.

"*Ya*, they are. I left a message for *mei mamm* and Lizzie last night. They left me messages earlier this morning. They're both excited to see the store." Mattie lifted a leather keychain designed in the outline of a cat from a box and inhaled the sweet, leathery scent. She flipped it over in her hand and ran her finger up and down the side of it. Both Leroy and Hank possessed an incredible amount of talent. This store was going to be a great success.

She sensed someone staring at her. When she looked over her shoulder toward the counter, Leroy nodded at her and she smiled before he turned his attention back to the battery-operated cash register.

She continued hanging key chains and then moved on to doorknob hangers with bells. Once they were all displayed, she hung up pet collars and leashes. Soon her cheeks were flushed, and perspiration beaded on her forehead.

"Are you feeling okay?" Tillie's eyes were wide.

"It's hot in here, isn't it?" Mattie wiped her hand across her brow. She started to sway and then grabbed onto the display, righting herself.

"Mattie!" Leroy rushed over with a stool. "You need to rest." Taking her hands, he steered her toward the stool. "Sit down. I've got you."

While gripping his hands for balance, Mattie lowered herself onto the stool. When would the room stop spinning?

"Tillie," Leroy called over his shoulder, "please get her a bottle of water from the cooler." Then he turned his focus to Mattie. "Are you all right?"

"*Ya.*" She released one of his hands and swiped her hand across her forehead. "It's just so hot in here."

"Here you go." Tillie opened the bottle of water and then handed it to Mattie.

"*Danki.*" Mattie took a long drink, enjoying the cold liquid on her parched throat. Then she held the cool bottle up to her cheek.

"You should go home and take a nap." Leroy crouched down beside her and touched her shoulder. "I'll help you back to the *haus.*"

"I'll be fine."

Leroy frowned. "You are too stubborn sometimes."

"I'm really fine. I'll just rest for a minute."

"Leroy!" Hank called from the doorway. "The vendor is here with the saddles. Do you have a minute?"

"*Ya,*" Leroy responded before turning to Tillie. "Please make her sit and rest for a bit. Maybe she'll listen to you."

"I'll do my best." Tillie turned to Mattie. "You can sit and supervise me. Sound *gut*?"

"*Ya.*" Mattie sipped more water.

Leroy studied her for a moment and then touched her cheek. "Don't overdo it. You need to rest for the *boppli.*"

"I know." She sighed. "I'll just sit here and give Tillie instructions if she needs them."

"Fine. If I find you overdoing it, then I will make sure you go in and take a nap."

Tillie rolled her eyes. "She's not three years old."

Leroy stood up to his full height and raised an eyebrow, and Mattie suppressed a grin. He crossed the store to the front door, where Hank stood talking to a man clad in jeans and a black T-shirt.

"He's awfully bossy," Tillie quipped.

Mattie chuckled. "He's worried about the *boppli.*"

"And he's worried about you too."

"I know." Mattie bit her lower lip. "Can I tell you something?"

Tillie raised an eyebrow. "*Ya,* of course you can."

She stared down at the bottle of water. "I'm a little *naerfich* about tomorrow."

"Why are you *naerfich?*"

"All these *Englishers* are going to be here tomorrow, and we don't know them." Her shoulders tightened. "How do we know one of the men who comes isn't violent, like the man who killed Isaiah? What if someone with a gun comes in and tries to hurt someone?" She shivered despite the humid store. "I abhor violence, and I can't help thinking someone else I love will get hurt by a violent person."

"*Ach,* Mattie." Tillie touched her arm. "I know you're

afraid it will happen again, but those events are rare. Don't live in fear of everyone because of what happened to Isaiah. Most likely the people who come tomorrow are kind people who appreciate our culture. They won't come here looking to hurt us or anyone else." She tilted her head. "You know Leroy and Hank will do their best to keep us safe."

Mattie's eyes misted over. "That's what Isaiah did, and he wound up losing his life helping someone else."

Tillie blew out a deep sigh. "I'm sorry. That was a wrong choice of words. Please don't live in fear. I'm sure we'll be fine."

"You're right." She forced a smile. "I won't let it ruin tomorrow."

"*Gut.*" Tillie touched her arm again and then moved over to the display. "Now, what were you working on before you decided to take a break?"

. . .

"Tillie! Mattie!" Hank called into the store later that morning. "Come down to the road. We're going to unveil the sign."

"Be right there." Tillie hung up another dog leash. "Do you feel well enough to walk down to the road?"

"*Ya*, of course." Mattie stood and placed the empty water bottle on the stool.

"I can't believe tomorrow is the grand opening," Tillie said as they walked toward the front doors. "It seems like we just poured the foundation for this building yesterday."

"It sure has gone quickly." Mattie did her best to sound enthusiastic despite her aching back and throbbing feet.

Tillie grabbed Hank's hand and then started down the rock driveway toward the road.

"Are you feeling better?" Leroy fell into step beside her.

"*Ya.*" Mattie looked up at him. The bright sunlight brought out the golden flecks in his dark eyes.

"Are you telling me the truth?" His lips quirked up. "Or do I need to make sure you take a nap?"

"I don't need a nap." She pointed toward the road. "Let's go before they uncover the sign without us."

Leroy held out his hand, and she took it. Mattie enjoyed the warmth and strength of his hand as they made their way down to the road. She and Tillie clapped as Leroy and Hank uncovered the sign, formally announcing the Bird-in-Hand Harness Shop.

"We've done it," Hank said, shaking Leroy's hand.

"*Ya*, we sure have." Leroy's expression brightened his entire face. He clapped Hank on the shoulder.

"*Danki* for supporting this." Hank pulled his wife into his arms and kissed and hugged her.

Mattie fidgeted with her apron as she looked up at Leroy again. Leroy suddenly pulled Mattie into his arms. She gasped, taken by surprise.

"I'm so *froh* you're here to celebrate with me," he whispered into her ear.

"Congratulations." Mattie rested her cheek on his shoulder and enjoyed the feeling of being in his arms, where she was loved and protected. She closed her eyes and relished his affection for a moment.

"Danki." He released her, and they stared at each other.

Was he disappointed in only receiving a hug from her? Did he expect her to kiss him with the same enthusiasm as Tillie kissed her husband while their neighbors watched?

She wanted him to kiss her. She longed to experience the sensation of his lips brushing hers. Her stomach fluttered and her cheeks burned with embarrassment at the thought of kissing Leroy.

"I think I'll head into the kitchen now and start baking the cakes and pies for tomorrow," Mattie blurted out. "Does that sound okay to you?"

"Ya." Leroy's smile was back. "That's a *gut* idea if you're feeling up to it."

"Ya, I feel much better. Resting on the stool helped." Mattie started toward the house, and Leroy walked beside her. "I was thinking about making *kichlin* and maybe two chocolate cakes as well."

"You'd better make three chocolate cakes."

"Why?" She shielded her eyes from the sun as she gazed up at him.

"One will be for me, of course." He smirked, and he looked so cute.

"All right." She chuckled. "I'll make you your own chocolate cake."

"Danki." He took her hand in his and squeezed it.

Mattie grinned up at Leroy before heading into the house. As she pulled out the baking supplies, she recalled how much she loved being in his arms. She again pondered what it would feel like to kiss him, and her pulse skittered.

Pushing those thoughts away, Mattie found her mother's recipes and concentrated on baking.

. . .

"Good morning. Welcome to the Bird-in-Hand Harness Shop," Leroy said as he greeted another group of customers the following morning. "Thank you for coming to see us today."

The customers had begun filing into the store only minutes after he hung the Open sign in the window. A quick informal survey of the customers revealed his advertisements in the local paper and tourist books had worked. Their new business was off to a promising start.

Leroy stood a little straighter as he scanned the store. Customers were clogged around the displays, investigating everything from key chains to the leather bags and saddles. He looked over at the counter to where Mattie was ringing up the merchandise while Tillie put the items in bags.

Mattie looked radiant in her purple dress and black apron. Although they continued to sleep in separate bedrooms, she was slowly warming up to him. She smiled more, and she eagerly prepared baked goods for the grand opening. A table with cookies and individually wrapped pieces of chocolate cake was set up in the corner, and customers had already picked over more than half of the baked goods. Yes, it was going to be a great day, and he was grateful to have Mattie by his side.

"Excuse me, sir." A woman clad in jean shorts and a

pink T-shirt featuring a drawing of a tabby cat tapped his arm. "Would you please help me figure out which size collar I should buy for my cat?"

"*Ya*, I'll do my best." Leroy rubbed the beard sprouting in his chin to keep from laughing. What did he know about cat neck sizes? "Let's look at the collar display. How old is your cat?"

"Well, my sweet little tabby, Lily, is about seven years old." She made a circle with her fingers. "I think her neck is about this big."

"Okay. Let's see what might work." Leroy helped the woman choose a collar and then asked a few more customers if they needed help.

Once he finished helping customers, he glanced over to where Mattie sat on a stool at the counter, sipping a bottle of water as Tillie helped a customer who was examining a leather satchel. Hank stood nearby, talking to a neighbor who had stopped by to see the store.

Leroy weaved through the knot of customers and came around the counter to stand next to Mattie. "How are you feeling?" She'd looked close to passing out yesterday. He wouldn't allow her to overdo it again today.

"I'm fine. The stool was a great idea. I can relax between customers." She leaned closer to him, and he inhaled the scent of her shampoo, which was nearly intoxicating to him. "We've been busy nonstop since opening. I think it's going to be a very profitable day."

Leroy leaned down on the counter beside her and folded his hands in front of him. "I know. *Danki* for helping."

She raised an eyebrow. "It's my job to help you."

"You could've insisted on staying home today to cook or clean."

Her pink lips formed a thin line. "I couldn't do that to you. I know how much this store means to you. And it means a lot to me too. I'm excited to be here with you, Tillie, and Hank." She set the bottle of water on the counter and then rested her hands on her protruding belly.

"Is he kicking?" Leroy was anxious to feel the child's movement.

"He?" Mattie gave him a coy smile. "What makes you so certain the *boppli* is a he? The *boppli* could very well be a she, you know."

Leroy was speechless for a moment as his chest squeezed. Mattie was teasing him! He loved when she allowed her sense of humor to come out. He had to keep this playful conversation going.

"It's just a feeling I have." He turned to face her. "There's only one way to find out for certain that it's a *bu*."

Mattie grinned. "I know. That would be by ultrasound, but I told the technician I didn't want to know."

"Okay." He rubbed the scruff on his chin. "So that means there are two ways to find out."

"What's the second way?" Her blue eyes challenged him.

"If the *boppli* has a strong kick, then it's a *bu*."

Mattie laughed. "You do realize that's not true, right? Both *buwe* and *maed* have strong kicks."

"Not always."

"All right then. You tell me if you think this is a *bu*." She grabbed his hand and placed it flat on her abdomen.

Leroy's skin tingled at her touch. He sucked in a breath as she placed her hand over his and he felt the *Bump! Bump!* He gaped at her as his emotions swirled with love, adoration, and exhilaration for her child that he would soon meet and raise as his own. He was going to have a real family.

Mattie giggled. "Doesn't it feel funny?"

Oh, how he loved the sound of her sweet giggle.

"Oh, how sweet. Is this your first?"

Leroy glanced to the other side of the counter at the woman wearing the cat T-shirt. He quickly stood erect and cleared his throat.

"*Ya*, it is." Mattie rubbed her belly.

The woman pointed to Leroy. "This is your husband?"

Mattie's cheeks blushed bright pink. "*Ya*."

The woman leaned toward Leroy. "I have four kids." She winked at him before turning back to Mattie. "How many children do you want?"

Mattie shrugged before turning toward Leroy. "We haven't really talked about it. Right, Leroy?"

"Right. We'll just wait to see how God chooses to bless our family."

"Oh." The woman frowned before placing two pet collars and four cat key chains on the counter.

Mattie rang up the items, and the woman paid while Leroy put them into a bag. After the woman walked away, Leroy turned toward Mattie. "Let me know if you need a break." He placed his hand on her shoulder, and she looked up at him. He was grateful she didn't jump at his touch like she had when she dropped the mug. "You can go to the *haus* and rest if you need to."

"I'm fine. I want to stay and help."

"Excuse me." A man in a western hat approached the counter. "Would you please help me with a saddle?"

"Absolutely," Leroy said. "Which one would you like to see?"

As Leroy followed the customer to the saddle display, he looked forward to more teasing and playful banter with Mattie.

CHAPTER 8

"Please come back to see us soon," Mattie told a customer as she handed him his bag. She looked toward the door and spotted her parents, Lizanne, and Lizanne's husband, Al, walking through the door. "You made it!"

Mattie rushed around the counter and hugged her mother and then her sister.

"Of course we made it," *Mamm* said with a chuckle. "We wanted to be here earlier, but your *dat* wasn't in a hurrying mood this morning."

Dat chuckled. "I was going as quickly as I could. It just takes me a little longer to get ready now that I'm getting older." He looked around the store. "This looks *wunderbaar*. I'm going to see how I can help Leroy and Hank." He walked off toward the far end of the store where Hank and Leroy were both helping customers.

"What can I do to help?" Lizanne rubbed her hands together. "Do you need a break?"

"*Ya*, that would be fantastic." Mattie kneaded her fingers into her lower back. "I thought I could make it out in the store all day, but I would like to go home and put my feet up for a while. Would you mind helping Tillie at the register?"

"Absolutely. That sounds like fun. Go on." Lizanne waved her toward the door. "Take your time. Tillie can train me, and we'll handle it."

"*Danki*, Lizzie." Mattie gave her a quick hug before following her mother out the door and up the rock path to the house. They climbed the back porch steps and entered the kitchen through the mudroom.

"May I make you some tea?" *Mamm* placed a bag on the counter.

"That sounds *gut*." Mattie started toward the counter. "I have a jar of *kichlin* over here I can—"

"Sit, Martha Jane," *Mamm* instructed.

Mattie bristled at her full name. *Mamm* used that only when she was very serious. "Okay."

"I'll bring them to you. I made a casserole for tonight." *Mamm* set the kettle on the stove. Then she put the casserole in the refrigerator and carried her bag and the jar of cookies over to the table. "I also brought you a gift."

"You did? Why?"

"Your *dat* and I haven't given you and Leroy a housewarming gift." *Mamm* pulled a purple gift bag out of her canvas tote bag and handed it to her.

"*Danki*. You didn't have to get me anything." Mattie fished through the sea of white tissue paper and pulled out a cross-stitch pattern in a loop. The design had a colorful butterfly bathed in purple, blue, and pink, and she read the words underneath it.

Happiness is like a butterfly:
The more you chase it, the more it will elude you,

but if you turn your attention to other things,
it will come and sit quietly on your shoulder.

Mattie studied the words, taking in their meaning, and tears filled her eyes. She flipped over the cross-stitch and found a note written in neat cursive writing: "*Mattie, may this warm your new home and your heart. All my love,* Mamm."

Mattie covered her mouth with her hand. "This is so *schee.* I love it."

"I saw it at the fabric store and thought of you. I hoped it might bring you some happiness and help to brighten your day."

She looked up at her mother. "*Danki.*"

"*Gern gschehne.*" She touched Mattie's hand. "This is more than merely a housewarming gift. You looked so *bedauerlich* the day of your wedding and then you seemed unhappy when I saw you at church with Leroy. I wanted to give you something that would cheer you up."

"I looked *bedauerlich* at church? I don't remember being sad that day."

Mamm touched her hand to Mattie's cheek as if she were a child. "I know *mei dochdern.* I can tell how you or Lizzie are feeling by just looking at your face or listening to your voice. You can talk to me, *mei liewe.* Tell me what's bothering you. Are you and Leroy having trouble adjusting to your new life together?"

Mattie opened her mouth to speak, but no words could escape past the knot of confusing emotion tightening her chest. She wasn't exactly unhappy, but she wasn't overjoyed either. She was just existing, trying her best to make things work with Leroy.

"I know you miss Isaiah, but you're not alone. Leroy will take *gut* care of you and your *boppli*."

"I know." She cleared her throat. "It just feels so strange to build a life with Leroy when I thought I would grow old with Isaiah."

The kettle began to whistle, and *Mamm* jumped up from the table. She returned with two mugs of tea and placed one in front of Mattie. Then *Mamm* opened the cookie jar and handed a chocolate chip cookie to Mattie before taking one for herself.

"Your relationship will grow over time."

"I hope so." Mattie bit into the cookie.

Mamm took a sip of tea. "It will. Leroy has been by your side ever since Isaiah died." She placed her mug on the table and leaned forward. "Leroy is a *gut* man."

"I know that," Mattie said. "We're making strides as a couple. I just hope we can build a real marriage."

"You have a real marriage. Leroy's feelings for you are genuine. When you were teenagers, I remember telling your *dat* Leroy would someday be your husband."

Mattie blinked. "You actually said that to *Dat*?"

Mamm took a sip from her mug. "*Ya*, I did. Your *dat* once remarked at how Leroy has always been so devoted to you."

Mattie sniffed as tears flooded her eyes. "I feel so inadequate." She laughed and wiped her tears. "Maybe it's hormones. I'm so emotional."

"You'll do fine. Leroy understands what you've been through. He will make you *froh* if you give your heart a chance to heal, but you have to give him a chance to show you."

"I will." She suddenly smiled. "Leroy and I started working on the nursery. It looks so *gut*. You'll have to go up and see it."

"I'd love to. The *boppli* will be here before you know it."

"I know. I'm going to set up a sewing room upstairs too. I want to make some things I can sell." She shared her idea about hosting dinners to make some extra money too. "Leroy thinks that would be a great idea."

"I do too. You and Leroy will build a *gut* life together. You'll make a *gut* team, and that's very important for building a solid marriage."

Mattie looked down at the cross-stitch and ran her finger over the words. Her mother was right. She needed to make the best of her new marriage and work hard to help create a solid base on which to build their life together. She picked up the cross-stitch and pointed toward the far end of kitchen. "I'm going to hang this over by the door. That way I can see it every day."

"I'm *froh* you like it." *Mamm* reached across the table and touched her hand. "Everything will be fine. Just give yourself time." She lifted another cookie. "After we finish our tea, you can show me the *boppli*'s room. Then we can get ready for the party tonight. It will be fun. I'm so *froh* you invited us to share the grand opening celebration."

Mattie squeezed her mother's hand. "I'm glad you're here too." Spending time with her mother always helped Mattie feel better.

. . .

"The shop is staying busy," Mose said as he sidled up to Leroy at the back of the store. "I don't think it's slowed down since I got here."

"*Ya*, it is." Leroy blew out a deep sigh. "I'm so thankful that people actually showed up on our opening day. I hope they keep coming back."

"They will. I have confidence you will stay busy. All these customers will tell their *freinden* and family members about this store."

"I hope so." Leroy recognized that thread of worry in his voice. "Did your furniture store start off busy and then stay busy when you and your *bruders* first opened?"

Mose stared off toward the front of the store as if reaching into the depths of his memory. "It started off busy."

"So you had a slow time?"

A smile tugged at the corners of Mose's lips. "We had some short periods that were slow, but then business picked up. I have faith that this store will be successful. Don't worry about that today, okay? Just enjoy the grand opening." He glanced around the store again. "You and Hank have done a phenomenal job here. I'm proud of you."

"*Danki*." Leroy's smile widened. How he'd wanted to hear his biological father say he was proud of him. He was grateful to hear Mose say it. Mose was the father he'd always longed for.

Leroy reached into the cooler and pulled out two bottles of water. "Would you like a drink?"

"*Ya. Danki.*" Mose took the bottle and opened it.

Al suddenly appeared beside Leroy. "You're giving out drinks? I'm parched."

"Here. Take mine." Leroy handed Al his bottle and swiped another one from the cooler.

"*Danki.*" Al opened the bottle and took a long draw.

Leroy looked toward the cashier counter and panic seized his chest. "Where's Mattie?"

"She went inside to rest," Mose said. "Ruth is with her."

"Oh. I hadn't even noticed she left." Leroy leaned against the wall as his shoulders relaxed. "I'm glad she's resting. She's been so stubborn lately and won't rest like I ask her to." He took a long drink from the water bottle.

Mose pressed his lips together. "Those Byler women are stubborn."

"*Ya,* that is the truth." Leroy rolled his eyes. "I thought Mattie was going to pass out from the heat yesterday. She refused to take a break. I had to instruct her to sit on a stool, and she still argued with me."

"It's those pregnancy hormones too." Mose smirked as he looked at Al, who was drinking from his water bottle. "You'll know what that's like someday soon too, Al."

Al spit out a mouthful of water and gasped before coughing.

Mose laughed a deep belly laugh, and Leroy joined in.

"I'm sorry, son." Mose clapped Al on the back. "I didn't mean to scare you."

Customers turned and eyed them with furrowed brows.

Leroy fought back his laughter and then cleared his throat. "I'm going to go help some customers." He was still grinning as he approached a customer standing by the display of horse blankets.

. . .

"We made it through the first day!" Leroy flipped the harness shop sign from Open to Closed. "What do you think, Hank?"

Hank clapped. "I think it was a great success."

"I'll say." Tillie laughed. "My feet are killing me."

"*Danki* for helping." Hank kissed her cheek, and Tillie beamed.

Leroy's chest constricted. He couldn't wait to see a day when Mattie reacted to his kiss with such delight. He peered out the front windows in search of Mattie.

The shop door opened and Joel, Al, and Mose appeared carrying chairs. Ruth, Lizanne, and Mattie followed with trays of food.

"Looks like they are ready to eat," Leroy announced. "Let's get the tables set up." He turned to Tillie. "There's a cooler on the floor in our mudroom. Would you mind going to get it? It shouldn't be too heavy."

"No problem." Tillie rushed out the door.

Leroy and Hank set up folding tables in the center of the store while the other men set up chairs and the women made a couple of trips into the store with food and drinks. Once the tables and food were ready, they all moved to sit down.

Mattie pulled up a chair beside Leroy and sat down

beside him. When everyone was seated, he gazed around the table and was overwhelmed with appreciation for his family and friends.

"I'd like to say something before we pray and eat." Leroy folded his hands on the table. "Thank you all for being part of this grand opening."

He looked at Hank across the table. "As you all know, I never had a *dat* to teach me a trade, and it was Hank's idea I work alongside him in his *onkel* Merv's shop to learn leatherworking. I enjoyed the work, and I appreciated being able to work with my best *freind*. Hank and I came up with the *narrisch* idea of owning our own shop when we were twenty. There was a time when I wasn't sure this would ever happen, but here we are today."

Tillie, Lizanne, Joel, and Dora clapped.

Leroy turned toward Mattie. "This has been a busy couple of months, and I just want to say *danki* to all of you for supporting Hank and me. I think the store is off to a great start, and we couldn't have made it without the love and support from our families."

Mattie touched Leroy's hand, and heat rushed to the place her skin brushed.

"I want to add I'm really grateful to have this opportunity," Hank chimed in. "Not everyone gets to do what they love as their profession. I'm so honored and thankful to have this store and work with my best *freind*." He smirked. "And after all these years, I'm still teaching him how to make leashes. I doubt he'll ever learn how to stitch a straight line."

"That's fine because you still can't cut straight," Leroy teased in response, and everyone laughed.

"But seriously," Hank said, "thank you all for being here to celebrate with us. Let's pray and then enjoy this *appeditlich* meal."

They bowed their heads in silent prayer and then began filling their plates with the casseroles Dora, Ruth, and Lizanne had brought to share.

"You have to try Leroy's root beer." Tillie opened the cooler. "It's amazing." She passed around mugs and then the bottles.

"Oh, I want some," Mattie said. "You make the best root beer."

"*Danki.*" He handed her a mug and then filled it for her. "Are you feeling okay?"

"*Ya.* I rested for a while before we started preparing the meal. I feel much better than I did yesterday."

"*Gut.*" Leroy forked some of the tuna casserole.

"You look great, Mattie," Dora said from across the table, where she sat beside Joel. "How are you feeling?"

"I'm fine, *danki.*" Mattie lifted the mug, cradling it in her hands. "I just tire easily, and my back and legs have been sore." She sipped the root beer and licked her lips. "This is fantastic," she said under her breath to Leroy as she placed the mug on the table.

"I keep telling her to rest, but she's stubborn," Leroy chimed in.

Mattie playfully swatted his arm. "I am not stubborn."

Her father chuckled. "Leroy, Mattie and Lizzie are just as stubborn as their *mamm.*"

"That's not nice, Mose." Ruth chuckled.

Leroy snickered, enjoying the teasing from his in-laws. Happiness covered him like a warm blanket as he glanced around the room. He finally had the two things he'd wanted most in life—his own business and a family.

He glanced over at Mattie, who grinned while talking to her sister. He couldn't wait to welcome her baby into the world. Once he had a child, his life would be complete. He was blessed beyond measure.

Before long the sunset stained the sky in vivid streaks of orange, pink, and yellow, and soon after darkness flooded the shop. Leroy and Hank flipped on the Coleman lanterns and they shared the pies and cakes Mattie and Tillie had baked for the party.

"This lemon meringue pie is *appeditlich*," Lizanne announced. "You're an amazing baker, Mattie."

"Danki." She smiled as pink colored her adorable cheeks.

"This pie is delicious," Dora chimed from across the table. "Would you share the recipe with me?"

"Absolutely. I'll write it down for you," Mattie offered. "Walk over to the kitchen with me before you leave."

"Danki. I'd love to try to make one. Do you like it, Joel?"

He nodded while chewing. "Oh *ya*. It's *wunderbaar*."

"Danki." Mattie looked up at Leroy.

Bliss bubbled up inside of Leroy as he gazed at his wife. Mattie seemed content and willing to be a part of his family for the first time since their wedding. He prayed they were finally making strides toward being a couple, a truly happy married couple.

Soon the pies and cakes were gone, and all the women but Mattie divided up the dirty dishes and carried them to Leroy's and Hank's houses while the men stowed the tables and chairs.

Mattie swept the floor. She stopped periodically to wipe her hand across her brow, and her cheeks flushed bright pink. She looked so cute that he couldn't take his eyes off of her.

When she turned toward the counter, Leroy walked up behind her and touched her arm. "I can clean that up Monday morning."

"How will you have time to clean if you have a line of customers waiting outside the door?" She challenged him with a hand on her hip. She was stunning standing before him with her sapphire eyes sparkling in the low light. He wanted to grab her and kiss her until she was breathless.

Would she push me away if I kissed her right now?

He shoved the temptation away.

"You know I'm right." She gestured around the shop. "You saw how busy this store was today. If we don't clean tonight, it won't be ready for your next rush of customers." She pushed the broom. "We have to make sure the harness shop looks nice and clean so the customers will tell their *freinden* about it."

"That's true." Leroy lingered by the counter as she moved the broom around the store. He longed to stare at her for hours and memorize every detail of her beautiful face. She looked even more attractive than she'd been as a teenager.

"Leroy," Hank called from the back room, "quit staring at your *schee fraa* and bring back those two chairs. We'd like to get home tonight, you know."

"You've always been a spoilsport," Leroy grumbled as he folded up the last two chairs.

Mattie glanced over at Leroy, grinned, and shook her head as she swept the floor.

After the shop was cleaned up, they headed out to the driveway, where Joel, Mose, and Al hitched up the horses and buggies. Leroy shook hands with the men, thanking them again for coming to the grand opening.

Ruth moved beside Leroy and touched his arm. She looked over her shoulder toward Mattie, who was holding a piece of paper while engrossed in a conversation with Lizanne and Dora. When she gazed up at Leroy, her blue eyes shimmered in the light of the lantern she held.

"Leroy," Ruth began, "I want to say *danki* for taking care of *mei dochder.*"

Devotion and gratitude welled up in Leroy, leaving him speechless for a moment. He could only nod in response.

"Promise me you'll be patient with her."

"*Ya*, of course I will. She means everything to me. Her well-being is paramount to me."

"*Danki.*" Ruth touched Leroy's arm. "You're a blessing to her. Just remember her life with Isaiah was part of her past, but her life with you is her future. *Gut nacht.*" Then she climbed into the buggy and waved before Mose guided their horse down the driveway toward the road.

Leroy waved good-bye to Joel and Dora and Lizanne and Al as their horses followed Mose's buggy down the driveway.

"It was a *wunderbaar* opening day." Hank walked over to Leroy. "We're off to a *gut* start."

"No, we're off to a great start," Leroy said, correcting him. "All our hard work is paying off."

"*Ya*, it is." Hank yawned.

Tillie looped her arm through his. "It's past your bedtime, Henry Ebersol."

"Yes, dear." Hank rolled his eyes, and Mattie giggled as she stood beside Leroy. "I'll see you both tomorrow. *Gut nacht.*"

"*Gut nacht*," Leroy echoed with a chuckle. "Sleep well. We all worked hard today. I locked up the store and made sure all the lanterns were turned off."

"*Danki.*" Hank yawned again.

Mattie hugged Tillie and said good night to her before she and Hank started toward their house next door. Leroy and Mattie walked in the opposite direction toward their house.

"*Mei mamm* said she and Lizzie washed the dishes and put them away." Mattie held a lantern that illuminated their path as she fell into step with Leroy. "I told her she didn't need to do that. I would've washed them on Monday."

Ruth's words swirled through his mind again, and he grinned.

"What was that smile for?" Mattie gazed up at him.

"Nothing. I'm just really *froh*." He looped his arm around her shoulders and braced himself for her rejection.

Instead, she leaned into him. His heart swelled with joy. This had to be a fantasy. Did Mattie love him like a wife should love her husband or was this some sort of cruel dream?

"I gave Dora a copy of that recipe for the pie. I hope she likes it."

"I'm sure she will."

Mattie still leaned against him as they walked together toward the back porch. "I'm so excited about the store. You and Hank have worked so hard on this. You earned it."

They started up the porch steps, still side by side. When they reached the back door, he wrenched it open, allowing her to step through first. He shucked his boots and hat in the mudroom and then went into the kitchen.

A cross-stitch hanging on the wall caught his attention. He read the inscription and then looked over his shoulder at Mattie standing in the middle of the room, watching him. "Where did this come from?"

"*Mei mamm* brought it as a housewarming gift." She touched her apron. "She said she saw it in a fabric store and thought of me. I wanted to hang it there so I can see it every day." She paused. "Is it okay that I hung it there?"

"Of course it is. I'm glad to see you decorating. I want you to make this *haus* your home. Hang anything anywhere you'd like. You don't need to ask me for permission."

"*Gut. Danki.*" A yawn overtook her pretty face, and she covered her mouth with her hand to shield it.

"You need to get to bed. I worked you hard today too." He took her arm and started to steer her toward the downstairs bedroom.

She gasped and then held up her hand. "Wait!"

Alarm shot through him. "Is something wrong? Is it time to go to the hospital?"

She laughed. "No, nothing is wrong, and I'm not in labor. I just remembered I have a few presents for you."

"Presents?" He raised his eyebrows.

"*Ya.* Just wait here." She rushed over to the refrigerator and pulled out a pie plate covered in aluminum foil. "I only had time to make one, and I wanted you to have it." She held out the plate.

Leroy pulled back the foil, revealing a perfect raspberry pie. He breathed in the sweet scent, impressed by both her baking skills and her thoughtfulness. She'd made this pie for him because he enjoyed raspberry pies. Was this a sign that her feelings for him were growing?

"*Danki.*" His voice quavered with overwhelming emotion.

"*Gern gschehne.*" She gnawed at her lower lip. "I wanted to use *mei mamm*'s recipes to make you something special. I'm sorry I didn't have time to make more. I promise you I will."

"It's perfect." He covered it.

"I also saved you one of the chocolate cakes." She opened the refrigerator door and pointed to the cake.

"*Danki.*" He touched his abdomen with his free hand. "I've already eaten too much tonight, and I want to enjoy them. Why don't we have the pie and cake for breakfast with *kaffi*?"

"Pie and cake for breakfast?" Both her eyebrows raised.

He shrugged. "Why not?"

"Okay." She took the pie plate from him and put it

back into the refrigerator, setting it on the shelf beside the chocolate cake. "I have something else for you too." She reached into the refrigerator and pulled out a large jar with a lid on it. "I believe you once told me you liked this."

Leroy took the jar from her and opened it. "What's this?" He leaned down and smelled it. "Peaches?"

"Peach salsa." Mattie threaded her fingers together as if she were praying. "Don't you like peach salsa? *Mei dat* does, and I was thinking that you did too." She bit her bottom lip. The hope in her eyes softened something deep in his soul.

"I do like it. *Danki.*"

"Oh *gut!*" She blew out a deep breath. "I bought the peaches at the market and chips too. I only had enough for you, so I saved it."

"That was so thoughtful of you." He handed the jar back to her, and she returned it to the refrigerator. "I'll have some with lunch tomorrow."

"That sounds perfect. I couldn't wait to give it to you, but I didn't want you to have to share it tonight." She closed the refrigerator door. "I wanted to do something nice for you since you worked so hard on the nursery. I really appreciate it."

"You don't have to keep thanking me for that. It's our *haus.* I want you to feel comfortable and *froh* here." He held his hand out to her, and she took it. It was as if a wall had broken down between them, and their relationship had grown by leaps and bounds in the past few days.

Leroy led her through the family room toward the downstairs bedroom. His pulse quickened as they stood in front of the bedroom door. Would she invite him in? He wouldn't allow himself to take advantage of her, but he would relish sleeping beside her throughout the night.

Mattie stopped in front of the door and placed her hand flat against his chest. "I'm so proud of you."

Leroy swallowed against his dry throat as he gazed down into her eyes. *I have to be dreaming. This can't really be happening.*

"You really worked hard to make the harness shop dream come to life," Mattie continued, clearly oblivious to the tornado of emotions swirling inside of him. "You always struggled and felt lost because you didn't have a *daed* to guide you. Your *onkels* were generous, but they were too busy with their own *kinner* to make time for you and Joel. Still, you took it upon yourself to learn a trade and turned it into a business. The items you and Hank created flew off the shelves today. You're so talented."

"Danki." He rested his hand on her cheek, and she closed her eyes as she leaned into his touch. This was too good to be true. This couldn't possibly be real.

"I'm so thankful you're here with me." His voice was low and husky.

Leaning down, he brushed his lips against her forehead and then trailed kisses along the side of her face and down her jaw, slowly making his way to her mouth.

With her eyes still closed, a soft gasp sounded from her mouth. His heart slammed against his rib cage and his pulse quickened. It was finally going to happen. He was going to kiss his wife.

His lips brushed hers and heat buzzed through his entire body. She rested her hands on his shoulders as their lips brushed once again, sending electric pulses into every cell of his being. When he broke the kiss, he took a step back from her and raked his hand through his hair.

Mattie stared up at him, her breath coming in short bursts and her cheeks reddening.

"I'm sorry." He held up his hands as if to stave off her anger or irritation. "I didn't mean to push you too far."

"It's okay." She reached behind her for the doorknob and pushed the bedroom door open. "I should go to bed. It's late. *Gut nacht.*"

Before he could respond, she slipped through the door, then closed it behind her. Leroy stared at her door for a moment, his thoughts and emotions whirling through him at lightning speed. The kiss had been incredible, even more wonderful than he'd ever imagined. He didn't want it to stop.

While they were making strides as a couple, he wanted their progression to come naturally. Although she didn't protest when he kissed her, the expression on her face told him he'd kissed her too soon.

He slowly made his way up the stairs. When he reached the bedroom, Leroy changed into boxers and a T-shirt and then flopped onto the bed. The evening had been euphoric with Ruth's encouragement regarding his marriage, Mattie's surprise gifts, and then Mattie's compliments about the harness shop. The kiss had also been perfect.

He buried his face into his pillow and tried desperately to forget the taste of her lips. He longed to kiss her again and again, but he didn't want to force her into intimacy with him.

With a groan, Leroy rolled to his side and closed his eyes, and the memory of her lips against his filled his mind. He loved Mattie with all his heart. He hoped someday soon she would love him back.

CHAPTER 9

"You don't have to go with me." Mattie placed a platter of bacon in front of Leroy. "I know you're busy. I can go alone."

"I want to go with you," Leroy insisted.

She filled his coffee mug and then sat down across from him. "I appreciate the offer, but the harness shop has been busy all week. I don't feel right about pulling you away right now. I'll be fine by myself."

"I've already discussed it with Hank, and I'm going with you. Today is Thursday, so he and Tillie can handle it fine. It would be a different story if it were a Saturday when tourists are more likely to come in droves."

Mattie nodded and then lowered her head for a silent prayer. She peered up when she heard Leroy shift in his seat. She folded her hands in her lap as she watched him fill his plate with scrambled eggs, fried potatoes, and bacon. Her gaze landed on his lips, sending a tingle skittering through her.

For the past few days, Mattie had found herself reliving the incredible kiss Leroy had given her Saturday night before she'd gone to bed. While the kiss had shocked her, she hadn't exactly disliked it. It had been a good kiss, and it had awakened feelings inside of her that she'd never before experienced for Leroy. These new feelings for him were strange and unnerving, and she didn't know how to handle them. This was foreign territory, and she wasn't ready for it.

Also, it was too soon after Isaiah's death for her to be kissing another man. While part of her longed for Leroy to kiss her again, another part of her wanted him to keep his distance. Thankfully, he hadn't tried to kiss her again.

"If we're going to raise this *kind* together, then I want to be involved from the beginning." Leroy's words broke through her mental debate. "That means I want to go to your appointments with you. I'll step outside if you need to have an exam. I respect your privacy if that's what you're concerned about. I won't do anything that makes you uncomfortable. I won't embarrass you."

"That's not what I'm worried about." She scooped eggs onto her own plate. "I don't want you to miss work for this. It's just a routine appointment."

"I'm going with you." His voice was kind but firm. "I thought we could go to lunch and maybe do some shopping after the appointment. Does that sound okay?"

Mollified, Mattie nodded. "It sounds nice, actually. Are you certain Hank and Tillie will be able to handle the shop for that long?"

"*Ya.*" He speared a few potatoes with his fork. "I told you we've already discussed it. I thought it might be *gut* for you and me to spend some time together. I promised to return the favor, maybe sometime next week. He and Tillie can run errands, and I'll manage the shop."

"Oh," Mattie said, surprised. He truly had planned this out well. "That sounds *gut*. I could help you when Tillie and Hank are out running errands. I'll run the register while you take care of the customers."

"All right. As long as your doctor says it's okay for you to work. We need to think about the *boppli*."

"That sounds *gut*." Mattie smiled.

. . .

"I have an appointment." Mattie stood in front of the reception desk at her doctor's office two hours later.

"Your name?" a young woman with strawberry-blonde hair and clad in purple scrubs asked.

"Martha Petersheim. I mean, Martha Fisher," she added quickly, aware of Leroy's intense gaze as he stood beside her. "When someone called me to remind me of my appointment a couple of weeks ago, I explained I've remarried and changed my name." She bit back the sigh threatening her lips. She hoped she hadn't hurt Leroy by using the wrong last name. She didn't want to hurt him by saying careless things.

"You may have a seat, Mrs. Fisher. We'll be with you shortly."

"Thank you." Mattie watched as Leroy crossed the waiting room area and sat down by the window. He patted the seat beside him, and she joined him.

As Mattie absently rubbed her abdomen, she held her breath and waited for him to express disappointment because she said her last name was Petersheim and not Fisher. Instead, Leroy picked up a magazine and began to thumb through it. She studied him, looking for any sign of hurt but found none.

Was he so deeply hurt he had to look away from her to keep his emotions in check? Maybe he was even angry. But she'd never seen him lose his temper. Perhaps he was fine and understood her mistake.

"Mrs. Fisher?" A nurse holding a clipboard stood in the doorway leading to the examination rooms.

Leroy stood and held out his hand to her.

Surprised, Mattie took it, allowing him to lift her to her feet. *"Danki."*

"Gern gschehne." His voice was soft and warm in her ear. He held her arm as they made their way across the waiting room, and he waited in the hallway as the nurse took Mattie's weight.

When they reached the examination room, Leroy stood outside while Mattie changed into a gown. He knocked on the door and then cracked it open. "Do you want me to wait in the hall?"

"No, you can come in and hear what the doctor has to say." She waved him into the room.

He hesitated for a beat and then walked in. After sitting down on a chair, he lifted another magazine from a table and flipped through it.

Guilt and regret warred inside of Mattie as Leroy perused an article. He seemed to be reading the words to avoid the elephant in the room. She couldn't take his silence or the guilt that drowned her.

"I'm sorry." The words exploded from her lips.

He peered up at her and arched an eyebrow. "What are you talking about?"

"I'm sorry for upsetting you out in the waiting room. You have to remember I was Mattie Petersheim for two years, and I've only been Mattie Fisher for less than a month."

He closed the magazine. "It's all right. This is all an adjustment."

"Right." The muscles in her shoulders relaxed slightly. He was going to forgive her, and maybe they would be okay.

A knock sounded on the door, and Dr. Carrie Sheppard stepped into the room. An attractive woman in her mid-forties, she had light-brown hair and warm hazel eyes.

"Hello, Mrs. Fisher." She shook Mattie's hand. "It's good to see you again." She turned to Leroy. "You must be Mr. Fisher."

"Hi." He shook her hand. "Nice to meet you."

"How are you feeling?" Dr. Sheppard asked.

"Fine." Mattie rubbed her lower back. "Just a little tired and sore."

. . .

"The doctor seemed pleasant." Leroy sat across from Mattie in a booth at the Bird-in-Hand Family Restaurant. "She said everything is going fine. That's *gut* news." He looked down to peruse the menu.

"*Ya*, it is. I can't believe I have only six weeks to go." Mattie skimmed the selections. Although she'd tried to prevent Leroy from going to the doctor's appointment, she was grateful he had gone with her. He was considerate enough to leave the room before the exam, and he was quiet and attentive while Dr. Sheppard spoke. It was as though Leroy sensed what she needed without her having to even ask.

She peered up at him as her mother's words from Saturday afternoon echoed through her mind: "*Your* dat *once remarked at how Leroy has always been so devoted to you.*"

"Do you know what you want for lunch?" His question broke through her thoughts.

"I think I'll have the meat loaf."

"Your usual. That sounds *gut*." His gaze moved back to the menu. "Meat loaf it is."

The waitress stopped by to take their order and then left.

Leroy leaned forward, resting his folded hands on the table. "Your doctor seemed very attentive."

"Dr. Sheppard is very nice." Mattie touched her cool glass of water. "She actually hugged me and let me cry on her shoulder when I told her Isaiah had died."

Leroy gave her a weak smile. "She seems compassionate and thoughtful."

"She is." Mattie sipped the water. "*Danki* for coming with me today."

"*Gern gschehne.* I'm *froh* I could go." He leaned back in the booth and eyed her for a moment. "Mattie, don't shut me out, okay? I want to be part of this."

"*Ya.*" She needed to change the subject, and she racked her brain for something to discuss. "I haven't made it out to the harness shop since Saturday. Is your key chain display empty yet?"

"No, but I've had to make more key chains. Hank and I are trying to keep up with the inventory in between customers."

"What's your biggest seller so far?"

Leroy gripped his suspenders as he considered the question. Mattie took in his face, studying his deep brown eyes. He was so attractive in that dark-blue shirt. Her mind wandered back to their kiss.

Would he kiss her again? And if so, how soon? She shivered with a mixture of fear and excitement at the notion. She was now Leroy's wife, and part of her wanted to surrender herself completely to him.

The waitress appeared with their food, and Mattie nibbled her meat loaf as Leroy continued to discuss the harness shop. She half-listened to him as her confusing feelings for him clashed inside of her.

"Are you feeling well?" Leroy's question hurled her back to the present.

"*Ya*. I'm just not very hungry."

"Oh. Do you want to go straight home and rest?"

"No, I need a few groceries. It would be helpful if we could get the shopping done today."

"All right. As long as you promise to rest when we get home." He gave her a sweet smile, and her heart seemed to turn over in her chest.

Was she developing romantic feelings for Leroy? Everything was just so confusing.

After lunch, the driver took them to the grocery store. They filled the shopping cart with food and supplies and then wandered over to the baby section.

While Mattie perused the displays of disposable

diapers, Leroy disappeared into a nearby aisle with the shopping cart.

"I'm going to get these," Leroy said when he returned. He held up a blue onesie and a pink onesie. "What do you think? This way we're covered whether it's a *bu* or a *maedel*."

Mattie chuckled. "All right." She kneaded her fingers on her lower back.

Leroy frowned. "Your back hurts again."

"It's okay. It seems to hurt constantly."

"Let's get you home." He looped his arm around her shoulders and guided her toward the checkout.

Leroy paid for their groceries and supplies and then they climbed into the van and headed home. Leroy insisted upon carrying in all the groceries while Mattie began stowing the food and supplies. She was putting a gallon of milk into the refrigerator when Leroy burst into the kitchen.

"I have a gift for you."

"A gift?" Mattie closed the refrigerator door and crossed the kitchen to where he stood beside a cradle. She gasped, running her fingers over the smooth oak wood. "This is so *schee*. Did you make it?"

"No, it was actually mine. *Mei daadi* made it shortly before I was born. I just cleaned it up and stained it. I've been working on it a little bit each night after we close the shop."

"I love it." Tears stung her eyes as she continued to run her fingers over the precious cradle. In approximately six weeks, she'd rock her newborn in it.

"I wanted to give you something special since you

made the *appeditlich* peach salsa, chocolate cake, and raspberry pie for me." He stood beside her. "You have a crib, but you don't have a cradle. You can keep the cradle in our room while the *boppli* is little." His eyes widened. "I mean your room."

While she'd heard him call the bedroom her room, she didn't correct him. She wasn't certain how long she'd want to stay in the room alone, and she didn't want to give him any false hope for their future as a couple. "*Danki.* I love it."

"*Gut.*" He breathed a deep sigh. "I was worried you wouldn't like it."

She tilted her head. "Why wouldn't I like it?"

"I don't know. Woodworking was never my gift." He ran his hand over the top of the cradle. "*Mei daadi* was a *gut* carpenter. I just tried to clean it up."

"It's perfect." Mattie rested her hand on his arm as admiration surged through her. "I can't wait to use it."

Leroy touched her cheek. "We can use it for all our *kinner.* We'll make it our family tradition. All our babies will sleep in this cradle." He stroked her cheek with the tip of his finger, and she enjoyed his gentle and affectionate touch. "That nosy woman in the store on Saturday asked us how many *kinner* we wanted. How many do you want?"

"I'm not sure." She looked down at her protruding abdomen as she caressed it with her hand. "Why don't we see how this goes first."

"That sounds like a *gut* idea." He nudged the cradle, and it rocked back and forth with a soft swishing sound. "Would you like me to put it in the nursery?"

"*Ya. Danki.* It's the perfect gift."

"I'm *froh* you like it. I'll take it upstairs."

As he carried his gift toward the stairs, Mattie hugged her arms to her middle and envisioned her baby rocking in the gorgeous cradle.

CHAPTER 10

Mattie brushed a paper napkin across her sweaty brow as the unrelenting August heat seeped into the kitchen through the open windows. She'd hoped for a cross breeze, but instead, the kitchen sweltered like the inside of an oven set to four hundred degrees.

"Did Tillie help you with the laundry today?" Leroy asked as they sat at the table.

"*Ya.* She also helped me cook supper. I'd be lost without her." She swiped the napkin across her brow again. If only she had a battery-operated fan that could move the air and offer some relief.

He set down his fork and leaned toward her. "You look miserable."

"I'm fine." She forced a smile despite her aching back, throbbing legs, and swelling feet. Her back pain had increased during the past month, and her feet and legs had also joined her list of complaints.

But she didn't want to burden Leroy with her issues since she'd already caused him enough stress with her manic moods. He seemed to walk on eggshells around her, giving her pleasantries and offers of help while she tried her best to complete her daily chores. Although he never raised his voice or lost his temper, she sensed his growing despondency because of her constantly erratic attitude.

Her gaze moved to the cross-stitch hanging by the back door. If only she could find some relief . . . or happiness. *You'll find it after the baby is born.*

"This is the best fried chicken I've ever had." His compliment yanked her from her thoughts.

"I'm glad you like it. I'll tell Tillie." She rested her hands on her abdomen. In approximately two more weeks she would be a mother. She wasn't certain she was ready for that responsibility.

"Is everything okay?"

"What?"

"You seem lost in your thoughts." He placed the fork next to the plate. "Do you want to talk about it?"

Mattie continued to move her hand over her abdomen. It had grown so much during the past month she was certain she resembled a cow instead of a young woman. "I'm just sore, but you're probably tired of hearing about my aches and pains."

"No, I'm not tired of hearing anything you want to say." He held his hand out to her, and she took it, enjoying the warmth and comfort of his skin against her.

Tears flooded her eyes, and he frowned.

"Did I say something wrong?"

"No." She wiped away an errant tear. "You said the right thing. I know I'm an emotional mess, and I'm sorry you have to deal with me."

"You don't need to be sorry."

"*Danki* for putting up with me."

A low rumble of laughter sounded from his throat.

"Are you joking? I'm *froh* to put up with you. You're my *fraa*, and you're entitled to be achy and emotional. Tell me what else is bothering you. Please talk to me."

"Okay." She sniffed. "The *boppli* hasn't been very active in the past couple of days. It's strange. I'm used to the *boppli* having the hiccups every morning and then kicking me most of the afternoon. I haven't felt much movement at all today. The last time I felt the hiccups was Saturday morning, and I think the last real kick was Saturday night."

He gaped. "Why didn't you tell me?" He glanced toward the clock. "The office is closed now, but I would've taken you in to see the doctor earlier if you'd told me. Do you want me to call the answering service and tell them what's going on?"

She waved off the idea. "No, it's not necessary. We can call tomorrow."

"All right." He leveled his gaze with hers. "We'll wait, but we have to call as soon as they open tomorrow. I'll go with you to the doctor's. Hank can handle the store."

Mattie yawned. "That sounds *gut*. I think the office opens at eight."

"You should go rest. I'll do the dishes."

"No, I can do them. You worked all day."

"You worked too." He reached over and squeezed her hand. "Remember what I said. We help each other, okay?"

Mattie's lower lip quivered, and she cleared her throat against the emotion lodged there. "Okay." *Hopefully someday I can find a way to thank him for all he's done for me.*

. . .

Leroy sat up straight in bed. The bedroom was shrouded in darkness. He rubbed his eyes as he turned toward the clock. It said 3:59.

The light tapping of raindrops sounded on the roof above him, and a spray of cool rain misted in from the window beside the bed and moved over his hot and clammy skin.

He yawned, wondering what had awakened him.

A noise resonated from downstairs. *What was that?*

He flipped on the lantern beside the bed and padded to the doorway. Leaning out into the hallway, he listened again.

"Leroy!" Mattie shrieked.

"Mattie! I'm on my way!" Leroy rushed down the stairs, his pulse pounding in his ears. "Where are you?"

"In the bathroom! Please hurry!"

Leroy ran to the door and then skidded to a stop. "I'm here. *Was iss letz?*"

"My water broke." Her voice was breathy and then she groaned. "The contractions have started." She groaned again. "It hurts."

Alarm shot through Leroy. He reached for the doorknob and then stopped. Should he go inside or give her privacy? "What can I do?"

"We need to go to the hospital." She moaned again. "Would you please call for an ambulance?"

"*Ya, ya,* of course." He pressed his hand flat against the door. "How long have you been calling me?" He squeezed his eyes shut, hoping she hadn't been screaming for an hour while he slept.

"It wasn't long. Maybe ten minutes."

"I'm so sorry." He hung his head. "I should've started sleeping on the sofa last week."

"It's fine. Don't worry about it." She sucked in a loud breath and then let out a long groan.

"Mattie?" He leaned against the door as his heart pounded.

"Please go call for an ambulance, okay?" Her words came in short puffs of air.

"Oh, right!" He pushed his hands through his messy hair. "Then I'll get dressed and grab your suitcase."

"Great."

"Hey, Mattie," he called as he walked away.

"What?"

"We're going to have a *boppli*!"

She laughed, and he grinned. "Quit talking and go call nine-one-one!"

Leroy chuckled as he rushed out the back door to the phone shanty. After placing the call, he hustled back through the house and knocked on the bathroom door.

"The ambulance is on its way." He leaned against the door. "How are you doing in there?"

"I'm still here." She sounded exhausted. "The contractions seem closer together. I wonder if this means it won't be long."

Excitement combined with fear twisted inside his gut. "I'll get dressed and then help you to the kitchen."

"That sounds *gut*." She sucked in another breath.

"Can I help you?"

"No, no. I'll be fine."

He hesitated, longing to take away her pain. "I'll be right back."

"Okay." Her voice seemed small, like a frightened child.

Leroy ran up the stairs, quickly dressed, and then jogged back down the stairs. After retrieving the suitcase Mattie had packed last week, he returned to the bathroom door. "I'm here. Are you ready to try to go to the kitchen?"

"*Ya*. Just give me a minute." After several moments she said, "You can come in."

Leroy entered the bathroom and took her hand. She was clad in a white nightgown, and her hair fell in waves to her waist. She was pale, and her face was twisted into a grimace.

"Do you want to get dressed?"

"No." She grabbed his arm, and he lifted her to her feet. "Would you please get my robe and a scarf for my head?"

"*Ya*, of course." He helped her to a kitchen chair, and after she gingerly lowered herself into it, he retrieved the robe and scarf from her room. He helped her cover her hair with the scarf. "Do you need anything?"

"Water, please," she whispered while wincing.

He brought her a glass of water, and her hand shook as she took a long drink. He was helpless as she squeezed her eyes shut and groaned. He was helping her into the robe when a knock sounded on the back door.

"I'll be right back." Leroy kissed the top of her head

and hurried to the door, where two paramedics, a tall man and a medium-height woman, stood on the back porch.

"Hi," Leroy said, opening the screen door. "My wife is in labor. Would you please help us get to the hospital?"

"You bet." The man turned to the woman. "I'll get the gurney."

"Okay." The woman smiled at Leroy. "Hi. I'm Christine. Where is your wife?"

"She's in the kitchen." Leroy led her to Mattie. He stood close by as Christine spoke to Mattie, checking her vitals and asking her how she felt.

"Trevor and I are going to get you to the hospital as soon as we can," Christine explained, squatting down beside Mattie. "You let me know if you feel any sudden changes or if the pain becomes unbearable."

"Okay." Mattie's voice was barely audible. She looked up at Leroy with wide eyes. "Can my husband stay with me?"

"Absolutely. I'll make sure he's with you the whole time."

"Good." Mattie held up her hand, and when Leroy took it, she squeezed hard.

Mattie needed him. Leroy's heart seemed lodged in his throat.

The male paramedic returned with a gurney, and soon Mattie was loaded up in the back of the ambulance. Leroy climbed in beside her, and she held out her hand to him once again.

"Leroy."

"*Ya.*" He leaned down.

"Please don't leave me."

"I promise I won't." He brushed a wisp of her hair back from her face.

Her eyes glistened, and he hoped she wouldn't cry. It would rip him to shreds if she cried. If only he could do more than just hold her hand.

"*Ich liebe dich*," he whispered, relieved to tell her his true feelings at last. "And you are going to be a *wunderbaar mamm*. Think about all you have to look forward to. Soon you'll be holding your *boppli* in your arms."

"*Danki.*" A tear trickled down the side of her face.

Leroy wiped the tear away with his fingertip as the ambulance roared to life. Then he sat in a seat beside her and held her hand as the vehicle steered down the driveway toward the road.

. . .

"Mrs. Fisher," a nurse said after Mattie was deposited in a birthing room at the hospital. "Let's get you changed into a gown so we can do an exam."

Mattie tightened her grip on Leroy's hand as he looked up at her. Her eyes were still wide. In fact, they hadn't gone back to their normal size since he'd helped her walk from the bathroom to the kitchen.

He pushed a golden lock of hair away from her face. "Do you want me to go and call your *mamm*?" He offered to leave to avoid her having to ask him to give her privacy. "Your parents should be up soon, and I know they'll want to be here for the birth of their first grandchild."

Mattie bit her lower lip. "Will you hurry back?"

"Of course I will, *mei liewe*." He leaned down and kissed her cheek. "I'll be right back." He crossed the room toward the door.

"Don't take too long," Mattie called after him.

"I promise I won't." Leroy rushed to find a phone in the lobby.

. . .

Leroy left messages for Mattie's parents, Hank, and Joel. He made a quick stop in the restroom and then purchased a bottle of water from a vending machine before hurrying toward the birthing room where he'd left Mattie.

When he entered the room and found it empty, his stomach seemed to plummet toward his toes as alarm gripped him. He glanced at the clock on the wall. He'd been gone for only twenty minutes. Where had the hospital staff taken Mattie and why had they moved her in such a short period of time?

He rushed out to the desk in the hallway, where three young women dressed in hospital scrubs were working. One spoke on the phone, another typed on the computer, and the third wrote in a notebook.

"Excuse me," Leroy said to the young woman dressed in purple scrubs with the notebook.

She looked up at him. "May I help you?"

"My wife, Martha Fisher, was in room five." He pointed in the direction of the room. "I just left her there twenty minutes ago, and when I returned, she was gone."

"What is her name again?" The young woman flipped through another notebook.

"Martha Fisher." He repeated the name through gritted teeth and then took a deep breath in an attempt to calm his frayed nerves.

"She was taken into surgery. You can have a seat over there and someone will update you soon." The woman gestured toward a waiting area with chairs, a table, and a television.

"Surgery?" Leroy's body thrummed with renewed worry and anxiety. "Why?"

"I'm not sure, but I will contact the nurses and see if I can get more information."

"But she wanted me to stay with her." His voice rose, and the workers nearby turned to look at him. "She wanted me to hold her hand. You don't understand. I have to stay with her. I promised I would be right back. You have to tell me where she is so I can be with her."

"I'm sorry. You can't go into the surgery room." She pointed to the chairs again. "You can have a seat for now. Would you like something to drink?"

Leroy held up the bottle of water. "I have a drink. Thank you." He walked past the bank of chairs and stared out the window at the dark clouds and steady raindrops. *This has to be bad. They wouldn't have whisked her away unless she was in danger.*

Leaning his head against the cool glass, he closed his eyes. *Please, God, please keep Mattie and the* boppli *safe. Please lay your healing hands on her and the* boppli *and give the surgeons strength and wisdom. Please, Lord, take* gut *care of her. I can't possibly live without her by my side.*

. . .

"Leroy!" Ruth rushed toward him. "How's Mattie? How's the *boppli*?"

Leroy turned as Mattie's parents approached. A tiny thread of relief moved through him. He was thankful not to be alone anymore. "I don't know much of anything. A nurse came out for a few seconds and told me there were complications, but that's all she said she was able to tell me. All I really know is that Mattie's in surgery. I haven't heard how she is."

For more than an hour, he'd paced and stared out the window, waiting and praying for news about Mattie and the baby. The anxiety was eating away at his insides, and all he could do was pray for her.

"I don't understand." Ruth looked at Mose and then back at Leroy. "Did she have to have an emergency caesarian section?"

Leroy clenched his jaw. "I don't know." He explained how he'd left to make phone calls and then returned to the birthing room only to find she was gone. "The nurse promised to bring me news when she had it, but she hasn't returned."

"We'll sit with you." Mose patted Leroy's shoulder. "Do you need something to eat?"

"No, *danki*. I can't eat."

"Let's sit down." Mose pointed to nearby chairs. "I'm certain everything will be just fine."

"*Ya*, I agree." Ruth's smile seemed forced. "My friend's *dochder* had complications with her first child, but everything turned out just fine."

Complications. What if Mattie or the baby weren't fine? What would he do then?

Have faith and pray.

"I talked to Lizzie," Ruth continued. "She and Al are on their way. They should be here shortly. Did you call Tillie and Hank?"

"*Ya.*" Leroy fiddled with his empty bottle of water, which crackled in protest. "I imagine they will come too."

"Oh, *gut.*" Ruth rubbed her hands together. "We can all celebrate the *boppli* together." She reached over and squeezed Mose's hand. "We're going to be grandparents. Can you believe it?"

"No. I don't feel that old."

He and Ruth chuckled at the joke, but Leroy couldn't find the strength to smile. His mind was tied up in worry as he sent more silent prayers up for Mattie and the baby.

. . .

Mattie glanced around the operating room. Her mind was fuzzy, and the pain in her abdomen and lower back was unbearable. What was happening?

A sea of people dressed in green scrubs rushed around her as monitors beeped and clicked. A young woman with big, green eyes stood at Mattie's side and whispered words of encouragement to her, but the words were garbled by the chaos around them.

Mattie picked up words now and then, such as "losing too much blood," "unresponsive," and "critical." Someone else hollered, "Nuchal cord!"

She didn't know what it all meant or what was happening to her. Maybe she had fallen asleep in the ambulance and she was just dreaming.

"Hang in there, Mrs. Fisher." The young woman beside her squeezed her arm. Her tone was too happy, as if she was forcing her pleasantness.

What was going on?

"Stay with us, Mrs. Fisher," someone near her feet said. "Be strong for us."

Mattie tried to nod, but her strength was nearly gone. She wanted to sleep. She needed sleep.

She could try to be strong again another day.

Maybe tomorrow.

Yes, being strong tomorrow sounded like a good plan.

"We're losing her!" someone yelled.

Mattie's vision blurred, and the room spun. She closed her eyes, and then everything went black.

CHAPTER 11

Leroy walked over to the reception desk with growing frustration and worry.

"Miss." He tapped his finger on the desk as the young woman looked up at him. "It's been two hours, and no one has told me what's happening. Would you please check on my wife? Her name is Martha Jane Fisher."

"Mr. Fisher?"

Leroy turned toward Dr. Sheppard's voice. She stood at the far end of the desk, and his stomach dropped when he saw her hazel eyes were red and puffy, as though she'd been crying.

Oh no. His chest seized with panic. *Please, God, let Mattie and the* boppli *be okay. Please protect them.*

"May I speak with you in private?" Dr. Sheppard pointed to a conference room.

"Of course." Leroy turned toward the reception area to where his family looked on, their brows furrowed and their faces contorted with concern.

Leroy was grateful everyone had come to sit and wait with him. Ruth, Mose, Tillie, Hank, Joel, Dora, Lizanne, and Al were all huddled together in a corner and had kept the conversation going during the past hour. Hank and Joel had worked to keep the mood light by sharing funny stories of their youth, and Leroy had even chuckled a few times.

But now dread pooled in the pit of his gut as he followed Dr. Sheppard into the small conference room.

"Please have a seat." She pointed to a table and closed the door behind them.

"Is Mattie okay?" His tone was thin and shaky as he sank onto one of the four hard wooden chairs.

She took a deep breath and stepped toward him. "Your wife will be fine."

"She *will* be?" Renewed frustration surged through him. "I've been waiting for two hours to get some news. When we arrived at the hospital, I left her in a room for twenty minutes, and when I came back, she was gone. No one has told me anything except to say she was rushed into surgery with complications."

His hands shook. "I need to know what's going on, and I want to know now. Please, give it to me straight."

"I'm sorry no one has kept you informed." She sat down and rested her elbow on the table, then suddenly wilted, resembling a tired woman instead of a confident doctor. "Everything happened so fast, and we were doing all we could to save both Mrs. Fisher and the baby."

"To save them?" Tears stung his eyes.

"Your wife lost a lot of blood, and we almost lost her. She's received two units of blood, and she's going to be fine. She's just very weak." The doctor worried her lower lip as if choosing her words with care. "I'm sorry, but the baby didn't make it."

"What?" He gasped as tears streamed down his cheeks. "We lost the baby?"

"Yes. I'm so sorry." She sniffed and wiped away a tear. "A team of doctors and I worked on him, but there was nothing we could do. The umbilical cord was wrapped around his neck twice. He suffocated before she even went into labor."

He wiped at his tears, and she handed him a nearby box of tissues. "How is Mattie?"

Dr. Sheppard paused again, and her eyes misted. "I haven't told her yet. She's still under sedation, and I thought you would want to be with her when I share this devastating news."

He nodded. "Yes, I do want to be there."

"I know this is a lot to process, so I understand if you need time before we go together to tell her. Take all the time you need, and I will take you to see her when you're ready."

Leroy cleared his throat. "I need to tell her parents first. They've been just as worried as I've been."

"I understand." She touched his hand. "I am so sorry. Please know we did all we could. When things like this happen, it reminds us doctors that we're only human. There's only so much we can do, but it still hurts us deeply. Losing a patient is a devastating loss to me, but I know it will never compare to how you and Mrs. Fisher feel. You have my deepest condolences and my prayers."

"Thank you." He brushed away another tear. "Thank you for saving Mattie."

She rubbed his arm. "I wish I could've done more. Have the nurses find me when you're ready to see your wife."

He followed the doctor out to the waiting area, where Ruth and Mose rushed over to him, their brows creased.

"What happened?" Mose asked.

"How's Mattie?" Ruth wrung her hands. "How's the *boppli*?"

"Mattie lost a lot of blood, but she's going to be okay." He paused as his body shuddered with raw agony. "But the *boppli* didn't make it." His voice cracked. "The umbilical cord was wrapped around his neck, and he suffocated."

"*Ach* no!" Ruth's eyes misted over with tears. "No, no, no!"

Mose encircled Ruth in a hug as she sobbed.

Leroy's eyes flooded with more tears as everyone else rushed to gather around them, all asking questions at once.

"Let's give him a chance to talk," Joel said.

Leroy took a deep breath and told the story again. Lizanne and Dora sobbed in their husbands' arms, but Tillie approached Leroy as she wiped away her own tears.

"How are you holding up?"

When Leroy shook his head, she pulled him into her arms, and, leaning down, he cried on her shoulder as Tillie rubbed his back.

"I'm so sorry." Hank's voice was soft by his ear. "I knew something had happened when you called me, but I didn't realize . . ."

"It's all right." Leroy stood up straight. Tillie handed him a tissue, and he wiped his eyes. He had to force himself to be strong. "*Danki*, Tillie."

"You need to go see her." Tillie's brown eyes shimmered

with tears. "Hank and I will take care of everyone else. You go take care of your *fraa*." She squeezed his arm. "She needs you."

"*Danki*." Leroy took a deep breath and walked over to the reception desk. "Dr. Sheppard said I should let you know when I'm ready to see my wife. Would you please tell her I'm ready now?"

. . .

"Mrs. Fisher?"

Mattie blinked her eyes open and stared up at a fluorescent light. She scanned the unfamiliar room just enough to realize it was a hospital room. She turned to her side to where Dr. Sheppard stared down at her, her lips pressed into a thin line. Leroy stood behind her, his dark eyes glistening with tears. Had he been crying?

Recognition filtered through her confusion, and she remembered everything that happened up until when she passed out.

"What's going on?" She attempted to sit up.

"Please, Mrs. Fisher, just relax." Dr. Sheppard placed her hand on Mattie's arm.

Leroy came around to the other side of the bed and touched her shoulder. The pain in his eyes sliced through her.

Something was wrong. Dread gripped her and her hands shook.

"Where's my baby?" Mattie's voice trembled. When the doctor didn't respond, she repeated the question, looking at Leroy. "Where is *mei boppli*?"

Dr. Sheppard's eyes shimmered with tears. "I'm sorry, but your baby didn't survive."

"What?" Mattie asked as confusion settled over her. And then the doctor's words echoed through her mind, and understanding shoved away her confusion.

Mattie gasped as terror and horror lanced through her chest, squeezing her lungs and stealing her words for a moment. "No, no, no!" she managed to say through a strangled breath. "You don't mean that. My baby has to be okay! You've made a terrible mistake."

Leroy sniffed and rubbed her arm as tears traced down his cheeks. "I'm so sorry, Mattie." His voice was thin and reedy.

Dr. Sheppard rubbed her fingers over her reddened eyes. "He was stillborn. The umbilical cord was wrapped around his neck."

"No," Mattie whispered as tears flowed from her eyes, dripping from her cheeks to her blue gown. She looked up at Leroy. "It can't be true."

He swallowed a sob.

"He suffocated in the womb. We tried to bring him back, but we couldn't." She looked away for a moment, then met Mattie's eyes again. "When we were delivering the baby, your incision tore because he was so big, and the arteries to the right and left of your uterus ruptured too. You lost so much blood so fast that we almost lost you as well. Thankfully, we noticed the tears quickly, and we were able to save you."

Sobs tore from Mattie's throat as she drowned in grief. This had to be a nightmare. This couldn't be real. She'd lost Isaiah and now their son was dead. *No, no, no!*

Certainly God wouldn't take both her beloved husband and their innocent son. What had she done to deserve this? How could she live when both her precious Isaiah and Jacob were gone?

Why, God, why?

Tears gushed from Mattie's eyes like a waterfall as agony shook her body to the core.

Leroy gently pulled her into his arms and rubbed her back until her sobs subsided.

"Oh, I'm so sorry," Dr. Sheppard said. "Would you like to see him?"

Unable to speak, Mattie nodded and pulled a tissue from the box beside her.

"I'll have the nurses bring him to you." Dr. Sheppard walked to the door and then turned to face them, dividing her sad expression between Mattie and Leroy. "Please know that we did everything we could. I wish I could have saved your son."

"We know," Leroy said softly as he moved his hand back to Mattie's shoulder.

Mattie dabbed at her eyes, but the tears refused to stop.

Dr. Sheppard stepped out of the room. As the door clicked closed, Mattie hugged a pillow to her chest and began to sob again. When would she awaken from this nightmare?

"We'll get through this." Leroy's breath was warm in her ear. "I promise you we will, Mattie."

Mattie kept her eyes focused on the pillow. It was all too much to take in and comprehend. How could her baby be dead? How did this happen?

Leroy sniffed as the room fell silent.

A few moments later, a knock sounded on the door.

"Come in," Leroy called.

A nurse entered holding the baby. He was wrapped in a white blanket trimmed in pink and blue. The nurse's expression was tentative as she approached them.

Mattie sucked in a breath.

"Would you like to sit in the recliner while you hold him?" The nurse nodded to the chair.

"That's a *gut* idea." Leroy took Mattie's hand. "Let me help you up."

Mattie allowed him to lift her and steer her to the chair. Once she was seated, Leroy covered her lap with a blanket and the nurse handed her the baby.

"He's beautiful," the nurse said. "He weighs almost nine pounds."

Mattie's lower lip trembled as she stared down at her son.

"Please let me know if you need anything. Just push the call button, and I'll come right away." The nurse excused herself and disappeared from the room, gently closing the door behind her.

Leroy moved to the window, and Mattie cuddled her son close to her chest. Tears spilled down her cheeks as her precious baby lay motionless in her arms.

Mattie touched his shock of blond hair and then ran her finger over his small nose, cheeks, and lips. He was perfect and beautiful. If only Isaiah were here to see his baby boy.

"Hi, Jacob," she whispered, her voice wobbly. "I'm your *mamm,* and I love you very much. Your *dat* was Isaiah.

Your *dat* wanted to name you after his *daadi*. He and his *daadi* were very close. You look just like your *dat*."

She touched his hair again. "Your *dat*'s hair was blond when he was born. It turned darker when he got older, but it was still blond in the sunlight."

She touched his tiny fingers. "I remember the first day I met your *dat*. We were playing volleyball on separate teams at a youth gathering, and he was wearing these really neat sunglasses. When the game was over, he walked over to me and asked me what my name was. When he smiled at me, he stole my heart. I knew then I wanted to marry him and raise a family with him. I know that sounds *gegisch,* but it was love at first sight."

She sniffed as more tears trickled down her cheeks. "Your *dat* died six months ago. He was at the bank and an angry man came in with a gun. You don't need to know the details, but he died helping someone else. He sacrificed himself. Isaiah was like that. He always put other people before himself.

"I'm sorry I couldn't save you, Jacob. I wanted you more than I can ever express. I've loved you since before you were born, and I will always love you, my sweet *bu*. Don't forget that, okay?"

Mattie leaned down and kissed his forehead, tears blurring her vision. She held Jacob closer and sobbed as agony tightened her chest and stole her breath.

. . .

Leroy swallowed his own sobs as Mattie cried. He'd moved to the window to give her some space while she held her child, but he couldn't take it any longer. He had to try to help soothe her broken heart.

"Oh, Mattie." He rushed across the room and fell to his knees in front of her. "Mattie, *mei liewe*. I'm so sorry. I'm so very sorry." He placed his hand on her shoulder.

She met his gaze with red, puffy eyes, and he touched her tear-stained cheek as renewed grief coursed through him.

"I'm so sorry," he whispered again. He longed to ease her pain, but there was nothing he could do or say to take away her agony. He could only offer her his heart.

"Isn't he *schee*?" She gave him a watery smile as she looked down at the baby. "He looks like Isaiah with his blond hair and little nose." She stroked the baby's face with a trembling hand. "He's a big *bu* too. I guess that's why my back hurt so much."

Leroy's words were stuck in his throat. He kept his focus trained on the child. How could he ever make this right? How could he ever help Mattie's broken heart heal after she'd lost both her husband and son?

Suddenly Ruth's words echoed through his mind. *"Her life with Isaiah was part of her past, but her life with you is her future."*

Strength flourished somewhere deep inside his soul. He would be her fortitude, her shoulder to cry on. He would show her he loved her no matter what they faced together.

"May I hold him?" He held his breath, wondering if she would reject his request.

Mattie glanced up at him and then nodded. She held out the baby to him.

Leroy stood and took the baby into his arms. He

lowered himself onto the corner of the bed across from her. He studied Jacob's tiny face, his nose, and his light hair.

Why did God take this little child before he had a chance to grow? He shoved the question away. It wasn't Leroy's place to question God's will.

"He is *schee*. You're right. He does look like Isaiah." He touched Jacob's tiny fingers and then rubbed his cheek. The child's skin was cold as though he were a doll.

"It's all my fault, you know."

"What?" His eyes snapped to her crumpled face.

"If I had told you on Saturday I hadn't felt him moving, we probably could have saved him." She leaned back in the recliner and cleared her throat. "I should have gone straight to the hospital when I realized something could be wrong, but I didn't. I let him die."

"Don't say that. You don't know that's true."

Mattie blew out a shuddering breath and then stared down at her lap. "God is punishing me."

"No, no, he's not. I don't understand why God allows tragedy in our lives, but I know he's not punishing you."

"He must be. He took Isaiah, and now he's taken Jacob." She met his gaze, and her face crumpled in despair. "I must have done something to deserve this."

"No, no, no." He shook his head. "You didn't do anything to deserve this. It just happened, and we'll get through it. I'm here, and I'll be by your side." He reached out to take her hand, but she pulled it back.

Mattie opened her mouth to respond just as the hospital door opened and an older nurse walked in. She wore blue scrubs and carried a clipboard and pen.

"Mr. and Mrs. Fisher, I'm so sorry for your loss." She came around the bed and stood by them. "My name is Tracey, and I'm completing your paperwork. I need to know the baby's name for his birth and death certificates."

Mattie lifted her chin. "Jacob Isaiah Petersheim."

"Fisher." Leroy ground out the word as frustration and hurt born of grief grabbed him by the throat. "His last name is Fisher."

Mattie turned toward him and frowned. "Fine. Jacob Petersheim Fisher."

The nurse blinked. "Would you please spell that for me?"

Mattie spelled it out, and the nurse thanked them before quickly leaving.

Leroy looked down at Jacob, and fresh grief strangled his resentment. How could he allow himself to be frustrated with Mattie when she just lost her son?

No, Jacob was *their* son. Leroy was supposed to be Jacob's father and raise him as his own. His dream for their family had been shattered too.

A single tear spilled down his cheek as he studied the boy, then ran the tip of his finger over the baby's face. "We'll never forget you, Jacob."

The door opened, and Ruth and Mose stepped in.

"*Ach*, Mattie!" Ruth rushed over. When her gaze fell on the baby in Leroy's arms, her tears began anew.

"Would you like to hold him?" Leroy held up the child, and Ruth nodded before taking him. "I'll give you some time alone."

He glanced over at Mattie, but her eyes were focused on her mother. He paused for a moment, then stalked out of the hospital room, down the hallway, and out the door to the parking lot.

The rainy, humid August morning air hit his skin like a hot shower. Confusion and despair coiled through his tight shoulders and stole his breath. How could he be Mattie's strength when he couldn't temper his own emotions?

Leaning against the brick wall behind him, Leroy closed his eyes. *God, show me how to help Mattie. Guide my heart and help me be the husband Mattie needs. I can't do this without you. Amen.*

CHAPTER 12

Mattie wiped away tears as her parents took turns holding Jacob and speaking softly to him. The entire scene was a surreal dream. No, it was a nightmare. Surely she'd wake up soon to find she was still pregnant with Jacob kicking inside of her.

If only she could pinch herself hard enough and wake up from this tribulation.

Mamm wiped away her own tears and then looked over at her. "I'm sorry. Your *dat*, Leroy, and I are all here for you. If you need to cry, then cry. Let yourself grieve."

Mattie wiped her face with another tissue. "*Danki.*" She looked toward the door and found that Leroy was gone. When had he left and where had he gone? Had he stormed out, upset with her about Jacob's name?

"I'm so sorry," *Dat* said, pulling a chair up next to her.

"*Dat.*" Mattie's voice broke as she turned toward him, and he gathered her into his arms as if she were a little girl.

Mattie closed her eyes and sobbed on his shoulder. Her parents' love was just what her battered and bruised soul craved.

• • •

Mattie walked slowly into the kitchen. Her legs felt like heavy blocks of wood and her abdomen and back were sore. When she touched her flatter belly, it was as though something was missing.

Something *was* missing. She was home from the hospital without her baby. Jacob was gone, and he left a hole in her heart when he died. She breathed out a shuddering breath and leaned against the kitchen table.

"Your *mamm* is here." Leroy hurried into the kitchen carrying her bags. "She came over this morning to do a few chores around the house. All you need to do is rest. Your *dat* is helping Hank in the harness shop so I can be with you too." He paused, his eyes searching her face. "Do you need anything? Maybe a glass of water? Something to eat?"

"Water would be fine. *Danki.*" She sank onto a kitchen chair at the table and rested her chin in her hand.

"Here you go." Leroy placed a glass of water on the table and then picked up her bag. "I'm going to put your things in the bedroom. Call me if you need me." Then he disappeared into the family room.

She took another drink and evaluated her life. The past twenty-four hours had been a whirlwind. It seemed as if Jacob had been born last week instead of only yesterday. She'd become a mother and then lost her baby in the same instant. She wanted to cry but had no more tears left in her to shed.

The *click* of the screen door drew her attention to the mudroom doorway.

"Mattie!" *Mamm* rushed into the kitchen and sat beside her. "I was in the harness shop with Hank and your *dat* and thought I heard the van pull up. I'm so glad you're home."

Mattie gripped the glass. "I saw the doctor this morning. She told me to take it easy. I should feel better in about six weeks." She gave a sarcastic snort. "I'm not sure if I'll ever feel better, though."

"You will, *mei liewe*." *Mamm* touched her arm. "It will take time, but your heart will heal. Just give yourself time to grieve."

"*Ya*." Mattie wiped her hand across her face and then stared down at the blue tablecloth. "Isaiah is gone, and now Jacob is gone. All I have left is time."

"Your life is not over." *Mamm* squeezed her shoulder. "You're not alone. You have Leroy."

Mattie glanced up to where Leroy stood in the doorway to the family room, watching her. The frown creasing his face cut her to the bone. Her mouth dried, and her heart twisted. He must have heard what she'd said. She sucked in a breath, waiting for his biting retort— the same kind of retort he made when she told the nurse the baby's last name was Petersheim. But he remained silent, his intense gaze focused on her.

"The bishop will be here later to discuss Jacob's service with us. I thought we could have it on Saturday."

"Saturday?" Mattie looked at her *mamm*. "Is that enough time?"

"*Ya*, we have two days to prepare. I've already started cleaning, and I'll work more this afternoon."

"*Danki*." Mattie's eyes stung with threatening tears. She'd buried her husband, and now she had to bury her son. When would her shattered heart ever heal?

Every cell in her body was completely exhausted. She needed rest. She needed time alone to process the grief that covered her like a heavy blanket. She pushed herself up from the table and started for the bedroom.

"Where are you going?" *Mamm* asked.

"To lie down." Mattie dragged herself forward.

She stopped when she approached Leroy and looked up at him. His attractive face was twisted with a deep frown and his dark eyes were misted with tears.

"I didn't mean what I said," she whispered, her voice trembling. "I know I haven't lost you."

"It's okay." He touched her shoulder. "Go rest. Let me know if you want something to eat."

"*Danki.*" She stepped into her bedroom and flung herself onto the bed before burying her face in the quilt.

When the door creaked open, she rolled onto her side and faced the wall. She didn't want any visitors. She wanted to cry and pray without an audience.

"Mattie." *Mamm*'s voice was soft as the bed shifted under her weight. "I know you're hurting, but you shouldn't take your grief out on Leroy." She rubbed Mattie's shoulder. "He wants to help you through this, and he's grieving too."

"I know that." Mattie rubbed her hands across her damp cheeks. "But I need to face this alone."

"That's not true." *Mamm* rubbed Mattie's back, making circles with her hands. "You and Leroy are a couple, and you should face your problems together as a united force." She paused. "I lost a *boppli* once."

Mattie gasped and looked at her mother. "What?"

"I had a miscarriage before Lizzie was born. I was

thirteen weeks along. I'd had some spotting and cramping, but the doctor insisted everything was fine. I lost the *boppli* in the middle of the night. It was terrible. I blamed myself, and I thought your *dat* and I would never have a child. I cried and I prayed a lot, asking God why he chose to take that child." She touched Mattie's face. "I know my situation was different because I lost the baby at thirteen weeks, but it was still a loss."

A tear slid down Mattie's cheek. "I'm so sorry. I had no idea."

"How could you know? I never told you about it because I didn't think you needed to know. Now seemed like the perfect time to tell you." *Mamm* gave her a weak smile.

"A few months later, I became pregnant with Lizzie. I was terrified the whole time that I would lose her, but I didn't. And then you came along three years later, and your *dat* and I were doubly blessed." She rubbed Mattie's arm. "My point is that you will get through this, but it will be easier if you let Leroy help you. He's desperate to comfort you, and you should let him. Allow him to feel useful and helpful."

Mattie's body trembled.

Mamm stood, pausing for a beat. "I'm going to do some more cleaning. Do you need anything?"

"No. *Danki.*"

"You should rest." *Mamm* started for the door. "Call me if you need me."

"I will." She sat up as her mother passed through the door. "*Mamm*. Wait!"

"What?" *Mamm* spun to face her.

"Would you please close the door?"

Mamm closed it and crossed to the bed. "*Was iss letz?*"

Mattie touched the stitching on the quilt. "I spoke to Dr. Sheppard this morning in private before Leroy came to pick me up."

"What did she say?" *Mamm* sat on the edge of the bed again.

"She said what happened to Jacob was rare, and there was nothing we could do to prevent it. It wasn't my fault." She glanced up at her mother and sniffed. "She said I can have more *kinner*. I just need to wait a couple of months to let my body heal, but I can try again."

Mamm touched her hand to Mattie's cheek. "That's *wunderbaar* news."

"I just don't know what I want. I'm so confused."

"You don't have to decide right now. Just rest and let your body and your spirit heal." *Mamm* kissed her cheek. "Take a nap. You'll feel better."

"*Danki.*" Mattie squeezed her mother's hand.

"*Gern gschehne.*" *Mamm* stood and walked out of the room, closing the door behind her.

Mattie looked at the bags sitting on the floor beside the bed. She stood and opened her tote bag and pulled out an envelope with "Leroy and Martha Fisher" written on the front in neat handwriting.

She opened it and an official government document fell out, saying "Certificate of Death for Jacob Petersheim Fisher." Fresh tears welled in Mattie's eyes as she ran her hands over Jacob's name. She peered in the envelope again and found his birth certificate and a lock of blond hair in a small zipper storage bag, along with his tiny footprints and handprints. Mattie wiped her eyes and then slipped everything back into the envelope.

When she opened the tote bag again, she found the pink and blue onesies Leroy had purchased at the grocery store only a month ago. Since *Mamm* had given Mattie a blue sleeper for Jacob to wear, Mattie hadn't needed to use the onesie. She found a flat box in her nightstand, and then she folded the onesies and placed them inside the box.

Mattie opened her hope chest and put the envelope and the box on top of a stack of linens she hadn't yet unpacked. Then she climbed into bed, closed her eyes, and fell asleep.

. . .

"How is she?" Leroy leaned against the kitchen doorway as Ruth walked through the family room.

Ruth frowned. "She'll be fine."

He cupped his hand to his forehead and gritted his teeth as guilt clawed at his shoulders. "I feel like I'm no use to her."

She chuckled and touched his arm. "You are the most patient man I've ever known, other than Mose."

He raked his hand through his hair. "I don't know how to help her."

She pointed to the kitchen table. "Sit."

He obeyed, slumping into a nearby chair as Ruth moved to the kitchen counter.

"Here." She placed a glass of milk and a plate of chocolate

chip cookies in front of him, and then sat down beside him. "Take a drink, have a *kichli*, and relax."

"*Danki.*" He took a long drink, placed the glass on the table, picked up a cookie, and took a bite. "I have no idea what to do for her or say to her now. She's lost so much. I'm never sure if I'm doing the right thing."

"You're doing just fine." Her smile faded. "You're the best thing that could've happened to her after losing Isaiah."

He shook his head as disappointment replaced his guilt. "I don't know where we go from here. We were both so busy preparing for Jacob, and now he's gone." He picked up the cookie crumbs and dropped them onto the plate. "I don't know how we can survive now that Jacob is gone. He was the glue that held us together as a couple. We were going to be a family, but now it's just Mattie and me."

"You're still a family whether or not you have *kinner*." Ruth leveled her gaze at him. "You are a *gut* husband and you will continue to be one. The two most important pieces you need for a marriage to work are love and determination. I believe you and Mattie have both, and you can work through this. In fact, you two may come out of this stronger after all you've endured. The most important piece is love, and it's apparent that you love her and always have. When you were teenagers, I would see you staring at her in church."

He cringed and swallowed a groan. "Was I that obvious?"

"*Ya*, and I always thought it was sweet. You were always her most loyal *freind*, and you stayed devoted to her throughout your teenage years. You remained her *freind* when she married Isaiah. You didn't let envy get in the way of your friendship, and you accepted Isaiah. That shows strength of character."

Leroy shrugged. "She chose him, not me. There was nothing I could do about it."

"Have faith in your marriage and in each other."

He frowned. "But it's always been a one-way street, Ruth. I love Mattie, but I don't think she loves me. It can't work if the marriage is one-sided."

Ruth squeezed his hand. "I believe there's a reason for everything under heaven. It was part of God's plan for you to marry Mattie, and I have faith that you will get through this."

Leroy picked up another cookie. "I hope you're right."

CHAPTER 13

Leroy waved as the last of the buggies carrying funeral guests steered down the driveway toward the road. He breathed in the sweet aroma of threatening rain and then looked up at the ominous clouds choking the sky. Lightning sparked, followed by the distant rumble of thunder. A storm was coming, which was a fitting complement to this bleak day. He walked slowly toward the porch, his boots crunching on the rock path.

The wake and funeral had worn Leroy out both physically and emotionally. He had stood beside Mattie through both events, and she had held on to him as though for dear life. Even during the graveside service Mattie held his arm as though he was the only thing holding her upright.

When the service was over, she sobbed in his arms. He was thankful she needed him, but he was emotionally drained from supporting her. He hoped he could continue to be her strength in the coming days. The pain of losing Jacob, the child he'd wanted, stabbed at his heart.

Give me strength, Lord. Help me be the husband Mattie wants and needs. Amen.

Leroy climbed the back steps and crossed the porch. He stopped at the back door and glanced toward the harness shop.

An image of the grand opening filled his mind— Mattie smiling and laughing as she swept the floor and then her sweet compliments about his talent and his hard work to make the harness shop a reality. That day had been nearly perfect, but it seemed as though it had been years instead of only a month since that day. He had to find a way to bring back her happiness, and he prayed he would see her smile again soon. But how?

As he leaned against the porch railing, a gentle breeze sprayed a light rain across his face. The cool wetness was refreshing, almost invigorating, after the hot, humid day he'd spent in the house for the funeral and then standing in the brutal sun for the graveside service.

Jacob Petersheim Fisher was buried beside his father while the community looked on and Mattie sobbed on Leroy's shoulder. He had to be strong for Mattie, but his own grief threatened to swamp his soul. Leroy closed his eyes as a frigid lump of ice seemed to swell in his chest. Lightning lit up the dark sky, followed by a louder clap of thunder. The storm was moving closer and preparing to bear down on Bird-in-Hand.

The back door clicked open, and Mose stepped out onto the porch, followed by Hank.

"*Ach*, it's raining now." He pushed his hat onto his gray hair. "I thought I heard thunder."

"*Ya*, a storm is headed this way." Leroy turned and leaned his lower back against the wet railing. "Are you getting ready to leave?"

"*Ya.*" Mose jammed his thumb toward Hank. "He's going to help me hitch up the horse and buggy."

"Oh, do you need help?" Leroy gestured toward the barn. "I could've done it for you."

"No, no." Mose clapped his hand on Leroy's shoulder. "You've been through enough today. You should go rest."

Hank nodded. "I'll help him. Go on inside."

"All right." As Mose and Hank walked down the path toward the barn, Leroy remained on the porch and breathed in the night air.

When the rain began soaking through his shirt, he pushed himself off the railing and headed in through the back door. He pulled off his boots and hat and then stepped into the kitchen, where Tillie stood at the sink, washing dishes.

She turned to face him. "Is everyone gone?"

"*Ya.*" He crossed the kitchen and stood by the table. "*Danki* for staying and helping to clean up."

"I don't mind. You know I'm always *froh* to lend a hand."

"Where's Mattie?"

She gestured toward the doorway. "I think Mattie and Ruth are in your bedroom. They were helping me clean up and then Mattie got upset again. Her grief seems to come in waves." She frowned. "I feel so bad for her. She rushed out of here, and Ruth followed her. I thought I should give them some privacy."

He rolled up his sleeves. "I'll dry and put the dishes away."

"Don't be *gegisch*. You can go sit with the men or check on Mattie. I can handle this."

"*Danki*. I don't know what I'd do without you and Hank."

"I already told you I'm *froh* to help. Stop thanking me." Tillie gave him a resigned smile. "You would do the same for Hank and me."

"*Ya*, I would."

"Go check on Mattie. I'll take care of everything here." She turned back toward the sink and continued her work.

He crossed through the family room to the downstairs bedroom. He knocked on the door and then stepped inside, where he found Mattie sitting on the bed and Ruth sitting across from her in a chair.

"Hi." He closed the door behind him. "Everyone is gone now. I just wanted to check on you."

Frowning, Mattie crossed her arms over her chest, blocking her black dress.

"I guess we should get ready to go." Ruth stood.

"*Danki* for being here, *Mamm*," Mattie said softly.

"Mose and Hank are hitching up your horse and buggy," Leroy said as Ruth walked to the door.

"Oh." Ruth looked back at Mattie. "I'll come and say good-bye before we leave." She looked at Leroy. "I'll give you a minute to talk alone."

"*Danki*," Leroy said before Ruth disappeared through the doorway and closed the door behind her. He sat across from Mattie. "How are you?"

"I don't know. I'm numb." She reached for him, and he hesitated. "What?" she asked.

"I'm all wet." He gave her a wry smile. "I was standing out in the rain."

"I don't care." She continued to hold out her arm. "Please hold me. I need you." Her pained expression twisted his insides.

"I'll always be here for you, Mattie." He pulled her into his arms and she sobbed on his shoulder. "Everything will be all right," he whispered, fighting back his own tears.

. . .

Mattie stared at the ceiling in the dark bedroom, with only a few faint slivers of light sneaking past the dark-green shades covering the windows. Her alarm had gone off more than two hours ago, but she couldn't bring herself to climb out of bed.

For the past three weeks, when the alarm sounded signaling the time she needed to get up and prepare Leroy's breakfast, she'd turned it off and rolled over, sleeping away the morning. She'd waited for Leroy to lose his patience with her and demand she complete her chores, but he hadn't. Instead, the delicious smells of breakfast foods had wafted into her bedroom, indicating that he made his own breakfast and left her in her room alone to rest.

Each morning when she finally hoisted herself out of bed and entered the kitchen, she found food waiting for her. Not only had Leroy made his own breakfast, but he'd made enough food for her.

While Leroy continued to complete his chores and then head to work at the harness shop every day, he gave her space and didn't push her. He continued to sleep in the bedroom upstairs without mentioning anything about their sharing a bedroom. He never raised his voice or questioned her despondency. Instead, he was patient, kind, and understanding. She didn't deserve his patience or his understanding.

"Mattie?"

She rolled to her side as Tillie's voice sounded from outside her bedroom door.

"Mattie?" Her voice was hesitant. "May I please come in?"

"*Ya.*" Mattie sat up and smoothed her hair over her shoulders. Her hand moved to her abdomen, which was now flat. The pain from the surgery had subsided, but she didn't feel like herself. She felt like a stranger stuck inside of her own body, someone she didn't know or understand.

The door creaked open, and Tillie stood in the doorway dressed in a blue dress with a black apron. Her pretty face was clouded with a frown as she crossed her arms over her chest. "How are you?"

Mattie shrugged. "I'm not sure."

"I'm here to help you." She stepped into the bedroom. "May I do your laundry for you?"

Mattie sighed. Their clothes hadn't been laundered in nearly two weeks. In fact, she hadn't done the laundry herself since before Jacob was born. Her mother had taken care of the laundry for her after the funeral, and Mattie hadn't touched the hampers since then.

"Did Leroy ask you to come over and do my chores?"

Tillie paused, resting her hand on the doorknob. "He didn't exactly ask me. He said he was worried about you, and I offered to come and help." She pointed to the bed. "If you get up, I'll strip the bed and remake it before washing your sheets too."

Mattie reluctantly nodded. "All right. *Danki*."

She stood and went into the bathroom, and after Tillie had stripped the bed, remade it, and emptied Mattie's hamper, Mattie slowly dressed and pulled her hair up. It was the first time she'd dressed in anything other than a nightgown since the funeral.

She entered the kitchen and found the remnants of breakfast—eggs, toast, bacon, and sausage—on a plate covered in aluminum foil on the counter. The rest of the dishes had been washed and set on the drainboard. Leroy had not only left her breakfast this morning, but he'd washed the dishes.

She picked up a cold piece of toast and bit into it. It tasted like sand and she dropped it onto the plate. She had no appetite. Nothing appealed to her. All she wanted to do was sleep.

"You need to eat something."

With a gasp, Mattie spun toward the doorway leading to the mudroom and found Leroy looking at her. His dark eyes focused on her with intensity as he frowned.

"It's *gut* to see you up and dressed." He walked over to her. "How do you feel?"

Mattie frowned as she peered up at him. "I'm not sure."

"You look exhausted." He touched her cheek and his eyes seemed to be full of concern. "You're so pale. You need to eat. You'll never get your strength back if you don't eat." He dropped his hand to his side and walked over to the stove. "Would you like a grilled cheese?"

"*Danki*, but I'm not hungry."

He looked over at her. "Let me make you something."

"You don't need to cook for me. I can do it."

He pointed to the table. "Sit. I don't mind."

"But you have work to do." She joined him by the stove. "I'll do it."

He studied her for a moment. "I don't mind taking care of you. I understand you need some time to heal and get your strength back."

Mattie swallowed against a lump swelling in her throat. "Did you ask Tillie to come and do the laundry for me?"

"No, she offered. She said she wanted to help you." He rested his hands on her shoulders and leaned down to her. "Let us help you. We want to take care of you."

Leaning down, he brushed his lips over her cheek. "Sit down and I'll make you a grilled cheese sandwich. I'll put tea on for you too."

She slumped into a chair at the table. Setting her bent elbow on the table, she rested her chin on her palm as he worked at the stove. When Leroy brought her the sandwich and cup of tea, she looked up at him. "*Danki.*"

"*Gern gschehne.*" He kissed the top of her head. "You get some rest. I'll be back in at lunchtime. Think about what you want for lunch, and I'll make it for you."

She bit into the sandwich, which melted in her mouth. "You shouldn't be cooking for me."

"Stop arguing with me." He touched her back. "I'll take care of you for as long as you need me to. I'll see you later." He walked out of the kitchen, the screen door clicking closed behind him.

She ate the grilled cheese sandwich and drank the
tea in the silence of the large kitchen. She was washing
her dish at the sink when she heard Tillie come in from
outside.

"Did you eat something?" Tillie asked.

"*Ya.*" Mattie turned to face her.

"*Gut.*" Tillie pointed toward the laundry room. "I
already have the sheets and linens hanging out on the
line. I'm going to clean the bathroom and sweep the
downstairs, and then I'll wash the clothes. You can go
take a nap if you'd like."

Before Mattie could respond, Tillie was gone.

Mattie wanted to run after her and offer to help, but
she had no strength. Her arms were heavy, and her legs
ached. Just washing the dishes had worn her out. She
pinched the bridge of her nose as guilt weighed heavily
on her shoulders. She was useless. Her husband had to
cook for her, and her best friend had to do her laundry
and clean for her.

After putting her dish and cup in the cabinet, she made
her way back to her room, to her freshly made bed. The
strong scent of vinegar filled her nose, and she glanced
toward the bathroom, where she heard Tillie cleaning.

Mattie heaved a heavy sigh, then climbed onto the
bed, rested her arm over her forehead, and gave in to her
urge to sleep.

. . .

Mattie awoke with a start and turned toward her clock.
Alarm coursed through her. It was nearly four in the

afternoon. She'd slept through lunch and the entire afternoon while Tillie had completed her chores. She had to at least attempt to do her own work. She couldn't depend on Tillie to continue to run the house for her while she slept her life away.

She hopped out of bed and hurried to the kitchen. She found pork chops in the refrigerator and surmised Leroy had planned to bake them for supper. She could show him she was still a hardworking and conscientious wife by making supper for him instead of allowing him to make another meal for her.

After breading the pork chops, she placed them onto a baking sheet and stuck them in the preheated oven. Then she peeled three potatoes and put them in a pot of water to boil in preparation for mashed potatoes.

A wave of exhaustion overtook Mattie after she set the table. She set the timer on the stove and then stepped into the family room and lowered herself into Leroy's favorite wing chair. She needed to sit and rest for just a few minutes before she continued preparing the meal. Leaning her cheek against the side of the chair, she closed her eyes.

She awoke with a start to the blare of the oven timer and smoke pouring from the kitchen. Panic constricted her chest, and with a gasp, Mattie jumped up and rushed into the kitchen. Smoke poured out of the oven, the water in the pot of potatoes had evaporated, and the bottom of the pot was black. She turned off the oven and the burner.

She grabbed an oven mitt and moved the burned pot to another burner. Then she held her breath as she removed the pan of pork chops, which were shriveled and charred. The smoke stung her eyes and stole her breath for a moment.

She grabbed two dish towels and waved them around the kitchen in an attempt to clear the smoke from the kitchen.

"Mattie!" Leroy burst through the back door. "Are you okay?"

She looked over at him, and tears stung her eyes. "I'm so sorry." Her voice was thick and sounded foreign to her.

"What happened?" He rushed over to her. "What burned?"

"Everything burned. I ruined the pork chops and the potatoes. I wanted to make you dinner, but I can't even do that right. I'm so sorry. I must have set the oven temperature way too high."

"Calm down." He looked at the stove. "Did you turn off the oven?"

"*Ya.*" She returned to waving the dish towels and attempting to send the smoke out through the opened windows.

"*Kumm.*" He grabbed her arm and led her through the mudroom.

"I need to clean up the mess." She tried to release her arm from his grip, but he held on to her tighter, moving her to his side. "I have to clean up the kitchen."

"Forget the kitchen." He looked down at her. "Supper doesn't matter. I'm just glad you're okay. I saw the smoke, and I thought my heart was going to beat out of my chest. Let's just let the smoke clear and then we'll

make sandwiches for supper. I don't care what we eat."
He steered her out of the house and onto the back porch.

She coughed and breathed in the fresh air.

"Are you sure you're all right?"

She nodded as a lump swelled in her throat. "I wanted
to make a nice supper for you. I've done nothing but
sleep since—the—well, since I got home from the hospital." She shook her head as despondency rained down
on her.

She glanced behind her at the clothesline and found
it was empty. Tillie had not only washed Mattie's clothes
and linens, but she had folded them and put them away.
Mattie had done nothing but slept today.

Her shoulders slumped. She wasn't living up to her
duties as an Amish wife. She had no purpose in this
household. She was no good for Leroy. She was nothing
but a burden.

"Mattie?" His eyes searched hers. "Are you upset about
more than the burned dinner? What are you thinking
right now?"

"I can't do anything right." Her voice quavered. "I can't
do my own chores." She pointed to the empty clothesline. "Tillie had to do our laundry." She gestured toward
the kitchen. "She cleaned our *haus*. I can't even cook a
meal without burning it and almost setting the kitchen
on fire."

He rubbed her arms. "It's not important—"

She held up her hand. "Please let me finish." She
took a tremulous breath. "I can't even give you a healthy
baby. I'm a failure as a *fraa*. You'd be better off without me."

His mouth formed a hard line. "Don't say that. I would not be better off without you. I need you, and you need me."

"No, you don't need me."

"Stop talking *narrisch*. You're just upset. I'll make us sandwiches, and we'll eat out here on the porch." He pointed to the glider. "Sit, and I'll bring you a mug of root beer and a sandwich. Just calm down. I promise everything will be fine."

She nodded, and he released her arms. As he walked back into the kitchen, she sank onto the glider. Her body trembled as the reality of her decision came into clear focus in her mind. She had to let Leroy move on with his life, and the only way to do that was to leave him and go back to her parents' house.

Wrapping her arms around her middle, Mattie pushed the glider into motion with her toe. She scanned Leroy's pasture and barns, committing them to memory. She would miss this house and this life that she and Leroy had attempted to build together. But she didn't belong here. Leroy deserved a wife who could give him what he needed, and she was only the shell of the woman she'd once been.

Mattie silently prayed that Leroy would forgive her for what she was going to do and that he would one day understand why she had to leave.

. . .

"Did Mattie call a driver to take her to the grocery store?" Tillie's voice rang through the harness shop.

"What do you mean?" Leroy asked, sitting up straight and turning from the worktable where he'd been creating a wallet.

She jammed her thumb toward the door. "I just saw Mattie climb into a van and leave. I would have done the grocery shopping for her or gone with her if I'd known she was leaving."

Alarm slammed through Leroy as he stood. "She didn't tell me she was going to the store. In fact, she was still in bed when I came to work this morning."

"Maybe she meant to tell you she was going." Hank straightened the display by the register. "She probably left you a note."

"I'll go check." Leroy rushed out of the harness shop and nearly ran up the path to his house.

He entered the kitchen and spotted a folded piece of paper on the table. When he picked it up, he realized it was a letter. His heart seemed to slam against his rib cage as he read it.

Dear Leroy,

    Danki for all the patience and love you've given me the past few months. You've gone above and beyond the call of duty of a *freind*. I can't thank you enough for opening your home and your heart to Jacob and me.

    I thought we could make this marriage work, but I'm not cut out to be your *fraa*. I'm no longer the strong woman I was before I lost Isaiah and Jacob. I thought I could pick myself up and move on, but I can't.

    When you married me, I needed a home and a *daed* for *mei boppli*, and you needed a *fraa* to help you run

your *haus* and your business. You've kept your part of
the deal, but I've failed you. I realized last night when I
burned supper that I have no purpose in our marriage.
You deserve a hardworking wife who will take care of
your *haus* while you work, but I just can't do it anymore. I don't have the strength or the determination
to move on without Jacob.

You're better off without me. I'm going to stay at
my parents' *haus* until I figure out what I'm going to do
next. I'm taking most of my clothes with me, but I'll
come for the rest of my things after I'm settled somewhere permanently.

I hope we can someday be *freinden* because I will
miss you.

Sincerely,
Mattie

Panic mixed with confusion seized Leroy. Mattie had
left him. Why hadn't he seen this coming?

Suddenly their conversation on the porch last night
echoed through his mind. She'd said she couldn't be
the wife he needed, but he had decided she was just upset
about the burned supper. Why hadn't he realized she
was serious?

He couldn't let her go. Their relationship had deepened with Jacob's death, and he was starting to believe
Mattie was falling in love with him too. The way she had
clung to him during the wake and funeral was a sure
sign Mattie's feelings for him were growing, right? Leroy
couldn't let his marriage dissolve the way his parents'
had. He had to go after her. He couldn't just allow her to

walk out of his life the way his father left his mother. He had to go get her, and he had to go now.

Gripping the letter, he walked back into the harness shop, thankful to find only Tillie and Hank there without any customers to listen in on their private conversation.

"She left me." His voice was thick with his swelling grief.

"What?" Hank stepped over to Leroy. "What do you mean she left you?"

"She's gone to move back in with her parents."

Tillie gasped, covering her mouth with her hand.

Leroy briefly explained their conversation last night after she'd burned dinner. Then he held up the letter and summarized what she'd written. "I'm going to go after her. I'll be back later today."

"Leroy, stop." Tillie grabbed his arm and prevented him from walking out of the shop. "Just let her go."

"What?" He stared at her. "How can I let her go?"

"Trust me." Her lips flattened into a frown. "It's the best way to handle this."

"I can't. I love her too much."

"I know you love her, but you need to give her time. I know how she feels. I've been there." She looked past Leroy. "Right, Hank?"

He nodded. "She's not thinking clearly now, but she'll realize she's made a mistake in a few days. Let her go to her parents' *haus* and sort through her confusing feelings."

"She's been through a lot." Tillie released his arm, and it fell to his side. "No one gives us instructions on how to handle grief. It's not our place to tell her how to feel or act after losing both Isaiah and Jacob only a few months apart." She touched his arm once again. "Just let her go."

Has everyone gone crazy? "I can't let her go. She's everything to me." His voice broke.

"She'll come back to you," Hank said.

"*Mei dat* didn't come back." He sank onto one of the stools in the work area and rested his forearms on the table.

Tillie sat down on the stool beside him. "She's just feels like she's drowning right now. When she comes up for air she'll realize you're what she needs. Have faith, Leroy, and rely on God."

He swallowed. "My worst fear was winding up like my mother, and here I am all alone in that big *haus*."

"Leroy, look at me," Hank said.

Leroy looked up at his best friend as he leaned against the wall. "What?"

"Mattie is not like your *dat*. She didn't meet someone else and leave you for that person. She's upset and confused. This too shall pass."

"*Danki.* I hope you're both right." Leroy looked down at the wallet he'd been creating. "I'm going to get back to work."

Giving Mattie space made sense, but how could he stay away from her? Closing his eyes, he begged God for the strength and wisdom to help Mattie's heart heal and to win her back.

CHAPTER 14

"Mattie? It's time for you to get up and face the world."

Groaning, she rolled over to her side and opened her eyes, staring at the plain white walls. It took a minute for her brain to register that she was on the sofa in her parents' little cottage.

"Lizzie?" Mattie sat up and faced her sister, standing in the doorway leading to the front porch.

"You do realize it's almost noon, right?" She jammed a hand on her hip. "*Mamm* said you refused to get off the sofa until nearly two o'clock yesterday afternoon and you ate very little all day. She's worried about you."

Glancing around the small family room that melted into the little kitchen, Mattie searched for her parents. "Where are *Mamm* and *Dat*?"

Lizanne pointed to the door. "*Mamm* is working in the garden, and *Dat* went to the furniture store."

"So *Mamm* sent for you so you could talk to me?"

"*Ya*, she did. I don't know why she didn't call me yesterday." Lizanne marched over to the window next to the sofa and opened the green shade, sending a flood of bright September sunlight into the room. Then she opened Mattie's suitcase on the floor and pulled out a green dress and apron before handing them to her. "It's Monday. This is the day the Lord has made. We will rejoice and be glad in it."

Mattie blinked against the bright sunlight. "Please don't trivialize my grief."

Lizanne frowned as she sat down on the sofa beside Mattie. "I'm not trivializing your grief. I'm sorry if it seemed that way."

"It's all right." Mattie pushed her long hair behind her shoulders and leaned back against the sofa.

"How are you feeling?" Lizanne folded her long legs under her blue dress and black apron.

"I'm tired." Mattie rubbed her abdomen, which seemed to get flatter with each passing day. "I feel like I could sleep my life away." *And my heart is broken beyond repair.*

"I'm worried about you." She touched Mattie's hand. "*Mamm* said you won't talk to her about what happened. You just said you needed to stay with her until you can figure out where you're going to live. I didn't know you were so upset. I would've come to visit you more if I knew you were so *bedauerlich*." Her blue eyes sparkled with tears.

"Don't be sorry." Mattie hugged a sofa pillow to her chest. "It's not your fault. You didn't know."

"What happened? Why are you staying here with *Mamm* and *Dat*?"

Mattie swallowed a deep breath and finger-combed her thick hair. "I don't know how to be a *gut fraa* anymore. I just can't do anything right. I'm a mess."

Lizanne gasped. "Why would you say that?"

Mattie studied the pillow in her arms as she explained what happened with the burned supper and her conversation with Leroy on the porch.

"*Ach, mei liewe.*" Lizanne touched her cheek. "You're not a failure. And the doctor said you can have a healthy baby. You just need to give your body time to heal. Give your heart time to heal too. Everything is going to be okay. It will just take a little time." She paused for a moment. "Leroy loves you and he needs you. You do belong with him, and he wants you with him."

Mattie touched the tag on the pillow. "No, I'm no use to him. It's better if I stay here."

"How long are you going to stay here and sleep on the sofa?"

She met her sister's intense stare. *Mamm* had definitely sent Lizanne to try to talk some sense into her. "I don't know. I haven't figured out where I'm going to go next."

Lizanne paused, twisting her lips. "I told you when Isaiah passed away that Al and I have plenty of room. You should move in with us. You can even have your old room back."

When they were married, Lizanne and Alvin took over the house and farm where Mattie and Lizanne grew up. Then their parents moved into the *daadihaus*.

"No. I don't want to get in the way of you and Al. You deserve your privacy."

Lizanne sighed and rolled her eyes. "We've been married for nearly two years. It makes more sense for you to sleep in your old room than for you to sleep on *Mamm*'s sofa."

"I'm fine here. I mean it, so don't worry about me." She didn't want to discuss this anymore. She pushed herself up from the sofa. "I'm going to take a shower and get dressed."

"Wait." Lizanne reached for her hand, but Mattie pulled it away. "I have one more question for you."

"I need a shower. We can talk later." Mattie started toward the bathroom.

Lizanne followed her. "Just tell me one thing."

"What?" She spun to face her older sister.

"Do you love Leroy?"

"I don't know what I feel about anything anymore." Mattie's voice trembled. "All I know is I need a shower." She headed into the bathroom and closed the door behind her, shutting out Lizanne and the rest of the world.

· · ·

Leroy blew out a frustrated grunt and slammed his knife down onto the worktable in the harness shop. He'd ruined another piece of leather.

Although he'd spent the morning attempting to create leashes and key chains, he destroyed each piece of leather he touched. He folded his arms over his chest and slumped on the stool. Today was a lost cause. Why had he bothered getting out of bed?

Because you can't sleep.

He hadn't slept since Mattie walked out on him Saturday morning. He'd lain awake, staring at the ceiling in the downstairs bedroom as his mind replayed snippets of his brief time living with Mattie.

He questioned and criticized himself endlessly, wondering if he had truly done his best to be patient, accommodating, and kind enough to Mattie. Perhaps he had somehow hurt her without realizing it. He tried to do everything right, but she'd still run out on him, leaving him with nothing but a broken heart and a big, lonely house.

What could I have done differently?

The questions and regret haunted him day and night. Since yesterday was an off-Sunday without a church service, he'd considered going to visit his brother, but he couldn't bring himself to face Joel and admit Mattie had left him. Instead, he'd spent most the day sitting in the family room, staring at the wall as the day crawled by at a snail's pace.

This morning he'd risen early, cared for the animals, and ate a piece of toast before dragging himself to the harness shop to sit in the workroom and ruin piece after piece of leather while Hank worked the front of the store.

He couldn't bring himself to face customers in his current mental state, and thankfully, Hank had left him alone after saying a brief good morning.

"Leroy?"

He looked up at Hank standing by the entrance to the work area. *"Ya?"*

Hank pointed toward the table covered in pieces of leather. "Are you going to murder all our stock or just the parts you find particularly offensive?"

Leroy rubbed at a knot in his shoulder without cracking a smile. Hank's jokes didn't amuse him at all today.

"I'm sorry. I thought I could work, but I'm not thinking clearly."

"It's fine. I was just teasing you." Hank leaned against the wall. "Are you hungry?"

"Hungry?" Leroy looked up at the clock on the wall. "It's noon already?"

"*Ya.*" Hank rubbed his brown beard. "Tillie would like you to join us for lunch. We can close the shop up for an hour, or she can bring it here."

"I don't think we should close the store and run the risk of losing customers. You go eat. I'll stay here and run things. I can sit up by the register so I don't miss anyone."

"I'm not going to leave you here alone while I go home to eat lunch. There's a way to enjoy lunch and not lose customers." Hank pushed off the wall. "I'll make a sign telling customers to knock on my door for service." He gestured for Leroy to follow him. "Come on. If I don't bring you home to eat lunch with us, Tillie will come and get you. You don't want me to send *mei fraa* after you, do you?"

"No, no, I don't." Leroy sighed and stood, pulled on his straw hat, and followed Hank to the front of the store. Then he leaned on the counter by the register and yawned while Hank quickly created a sign for any customers who came while they ate.

Once the sign was taped in the window, they exited the store and Hank locked the door behind them.

Leroy covered his mouth with his hand to shield another yawn as they climbed the porch steps of Hank's house.

Hank held open the back door. "Did you sleep at all last night?"

"I slept a little."

Hank motioned for him to step into the mudroom. "A *gut* lunch will give you some more energy."

I doubt it. Leroy hung his straw hat on the peg by the back wall. Then he stepped through the mudroom and into the kitchen.

"Leroy!" Tillie stood by the kitchen counter holding a pitcher of water. "I'm so glad you could join us for lunch." She pointed to the table, which was already set for three. "Wash up and then have a seat. We have plenty of lunch meat and rolls."

"Danki." So this lunch was planned because Tillie and Hank were worried about him. Leroy had turned down their offers for supper last night, but they had still found a way to invite him over to eat with them.

Hank and Tillie were a blessing in Leroy's life, and he was grateful Hank had bought the house next door to his. Leroy washed his hands at the sink and then sat at the table. He scanned the platters on the table, taking in the variety of lunch meat and condiments, and his stomach growled, alerting him to how little food he'd eaten since Saturday morning.

After washing his hands, Hank sat down across from him. "I hope you're hungry. I can't eat all this lunch meat myself." He smiled, and Leroy longed to return the gesture but couldn't.

"We don't have to eat it all in one day." Tillie sank into the chair beside Hank. "I just picked it up this morning."

Leroy hoped Tillie hadn't made a special trip to the

market just for him, but he had a sneaking suspicion she had.

After a silent prayer, Tillie and Hank each took a roll from the center of the table and began to build sandwiches. Leroy chose a roll and then silently debated what type of meat to put on it.

Tillie spoke.

Leroy looked up and met her gaze. "What did you say?"

"I asked if you've slept." She opened a jar of mayonnaise. "You look exhausted. You have dark shadows under your eyes, and you're a little pale. You look as though you haven't slept since Saturday. Am I right?"

He swallowed a snort. *Actually,* mei fraa *left me and I've never been better.*

But Tillie didn't deserve a biting response. She'd been like a sister to Leroy since Hank had met her. She always went out of her way to include Leroy as part of their family. No, she didn't deserve his sarcasm. She was entitled to his honesty.

"No, I haven't slept much at all." He piled roast beef, ham, turkey, and cheese onto his roll. After adding a piece of lettuce, he grabbed the mayonnaise and mustard. "I just stare at the ceiling all night and wait for my alarm to go off."

"Have you heard from her?" Tillie asked.

Leroy shook his head as he spread mayonnaise on the roll. Then he added the mustard and closed the sandwich.

"Have you reached out to her?"

Leroy looked over at her. "I thought I should give her some space. Isn't that what you suggested I do?"

"She's had more than twenty-four hours to think about you." She cut her sandwich in half and then peered up at him. "I think it's time you reach out to her and tell her how much you miss her." She frowned. "I hope this doesn't come across as forward, but you look terrible. It's apparent you're suffering. I'm certain she's miserable too. If you leave her a message then she'll know you haven't given up on your marriage."

Leroy stilled. "I haven't given up, but I'm also realistic. The letter she left me made it clear she wanted to go to her parents' *haus*."

"I didn't say you've given up," she countered. "I only meant she might take your continued silence to mean you don't think you can work things out."

Suddenly a memory washed over Leroy. He was five, and he was sitting on the top step of a spiral staircase while listening to his parents' loud voices boom below him. Tears streamed down his face as his mother begged his father not to leave. After several moments, the back door slammed, and *Mamm*'s wailing echoed throughout the house.

His stomach tightened, and his appetite dissipated. All he'd ever wanted was a loving wife and a family. Why couldn't he have that with Mattie? How had he managed to wind up as lonely and broken as his *mamm*?

"I'm sorry." Tillie scowled. "I didn't mean to overstep my boundaries. It just breaks my heart to see you and Mattie suffer like this."

"*Danki*, but how do I convince her to come back to me?" Leroy asked.

"Tillie already gave you the first step." Hank placed

his sandwich on his plate. "Call her and leave her a message. Tell her exactly how you're feeling and then let her reach out to you. If she doesn't reach out to you, then do something else to show her you still care." He lifted his sandwich. "Give her a call and let the Lord handle the rest."

Leroy nodded and then forced himself to take a bite of his sandwich. It tasted like sawdust in his mouth, despite the fresh lunch meat. They ate in silence for several moments, and he hoped one of them would change the subject. He was tired of being the focus of the conversation.

"I saw *mei mamm* at the market," Tillie began, and Leroy was grateful for the change in subject.

"Oh *ya*?" Hank asked. "How is she doing?"

"Fine. She said *mei dat* is feeling better. He's finally over that terrible summer cold. Summer colds are the worst."

Leroy lost himself in thoughts of Mattie as Tillie talked on about her parents. When their lunch was finished, he thanked Tillie for the meal and then followed Hank out toward the harness shop.

"I'm going to make a phone call," he called over his shoulder as he continued on toward his house.

Hank gave him a knowing smile. "*Gut* idea."

"I hope so," Leroy mumbled as he headed toward the phone shanty.

. . .

Mattie stood in front of the bathroom mirror and studied her reflection. Although her face was pale and her eyes seemed dull, the hot shower and clean dress and apron had refreshed her. Yet her heart remained heavy with grief for not only her loss of Isaiah and Jacob but also for the loss of Leroy's friendship. But she had to continue to believe she made the right choice.

As Mattie opened the bathroom door, voices drifted into the hallway. She froze, listening to her mother and sister speaking in the nearby kitchen.

"I'm just relieved you got her off of the sofa," *Mamm* said. "It's okay if you had to upset her to get her to take a shower. I tried all day yesterday to convince her to get up, but she refused to budge. I brought her a plate of food, and she only ate a few crackers. Maybe she'll start a sewing project or work in the garden since she's dressed."

"I don't know if she'll do any chores." Lizanne blew out a deep sigh. "When I asked her if she loved Leroy, she refused to answer, beyond saying she didn't know how she felt. She seems like she has a lot of emotions to work through. How long are you going to let her stay here?"

"I don't know. I can't allow her to stay too long. She has to go back to her *haus* and work things out with her husband. That's the right thing to do. There are no other options. She can't stay here forever. She has to face her problems with Leroy like an adult."

Mattie hugged her arms to her abdomen as her stomach growled. *Mamm* was right; she hadn't eaten much yesterday. Her stomach was hollow. She needed food.

Her stomach gurgled and she stepped into the kitchen, where her mother and sister were sitting at the table.

She nodded a greeting to them as she moved to the counter and found a loaf of bread. She buttered a slice and then smeared her mother's homemade strawberry jam over it before sitting at the table across from them. They exchanged surprised looks as she ate without saying a word.

"It's *gut* to see you up and dressed," *Mamm* finally said.

Lizanne carried *Mamm*'s and her mugs to the counter and began washing them. "Would you like me to make you something else to eat?"

"No, *danki*," Mattie said. "This is *appeditlich* with *Mamm*'s strawberry jam."

"I'm so *froh* you like it." *Mamm*'s expression became serious. "How are you feeling?"

"I'm all right. I'm just tired."

Mamm frowned. "I'm sorry you've been through so much, but I promise you it will get better. Just give yourself time to heal emotionally and physically."

Renewed grief radiated through Mattie's belly. She fiddled with the napkin in her hand.

Mamm gestured toward the doorway leading to her bedroom. "Lizzie and I are going to work on a quilt if you'd like to join us. It's one that a customer ordered, and it needs to be done next week. You can help with the stitching if you'd like."

"I'd love to," Mattie said. "I'll join you after I finish eating."

"Great." *Mamm* stood and looked over at Lizanne. They seemed to share a silent conversation before they both stepped toward the bedroom.

Mattie finished eating and then washed and stowed her plate and utensils before slowly walking to the bedroom where her mother had a small sewing area set up in the corner. Although her parents had planned to retire when they moved into the *daadihaus*, her father still worked part-time in his furniture store and her mother continued to take custom orders for quilts to keep busy and make a little extra money.

Her mother and sister sat together while working on a beautiful wedding ring-patterned quilt accented with purple material. She stood in the doorway for a moment, and Lizanne looked up.

"Mattie." Lizanne gestured for her to come in. "Come on in. Do you want to work on this quilt or maybe start on another one?"

"Do you need my help?" Mattie pulled a chair up to them.

"You can work on something else if you want. You once told me quilting helped you when you were upset. You can create something new if you'd like." *Mamm* pointed toward the far end of the room. "My box of material is back there."

Mattie looked toward the back of the room to see the large cardboard box with "*Ruth*" written on the side in *Mamm's* elegant writing.

"May I make a lap quilt?" The idea popped into Mattie's mind and took hold of her.

"*Ya*, of course." *Mamm* didn't look up from the wedding ring quilt.

Mattie crossed the room and peeked into the box, which was stuffed full of material of all colors. She picked through it until she found enough different shades of tans and browns for the lap quilt she had in mind.

"What pattern are you going to make?" Lizanne asked as Mattie sat at the sewing table across from them.

"I'm going to make a log cabin." She held up the material. "I thought tans and browns would look *gut*."

"Oh, I love it. Is it going to be a gift?"

"I'm not sure yet. I just want to make it."

They worked silently for several minutes. Mattie found a notepad and pencil and drew out her design.

"Mattie." *Mamm* finally broke the silence. "I know you're upset, and my heart goes out to you."

Mattie closed her eyes while keeping her back toward her mother. She wasn't ready for a lecture. It was too soon. Her pain was still raw.

"But you can't hide here forever. You need to be a *gut fraa* and go back to your husband. You lived together for almost three months, but that's not enough time to form a marriage. Besides, it's not right to live apart. You're joined for life now."

"I know that," Mattie responded through gritted teeth. "But I'm not in any frame of mind to be a *gut fraa*." She looked over her shoulder at her mother and sister, who both gazed at her with bright, intense blue eyes. "I'm not the same person I was when I married Leroy. He's entitled to a true *fraa* who can take care of him. I can't even take care of myself right now."

Lizanne gave her a muted smile. "Let him take care of you for a while."

"Lizzie is right," *Mamm* chimed in. "Let him take care of you."

Mattie sighed. She just wanted them to drop the subject and let her work it out on her own. She turned her attention back to her quilt project, hoping it would help to heal her heart and soul.

CHAPTER 15

"Oh, Ruth, someone should check the phone messages." *Dat* turned toward Mattie as he sat across from her at the table later that evening. "Would you mind checking them after supper?"

She chewed her pot roast. "I don't mind."

"*Danki.*" *Dat* gave *Mamm* a meaningful stare, and Mattie raised her eyebrows in question. Were they plotting something?

"How was work?" *Mamm* asked about the furniture store *Dat* ran with his three brothers, their sons, and Al.

"It was *gut.* The store is busy. I took another order for a bedroom suite today. That's four orders for bedroom suites just this month."

"Oh, that's *wunderbaar!*" *Mamm* exclaimed.

Mattie moved the green beans around on her plate. Was the harness shop staying busy too? Was Leroy sleeping well, or had he tossed and turned as much as Mattie did every night? Her heart always hurt when her thoughts turned to Leroy. She sighed and speared a green bean and then lifted it to her mouth.

She blinked as she chewed. Her stomach soured when she swallowed the green bean. Would she ever find a way to move past her grief and live once again?

She glanced up at her parents, who were still discussing the furniture store. Relief washed over her as they spoke. She was grateful to not be the center of their attention. She couldn't handle any more opinions or advice today. She just wanted to be left alone to contemplate her thoughts and confusing emotions.

When they were finished with their meal, *Dat* went outside to help Al care for the animals, and Mattie helped *Mamm* clear the table.

"You can go check the messages," *Mamm* said as she began to fill up the sink with water.

Mattie hesitated. Her parents were awfully eager for her to listen to the messages, but they wouldn't stop nagging her until she did as they asked. "All right."

Mattie wiped her hands on her apron and headed out the front door toward the phone shanty beside the barn. She dialed the number for her parents' voice mail and listened. She wrote out three messages for her mother—two were from friends inviting her to a quilting bee and the third was from a customer checking on her quilt order.

She was finishing up the note to her mother regarding the quilt order when another voice sounded in her ear. Her heart thudded and her knees wobbled.

"Mattie." Leroy's voice was low and seemed to strain with emotion. "I've been sitting here staring at the phone for several minutes now trying to figure out what to say to you. I've dialed this number three times and then hung up like a coward."

He blew out a loud breath. "There's so much I want to tell you, but I don't know how to put it all in coherent sentences. I was devastated when I found your letter.

I had no idea how serious you were when you said you were a failure and I would be better without you. I thought you were just upset about the burned dinner. I didn't know you really believed that. I'm not better off without you. In fact, I'm a mess without you."

He paused again as if gathering his words and perhaps also his courage. "You're *mei fraa*, and I care deeply for you. I'm sorry if I didn't make my feelings clear to you. I understand you need time to rest. I'll handle all your chores for you until you're ready to do them. I won't put a deadline on when you're supposed to go back to a regular schedule. There is no timetable for this sort of thing. No one has instructions on how they're supposed to feel or when they're supposed to feel whole again after something like this happens."

Mattie's eyes prickled with unshed tears. Regret churned in her belly.

"Please come home to me." He blew out another breath. "I need to talk to you in person, so I can make sure you understand I will give you all the time you need. This is your *haus* now. Let's work this out and build a life together."

A tear slipped down Mattie's cheek, and with a sniff, she wiped it away.

"We can get through this together. I promise you that I will try harder next time. You're *mei fraa* now. You're the most important person in my life. Call me or come and see me. I'm waiting for you."

The message clicked off, and Mattie stared at the top of the desk before hitting the button to erase it. Leroy's voice and pleading words touched something deep inside of her, but she wasn't ready to face him. She couldn't admit to him that she didn't know who she was or where she belonged. She didn't know when she'd be ready to go home to him. Right now she just wanted to be alone.

She gathered up the notes she'd taken on the notepad by the phone and then went back into the kitchen, where *Mamm* was drying dishes.

"You had three messages." Mattie set the messages on the end of the counter, picked up a dish towel, and began drying utensils.

"Danki." *Mamm* looked down at the messages. "I'll call them back tomorrow. Were there any other messages?"

"There was a message for me. I listened to it and then erased it." Mattie put down the dish towel and placed dry dishes in the cabinet, careful to keep her focus on them. She didn't want to discuss this with *Mamm*. It was already too painful to think about it, and talking about it would just drive the confusing emotions deeper into her soul.

"Who called you?"

Mattie retrieved her dish towel, gathered a handful of utensils from the drainboard, and moved the towel over them. "Leroy."

"What did he say?"

Mattie looked up at her mother. "Don't you already know the answer to that question?" She immediately regretted snapping at her mother, who had always supported her and her sister.

Mamm raised her eyebrows. "How would I know what Leroy said?"

"Isn't that why *Dat* sent me out to listen to the messages?"

She leaned her hip against the counter. "By the expressions on your faces during supper, you and *Dat* seemed to know there was a message for me."

Mamm frowned. "Your *dat* listened to the messages when he got home. He said he didn't listen to the message from Leroy because it was private. He saved the messages and then told me he was going to ask you to go out and listen so that you could hear it." She touched Mattie's arm. "I'm sorry *Dat* misled you, but we were worried you wouldn't listen to his message if he told you Leroy left one for you."

They were right. Mattie would've hesitated if she'd known Leroy had left a message. She wasn't emotionally ready to hear from him since she was certain she'd hurt him when she left. His grief over her leaving just added to the bereavement that was already weighing so heavily on her heart. She returned to drying the utensils, dropping the dry pieces into a drawer.

"What did Leroy say?"

Mattie kept her focus on the drawer. "He wants me to come home." She couldn't share the entire message with her mother. She squeezed her eyes shut as tears threatened to fill her eyes.

"That's *gut* news." *Mamm* moved closer to Mattie. "Did you call him back and leave him a message?"

Mattie shook her head and dropped a spoon into the drawer with a loud *clunk*.

"Are you going to call him or go see him?"

Mattie pressed her lips together. *Mamm* needed to stop pressuring her to talk to Leroy. She'd talk to him when and if she was ready.

Mamm's gaze dropped to the sink, and they finished cleaning up the kitchen in silence.

"I'm going to go lie down." Mattie exited the kitchen.

Mattie sank onto the sofa and touched her abdomen. Her eyes filled with tears as her thoughts turned to Jacob. What would her life have been like if he'd lived? She imagined living in Leroy's house with Jacob. They would've been a family. Oh, how she wanted a family.

"Mattie?"

She wiped her eyes and looked up at where *Mamm* stood holding an envelope.

Mattie sat up straight and patted the sofa beside her. "I was just lost in my thoughts."

"I understand." *Mamm* sat on the edge of the sofa and turned to face Mattie. "I want to share something with you. Did I ever tell you about *mei bruder*, Elias?"

"*Ya*, I think so. He died in a farming accident when you were twenty."

"That's right." *Mamm*'s blue eyes misted. "It was terrible. The farm was having a bad year, and it was just devastating for my family. We went through a really rough time." She examined the envelope in her hands. "I almost didn't marry your *dat* because of it."

"What?" Mattie gasped. "What do you mean?"

"Your *dat* was best *freinden* with *Onkel* Elias. In fact, that's how I met your *dat*. Your *dat* used to tease me all the time, but it wasn't mean-spirited." She chuckled. "He always frustrated me because I thought he was so handsome and funny, but he only seemed to see me as Elias's younger *schweschder*. It took me awhile to realize he teased me as a way to flirt with me."

"*Buwe* are so *gegisch* sometimes."

"*Ya*, they are."

"So what happened?"

"It took him awhile to ask me to be his girlfriend. I was so *froh*." *Mamm* had a faraway look in her eyes. "I could hardly contain my smile that night he took me for a ride in his buggy and admitted he'd always liked me but was too *naerfich* to say anything. He had no idea how I felt about him, even though I thought it was written all over my face. I suppose sometimes we think we're open with our feelings, but we aren't."

Mattie bit her lip as Leroy's words from the message echoed through her mind: "*You're* mei fraa, *and I care deeply for you. I'm sorry if I didn't make my feelings clear to you.*"

"Your *dat* and I were so *froh* together. We went for long walks on my parents' farm and we had picnics by the pond behind his parents' *haus*. We talked for hours and held hands. We dated for a few months, and then he asked me to marry him." *Mamm*'s smile collapsed. "And then Elias died, and I had a difficult time coming to terms with my grief. Elias and I were very close. I couldn't handle all of it, and I avoided your *dat*. I didn't know what to say to him, and I thought he could never understand my grief. I just cocooned inside of myself and shut him out."

"Did you delay your wedding after *Onkel* Elias died?"

"We did. I told him I wasn't sure I wanted to get married. I couldn't imagine leaving my parents. I thought they needed me to stay and help them with the farm." *Mamm* held out the envelope. "Your *dat* saved this. I thought you might like to read it."

Dear Mose,

As I write this letter, I'm watching the sunset outside my bedroom window. The sky is bathed in *schee* shades of purple, orange, magenta, and yellow, reminding me of that walk we took around your *dat*'s pond a few months ago. That was the perfect evening. The air was warm, and the birds were chirping their *froh* songs as we talked.

I've done a lot of thinking since our argument yesterday. I've realized now that you were right when you said bad things happen but we can't let them tear us apart. This has been both a terrible year and a *wunderbaar* year. I never imagined I would lose my *bruder*, and I had no idea his death would take such a toll on my parents. Yet I also never imagined that you and I would fall in love. For years you only saw me as Elias's younger *schweschder*, and I never expected to become more than that to you. You surprised me the day you asked me to go for a ride in your buggy so we could talk alone.

When you said I shouldn't let my grief stop me from marrying you, I was hurt. At first I thought you didn't understand how I was feeling. I was angry since you and Elias had been best *freinden*, and I thought you didn't care about Elias and were disrespecting his memory. Then I realized you do care about Elias. You were trying to tell me that even after we're married we will always keep Elias's memory close to our hearts. And Elias would want us to be *froh* together. He would bless our relationship.

Mose, I'm writing you tonight to apologize to you and to give you my answer. *Ya*, I will marry you in the fall. I always have loved you. I even loved you when you used to tease me and tell me I was nothing but a *gegisch maedel*.

Danki for not giving up on me. I can't wait to see you again. I'm going to make you another raspberry pie so we can share it while we discuss our wedding plans.

Love always,
Ruth

Mattie sniffed and brushed the back of her free hand over her eyes as she stared down at the letter. The words soaked through her and tugged at her heartstrings.

"I was devastated when I lost *mei bruder*. And seeing that loss reflected in my parents' eyes drove it deeper into my soul. I thought I couldn't go on, but I made room in my heart for your *dat*." *Mamm* rested her hand on Mattie's arm. "When he said I shouldn't let my grief stop me from marrying him, I was upset. I thought he didn't understand my grief, but I realized I was wrong. I thought he didn't care about *mei bruder*, but I had completely misunderstood him. And your *dat* and I helped each other through our grief. Despite what we'd been through, we still built a life together."

"So you're saying I should go home to Leroy and then let him help me through my grief for Jacob and Isaiah."

"*Ya*, that's right."

Frustration swamped Mattie. "I'm sorry you lost your *bruder*. I know that was difficult, but it's still not the same kind of loss."

"I understand what you're saying." *Mamm* paused. "Grief is difficult no matter whom you lose, but with

God's help, you can find a way to move on with your life. You'll never forget Isaiah or Jacob, but your heart will heal as time goes on.

"You're not alone. Leroy is waiting for you. He wants to make things work with you. You should reach out to him and talk this through." *Mamm* squeezed her hand.

"I don't know how to talk to him about everything I'm feeling," Mattie whispered as tears streamed down her hot cheeks. "I don't know how to move on."

"I understand how you feel. Your life has been turned upside down, and you're trying to figure out where you fit into the community now. I didn't know how to be an only child after Elias was gone, but I figured it out. My parents and I relied on God. With prayers and help from the rest of the community, we slowly got back to the rhythm of life." *Mamm*'s voice quavered, and she wiped her eyes. "Seeing my parents grieve for Elias was difficult, but God healed their hearts. You need to give God a chance to heal yours."

Mattie nodded to satisfy her mother, but she couldn't comprehend how to navigate her complicated relationship with Leroy.

. . .

Leroy crawled into bed and pulled the quilt up to his chin. He inhaled the lingering scent of Mattie's shampoo and his heart sank down to his toes. After he'd taken care of his animals, he'd checked his messages. It was the fourth time he'd checked them since he'd left his rambling message for Mattie. She still hadn't called him back.

Leroy settled onto his back and looked up at the ceiling. There had to be a way for him to convince Mattie to come home. Their friendship had to be strong enough to weather this difficult season in their lives. Their marriage was worth saving. He needed help.

Closing his eyes, he sent a prayer up to God, asking for assistance. Surely God could warm Mattie's heart and guide her home to Leroy.

CHAPTER 16

"I hope you two are hungry!"

Leroy looked up from the worktable at the back of the harness shop as Tillie approached with a tray of food on Thursday afternoon. He closed the accounting book and set it to the side. "What do you have there?"

"I brought you and Hank lunch. I have roast beef sandwiches, chips, and brownies." She set the tray on the table and handed Leroy a bottle of water.

"Danki." He opened the bottle and took a long drink.

Hank came up behind her and squeezed her arm before sitting down on a stool. *"Danki.* You read my mind. I was just going to ask Leroy to join us for lunch."

Tillie smiled at Hank as she handed him a sandwich. "You know we always have enough food for Leroy." She gave Leroy a sandwich and then perched on a stool beside him.

"I appreciate it, but you really don't have to worry about feeding me. I'm capable of taking care of myself." His friends meant well, but Leroy didn't want to be their charity case. He was a grown man and was capable of cooking for himself. After all, he'd lived alone for three years, and before that, he took care of his mother too.

After a silent prayer they began to eat their lunch. Leroy took a bite of his sandwich.

"How are you doing?" Tillie opened her bottle of water.

He finished chewing and swallowed. "I'm fine."

Tillie leveled her gaze with Leroy's and he sighed. She wanted to know how things were going with Mattie. If only he had something good to report.

"I haven't heard from her." He set his sandwich on his plate. "I've left her a message every day since Monday, and she hasn't called me back." He glowered. "I don't know what to do. I'm worried about coming on too strong, but if I sit back and do nothing, she might think I don't really care about her no matter how many times I've told her I do."

Hank frowned. "I'm so sorry. I thought she would've come back by now. I'm surprised she's been gone this long."

Tillie tapped a finger to her chin as if contemplating something, but she remained silent.

"Now I truly understand how *mei mamm* felt when *mei dat* left." Leroy lifted his sandwich and sadness raised its ugly head once again. He looked at Hank. "Was Mattie always this stubborn when we were *kinner*?"

Hank laughed. "*Ya*, she was. How can you forget? Remember that time she accused Amos Glick of copying off her paper in school? He insisted he didn't, but she wouldn't let up. I think he finally apologized just so she'd let it go."

Leroy chuckled. "*Ya*, I do remember that."

Tillie clucked her tongue. "You three have the best memories."

Leroy's smile dissolved as he placed the sandwich back on his plate. "*Ya*, we do. That's why I don't understand why she's given up on us so easily. Doesn't our past mean anything to her? We've shared so much together. Why can't she allow herself to consider what our future together could be?"

"I think you need to give her more time," Hank said.

Leroy took another bite of his sandwich. "I'm thinking about going to visit her. She might be more open to talking to me if she looks me in the face. She can't ignore me if I'm standing in front of her."

Tillie snapped her fingers.

Leroy turned toward her. "What?"

"I've got it. I'll be right back." She placed her napkin on the table, stood, and then hustled out the door.

Leroy looked at Hank. "What was that about?"

"Who knows? We've been together five years, and she still surprises me. I have no idea what she's thinking half the time." Hank picked up his sandwich and took another bite.

Leroy grabbed a handful of chips and began to eat them. "The store has stayed busy this week. According to the books, we're making a profit."

"That's *gut* to hear." Hank lifted his bottle of water in a silent toast. "Hopefully we're going to be just as successful as *mei onkel*."

"That would be fantastic." Leroy gestured toward the displays at the front of the store. "We're running low on key chains and reins. I'll have to make some later."

"I'll do it after I finish the books."

The front door opened and Tillie rushed back through

the store. "I found it!" She placed a basket on the table. "This is for you." She pushed it toward Leroy.

Leroy examined the large, brown, woven-wood basket with a two-hinge lid and two handles. He raised an eyebrow with confusion. "It's a nice basket."

"It's perfect. Look." She lifted the lid and pointed to the inside. "It's big enough for you to put a Pyrex serving dish inside of it. You can have it. It's been on my shelf for years, and I never use it. You might want to just wipe it down with a damp cloth. It's a little bit dusty."

"*Danki*. That's great, Tillie."

She pursed her lips and rested a hand on her small hip. "You don't understand what I'm suggesting, do you?"

"I'm sorry, but I don't." Leroy glanced at Hank, who shrugged before eating a chip.

"Didn't you tell me Mattie loves your cooking?" Tillie asked and Leroy nodded. "You can take her a meal in this. She'll be overwhelmed by the gesture."

The plan clicked into place in his mind. "*Danki*. That's a great idea." Then he frowned. "What if she refuses to see me?"

"Write her a letter and put it inside with the food." Hank pointed to the basket. "She'll be too curious not to read it."

"*Ya*." Tillie sat down on her stool. "That's a fantastic idea."

Leroy considered their suggestions as he fingered one of the basket handles. "Do you think I was wrong to ask her to marry me?"

Hank raised his eyebrows. "Why would you ask that?"

"I don't know." Leroy picked up his cool bottle of water. "Last night while I couldn't sleep I started thinking about how Mattie and I wound up in this mess. I spent most of my life wondering what it would've been like to have a *daed* in my life. When Isaiah died, I felt as if God wanted me to take care of Mattie and her baby so her child could have a *daed*. I was so certain God had called me to be the *daed* Isaiah couldn't be."

He lifted the bottle. "But now here we are living separate from each other. Jacob didn't need a *daed* after all. If I hadn't asked her to marry me, then she'd be free to find someone she truly loved."

Tillie shook her head. "She will come back to you."

"I don't know if that's true if she won't even respond to my messages." He set his bottle down on the table. "If she misses me as much as I miss her, then why hasn't she called me back?"

Tillie touched his arm. "Make her a meal and write her a letter that comes straight from your heart. It will work. Have faith."

The words soaked through him. He hoped she was right.

. . .

Mattie worked on stitching her quilt in her parents' bedroom. As her fingers moved, her shoulders loosened slightly and her mind swirled with thoughts.

Mamm appeared in the bedroom doorway. "You have a visitor."

"I do?" She placed the quilt on the table. "Who is it?"

"Leroy."

Knots clenched in her shoulders. "I can't talk to him. I just can't."

"You need to come and talk to him. He came all the way out here to see you, and he brought you something."

"What did he bring?"

"I'm not going to tell you. Come and see for yourself." *Mamm* turned and disappeared into the hallway.

Mattie sat frozen in the chair as emotions battled inside of her. Part of her wanted to run out to the kitchen and hug Leroy while apologizing for hurting him. The other part of her wanted to hide in her parents' bedroom until he left.

She remained in her seat for several moments and then slowly stood and padded to the doorway. She leaned against the doorframe and listened as Leroy spoke to her parents.

"How is she doing?" Leroy's voice was soft.

Mattie closed her eyes and imagined him standing there. She envisioned his face with his dark eyes and chiseled features. Had his beard grown since she'd left six days ago? It seemed as if it had been months since she'd seen him.

"She's having a difficult time." *Mamm*'s voice was equally soft. "I've been encouraging her to reach out to you."

"*Danki.*" He blew out a loud breath. "I don't want to push her too hard, but I'm afraid she'll forget about me if I don't at least try to talk to her."

"You don't need to worry," *Dat* chimed in. "I have a strong feeling everything will work out just fine."

"I do too," *Mamm* insisted.

"I hope you're both right." Leroy's tone was forlorn.

Mattie hugged her arms to her middle, fighting back the guilt ensnarling her. Her parents would never see things from her point of view.

"Well, I can't make her see me." Leroy sounded weary. "Would you be sure she gets this?"

"Of course we will," *Mamm* promised. "I'll also tell her she needs to go see you next."

"*Danki*, Ruth. I appreciate it. *Gut nacht*."

"I'll walk you out," *Dat* offered. "Tell me all about the harness shop. How's business going?"

Mamm said good night to Leroy, and soon the door opened and then clicked shut as her father's voice disappeared outside.

Mattie couldn't stand it any longer. She had to see him. She rushed through the family room and out the front door to where her father and Leroy stood on the front steps.

"Mattie," Leroy said, his eyes brightening as he looked at her. "I didn't think you were going to see me."

Dat shook Leroy's hand. "*Gut* seeing you, Leroy. Don't be a stranger." He turned to Mattie. "I'll give you two some privacy." Then he headed inside, the screen door clicking behind him.

Mattie ran her sweaty palms down her apron and looked up at him. "I was surprised you came to see me."

He pointed to the glider behind them. "Do you want to sit and talk?"

"*Ya*." She sat down, and he sank down beside her, jostling the glider into motion.

They were silent for several moments, and she searched her mind for something to say. She looked out toward the driveway and noticed the van sitting out by the road. He'd hired a driver to bring him out to see her tonight. Her heart warmed.

"Have you gotten my messages?" His question broke through the awkward silence.

She kept her eyes focused on the van. "*Ya*, I have. I just didn't know what to say."

"How have you been?"

"Okay, I guess." She looked up at him, taking in his dull eyes and the circles underneath them. He must have been suffering from insomnia too. "And you?"

"I miss you. I want you to come home with me."

"I can't." She started to stand, but he reached out and grabbed her hand. The feel of his warm skin against hers sent tingles dancing up her arm.

"Wait." His eyes widened. "I didn't mean to chase you off. You can come home whenever you're ready."

"*Danki*," she said, and he released her hand. "I need to go. *Gut nacht*."

She hurried into the house and then looked out the screen door as he loped down the driveway and climbed into the van. The engine rumbled as Leroy's driver left to take him back home, and her heart sank. She didn't know what to say to him, but she also didn't want him to leave. When would she stop being so confused?

Mamm frowned as Mattie walked toward the kitchen. "You didn't talk to him for very long."

She ignored the comment and approached the table where a picnic basket sat. "What's this?"

"Leroy left it for you."

"He brought me a basket?" Mattie lifted the lid, and the aroma of freshly baked goods wafted over her. She stilled when she found something written inside the lid.

In Leroy's neat, familiar penmanship, she read, *"2 Corinthians 1:7: And our hope for you is firm, because we know that just as you share in our sufferings, so also you share in our comfort."*

The scripture touched something deep in her soul.

"What is it?" *Mamm* sidled up to her.

"He wrote a scripture on the inside of the lid." Mattie pointed to it, and *Mamm* read it.

"That's lovely. Leroy is so thoughtful. What else is in there?"

Mattie pulled out an envelope with her name written on the front. She also found a loaf of bread and a storage bag filled with chocolate chip cookies. Her favorite.

"What a lovely gift." *Mamm* moved to the counter and began searching through her small plastic box filled with coupons. "He put a lot of thought into that."

Mattie didn't respond as she sank onto a kitchen chair. She opened the envelope and read the letter inside, which was also written in his handwriting.

Dear Mattie,

I know you're upset with me. It seems that no matter what I say, it's the wrong thing. I hope you know I care about you.

Please come home. We're married now, and we need to build a life together. We can't work things out if you continue to stay at your parents' *haus*.

I've left you a message every day since you left me. I miss you. The *haus* is too quiet, and I feel incomplete without you by my side.

We need to talk. Please call me or come to see me. I'll be here waiting for you.

Love,
Leroy

Mattie stared at the letter as tears burned her eyes.

"Are you okay?" *Mamm* asked.

Mattie nodded and stood. "I'm going to work on my quilt." She grabbed the bag of cookies and then hurried to her mother's room. She found a notepad and pen on her mother's dresser and then sat in the chair by the sewing machine.

She read his letter over and over again until a response formed in her mind. Then she wrote him a letter and sealed it in an envelope. Leaning back in her chair, she opened the storage bag and pulled out a large cookie. She took a bite and then moaned. The cookie was sweet and moist. Just perfect.

"Perhaps you should have opened a bake stand instead of the harness shop, Leroy," Mattie whispered with a grin.

She finished the cookie and then took another. She closed her eyes, and an image of Leroy standing at the counter while mixing up cookie dough filled her mind. She could envision his face, his deep brown eyes, and his wide, muscular shoulders.

Her eyes flew open and she gasped, wondering if the romantic feelings she thought she might be developing for Leroy before Jacob died had returned.

Mattie stood and walked to the kitchen, thankful to find it empty. Her parents must have gone out to the porch to sit as they often did on nights when the weather was warm.

She found the basket empty on the counter and the loaf of bread sitting next to it. She slipped the envelope into the basket and then hustled back to her quilt. She needed to release some of her confusing emotions.

As soon as Mattie sat down at the sewing table, she went to work, trying to ignore the longing that had taken hold of her when she read Leroy's letter.

"Mattie."

She looked up from the quilt and found *Dat* standing in the doorway. "Hi."

"Did you get the basket?" He jammed a thumb in the direction of the kitchen.

"*Ya*, I did."

He rested his forearm against the doorframe and paused for a beat. "I remember when Leroy's *daed* left his *mutter*. Leroy was about five, so you must've been four."

She gripped the quilt and held her breath, hoping her father wouldn't lecture her.

"Leroy's *mamm* was devastated." *Dat* didn't seem to notice Mattie's anxiety. "She never recovered emotionally, and she struggled to be both *mutter* and *daed* to Leroy and Joel."

"I know. Leroy used to talk about his *daed*'s abandonment when we were *kinner*. I was the only one he trusted, and he told me how much it hurt his *mamm*, his *bruder*, and him when his *daed* left them. He told me he used to hear his *mamm* crying at night, and it broke his heart."

"I remember that. She used to cry at church sometimes. I never understood how his *daed* could walk away from his family and never look back. It's not my place to judge him, but I truly can't comprehend it."

"I understand."

"I know you're grieving for Jacob and Isaiah." His hazel eyes glimmered in the low light of the lantern sitting on the table by the door. "Your *mamm* and I are grieving too. We loved Jacob and Isaiah. Your *mamm* and I are so sorry you've been through so much, and we both want to help you through this. There's only so much we can do, though. We love you and we support you, but you need more than us." He paused. "Leroy is a *gut* man. He's suffered loss in his life too. He lost his *daed* and *mamm*, and he also lost Isaiah and Jacob."

Mattie remained silent while digesting her father's words.

"I understand you need to take some time, but don't forget that you have a husband who cares about you."

"I won't," she promised, her voice wobbling. As he turned toward the hallway, she said, *"Dat."*

He faced her. "What?"

"I put a letter for Leroy in the basket. Would you please take it to him tomorrow?"

"Ya, I need to go to the hardware store. I'll stop by his shop."

"Danki." Mattie heaved a deep breath and then returned to sewing.

When she went to sleep on the sofa later that evening, she dreamt of baking cookies with Leroy.

CHAPTER 17

Leroy's eyes widened, and a gasp escaped his throat when Mose Byler stepped out of a van and walked toward the front of the harness shop the following morning. *The basket worked! Tillie is a genius!*

"Mattie." He nearly tripped on his way to meet Mose at the door.

"Where's the fire?" Hank smirked as he stood by the saddle display.

"Mose Byler is here," Leroy tossed over his shoulder. "I'm going to see if Mattie is with him. I'll be back."

"Take your time," Hank responded.

"Hi, Mose." Leroy pushed open the door. "How are you?"

"I'm fine." Mose held up the basket. "Mattie asked me to bring this to you."

"Oh." Leroy's excitement deflated. "She didn't come with you."

"No." Mose frowned. "I'm sorry, son."

"It's not your fault." Leroy took the basket from him. "*Danki* for bringing this over to me."

"*Gern gschehne.*" Mose rested his hands on his suspenders. "There's a letter in the basket for you."

"She wrote me a letter?" Leroy hated the thread of desperation he heard in his voice.

"*Ya.* Ruth told me Mattie read your letter and immediately wrote a reply. I think your letter touched her."

Their short conversation on the porch last night had left him yearning for more time to talk to her. He needed to hear her voice and he needed to encourage her to open up to him. "What do you mean?"

Mose pointed to the basket. "I mean that sending over the basket with the bread, *kichlin,* and letter was a *gut* idea."

"Why was it such a *gut* idea if she didn't even come with you to return it to me?" Frustration washed over him.

Two customers looked over at Leroy as they walked past and pulled open the door.

Mose motioned for Leroy to follow him to the corner of the building, away from the entrance to the shop and curious eyes. Leroy followed him with the basket dangling from his hand.

"It was a *gut* idea because you got her attention. You had left messages, but she didn't respond to you. But she spoke to you on the porch last night." Mose tapped the basket lid. "And there's a letter inside this basket. She's finally opening up to you. It's going to take time, but you're getting through to her."

Why hadn't Leroy come to that conclusion on his own?

"I know you're anxious for Mattie to come home to you," Mose continued. "I'm certain you're hurting just as much as Mattie is, but I think you're doing everything right."

Leroy sighed. "How long do you think it will take?"

"Well, she's just as stubborn as her *mamm*. Ruth made me wait awhile before she would agree to marry me, but as you already know, she eventually came around and told me yes. You just have to have faith that God will work this out."

"Danki." He wasn't certain he agreed with Mose's positive words. "I appreciate it."

"Will we see you at church Sunday?"

"Absolutely. Will Mattie be with you?"

"Ya. I'll make sure she comes with us."

"Gut." His insides thrummed with longing. He hoped Mattie would speak to him again. He couldn't even fathom what the community members would say or think when he and Mattie arrived at church in separate buggies.

He pushed that idea out of his mind. He couldn't waste any time worrying about what other people thought of his marriage. All he could do was work hard to fix whatever had gone wrong between Mattie and him.

"I'll see you tomorrow, then." Mose shook his hand. "Take care."

Leroy waited until after Mose's driver had steered the van onto the main road before opening the basket.

While leaning against the side of the building, he opened the envelope addressed to him and read the letter written in Mattie's pretty penmanship.

Dear Leroy,

Danki for bringing the letter, bread, and *kichlin* over to me last night. The bread and *kichlin* smell so *appeditlich*. I can't wait to try them. I'm sure they'll be fantastic since you are an amazing cook.

It was nice seeing you tonight. I'm sorry I haven't called you back. To tell you the truth, I was too much of a coward to call you back. As I told you on the porch, I just don't know what to say to you.

You believe we belong together, but I would be lying if I told you I agree with you. I don't think we can work this out. Your life is better without me there.

You are a kind, generous, and thoughtful person. I'm sorry for hurting you. I was grieving when I left you, and I still am. No matter what Dr. Sheppard said, I'm responsible for Jacob's death. As his *mutter*, it was my job to keep him healthy and alive, and I failed. I failed Jacob and I failed you and Isaiah when I let Jacob die inside of me.

I'm sorry for holding you back, and I'm sorry for disappointing you. I hope you understand. It's just better if we stay apart.

Sincerely,
Mattie

Leroy's hand shook as he read and then reread the letter once more. Mattie still wasn't coming home. How could he get through to her if she'd made up her mind?

He shoved the letter back into the envelope and then strode down the path to Hank's house. He climbed the back porch steps and knocked on the door.

Tillie appeared, wiping her hands on a dish towel. She tilted her head as she opened her door. *"Was iss letz?"*

"Do you have a minute? I need to talk to you."

"Of course." She motioned for him to follow her into the house.

"Mose stopped by," he explained as they walked through the mudroom and into the kitchen. Then he summarized Mattie's letter. "I don't know what to do. I want to work things out, but how can I if she refuses to even consider coming home to me?"

She folded her arms over her apron. "That's easy."

"It is? I've missed something."

"What did you send over yesterday?" She pointed to the basket.

"Homemade bread and chocolate chip *kichlin*. Her favorite."

She paused, tapping her finger to her lip. "I think you should try something different. Don't bake for her."

He raised an eyebrow. "You think I shouldn't bake for her?"

"No." Tillie snapped her fingers and grinned. "Make her something personal. Something from your heart that shows her how you feel about her."

He nodded as ideas swirled through his mind. "That's a *wunderbaar* idea."

"Give the basket and the gift to her tomorrow at church in person. That way she has to talk to you. It would be rude to turn you down if you're standing right in front of her."

"And you think it will work?" He cringed at the despair radiating in his voice.

Her smile was smug. "I'm positive it will work. Let me know if you need any help. I'm rooting for you and Mattie."

"I am too."

· · ·

Mattie smoothed her hands over her black dress as she walked beside her mother toward Eva Zook's house. In keeping with tradition, she would visit with the other women in the congregation before the church service began in the barn. She'd wanted to stay home today, but her parents insisted she join them without even asking her why she wanted to stay home. They couldn't understand why she needed time alone. They wanted her to just pick up and move on, but it wasn't that easy.

Biting her lower lip, she continued toward the house as she scanned the groups of men standing by the barn in search of Leroy. Last night she'd lain awake on the sofa, envisioning what she would say to him if he approached her today, and she came up short. She had nothing to say to him since she'd included everything she'd wanted to express to him in her letter. She hoped she could avoid him, but that would be impossible. Their congregation included only fifty families, and they were bound to see each other at some point.

Mattie followed her mother into the kitchen, where the women stood in a circle and greeted each other. She folded her arms over her middle and glanced around the crowd of familiar faces. She'd grown up in this congregation and considered many of the women members of her extended family.

"Mattie!" Lizanne emerged from the sea of faces and enveloped her into a hug. "How are you, *mei liewe*?"

"I'm fine." Mattie held on to her sister. While she trusted Lizanne with her private thoughts, she didn't want to go into the detail of her emotions in public.

"I wanted to come see you before today, but I've been caught up in a few quilt orders. I want to talk to you when we get a moment." Lizanne seemed to search Mattie's face and then she lowered her voice. "How are things with Leroy? Have you spoken to him?"

"Well, I—" Her words were cut off when one of her mother's friends approached.

"Mattie!" Lynn Esh rushed over, her face twisted in a frown. "How are you? You've been through so much. You poor thing." She squeezed Mattie's hand.

"Oh, Mattie, there you are. How are you?" Eva Zook joined them. "I was wondering if you would come to church today. *Ach*, you look so tired. You have dark shadows under your eyes."

"Oh, Mattie." Mary King walked over and stood by Eva. "I've been praying for you. I'm so sorry about Jacob. I can't imagine how you must feel. How are you feeling?"

As two more women approached, asking how she was in unison, Mattie glanced out the kitchen window toward her father's buggy. Could she run to it and hide?

She didn't want their attention or their condolences. She just wanted to go home and hole up by herself on the sofa. But it was too late. Now she had to face her congregation. She cringed as more women joined them.

"*Danki* for your concern, but let's give Mattie some space," *Mamm* said, taking one of her arms. "She needs some air."

Lizanne took Mattie's other arm and they led her to Eva's family room, where they released her. Thank goodness her mother and sister understood she needed to get away from the attention.

"*Danki*," she said, scrubbing a hand down her warm face. "I guess I should have stayed home."

"No, don't say that." *Mamm* rubbed her back. "It will get better. I promise."

Lizanne gave her a muted smile. "Everyone is concerned about you because they care about you."

"I know." Mattie gave a resigned sigh as guilt nipped at her once again. "I just don't want to talk about it. I want to go to the service, have lunch, and then go home without having to lie to everyone and say I'm okay."

"Just stay with *Mamm* and me." Lizanne hugged her again. "We'll be your support. Right, *Mamm*?"

"Of course," *Mamm* agreed.

The clock in the kitchen chimed nine, and Mattie let out the breath she hadn't realized she'd been holding. She walked to the barn with her mother and sister and sat between them in the married women section.

She folded her hands in her lap and stared down at the skirt of her black dress. She'd worn black today both to remember and to mourn Jacob. It had been only five weeks since her baby had been born. Somehow it seemed like several months had passed since that heartbreaking day.

"Leroy is here," Lizanne whispered.

Mattie squeezed her eyes shut to force herself not to look up. She wanted to look at him and she wanted to avoid him all at once. Why did that man keep her insides tied up in knots?

"He's looking over here," Lizanne whispered.

"Stop," Mattie said, seething. "I don't want to look at him."

Lizanne leaned in closer. "Have you spoken to him?"

"Briefly on the porch the other night. We've also written letters to each other."

"You've written letters?"

While speaking softly in an effort to keep the conversation private, she explained the basket and the letters. Lizanne listened with her eyes wide.

"You had *Dat* deliver the basket for you yesterday?" Lizanne asked.

"*Ya.* I'm hoping he read my letter and will respect what I said. I think he's better off without me."

Lizanne rubbed her chin as if considering what Mattie had said. "What did *Dat* say when he got home?"

"He didn't say much, except Leroy was disappointed I didn't go with him to deliver it."

"Huh." Lizanne glanced across the barn toward the section where the married men sat.

"Tell me you're not looking at Leroy right now."

Lizanne waved off her worry. "He's busy talking to Hank and Al. He doesn't see us talking." She turned back to Mattie. "Are you going to talk to him today?"

Mattie blinked. "I don't know." *I hope not.*

"May I join you?"

Mattie looked up as Tillie pointed to the empty space next to Lizanne.

"Hi, Tillie." She swallowed as she looked at Tillie's pretty smile. Tillie knew she'd left Leroy. Did she believe Mattie was a horrible person? She held her breath, waiting to see if Tillie would ask how she was like everyone else had.

"*Gude mariye.* It's *gut* to see you."

"*Danki.*" Mattie waited for her to say more.

"*Gude mariye.*" Tillie greeted Lizanne and their mother. "I was concerned Hank and I were going to be late this morning because we didn't leave the *haus* as early as we planned. We got here just in time." She picked up a hymnal from beside her on the bench. "The hymn is just about to begin."

Just then a young man sitting across the barn, who had been chosen as the song leader before the service began, sang the first syllable and then the rest of the congregation joined in to finish the verse.

Mattie lifted a hymnal and then fumbled with the pages until she located the correct song. She tried to redirect her attention to the hymn as she studied the words, but her traitorous thoughts whirled through her mind. Leroy was sitting across from her in this large barn, and she couldn't stop her eyes from seeking him any longer. She peered across the barn, and against her better judgment, her eyes immediately honed in on Leroy.

Her legs trembled, and she drank in the sight of him as though she hadn't seen him in years. His deep brown eyes were focused on the hymnal in his hands, and his mouth moved along with the song. The stubble on his jaw had transformed into a thick beard.

As if sensing her eyes looking at him, Leroy lifted his eyes, and their gazes locked. Mattie stilled, and her breath hitched in her lungs. It was as though she was seeing him in a new light. Leroy was handsome, really handsome. How had she missed this detail in the past?

Breaking their intense gaze, he looked down at the hymnal and continued singing.

Lizanne leaned in close to Mattie and patted her hand.

With her words stuck in her throat, Mattie could only nod in response to her sister's thoughtful gesture before turning her focus to the hymnal again.

While the ministers met in another room for thirty minutes to choose who would preach that day, the congregation continued to sing. Mattie followed along with the words and sang softly to herself. During the last verse of the second hymn, she looked up just as the ministers returned to the barn. They placed their hats on two hay bales located at the back of the barn, indicating that the service was about to begin.

The chosen minister began the first sermon, and Mattie did her best to concentrate on his holy words. She folded her hands in her lap and studied them. She tried to keep her focus on what the minister was saying, but it kept drifting to Leroy. Her eyes defied her and stole glances across the barn at him. He sat with his head bowed, staring at his hands in his lap. She bit her lip, curious about his thoughts. Was he thinking about her or maybe the letter she'd written to him?

While the minister continued to talk in German, Mattie lost herself in memories of the last year, of sitting with the other married women in the church district near the home she and Isaiah rented. She missed the Sundays when they would spend the afternoon visiting friends or with her parents and sister, or take walks and talk about the house they planned to build. She relished those special memories.

She redirected her thoughts to the sermon, taking

in the message and concentrating on God. She contemplated God's plan for her, wondering if he wanted her to reconcile with Leroy. But how could she reconcile with Leroy if her heart had been shattered when she lost Isaiah and Jacob?

The first sermon ended, and Mattie knelt in silent prayer between her sister and mother. She begged God to lessen the raw pain of losing Isaiah and Jacob. She also asked God to heal Leroy's heart. After the prayers, the deacon read from the Scriptures, and then the hour-long main sermon began. Mattie willed herself to concentrate, listening to the deacon discuss the book of John.

Relief flooded Mattie when the fifteen-minute kneeling prayer was over. The congregation stood for the benediction and sang the closing hymn.

While she sang, her eyes moved again to Leroy. It seemed natural for her to gaze at him as he sang along with the hymn. Could he sense her eyes focused on him? When his gaze met hers, her cheeks burned. She stood frozen, entranced by the ferocity of his gaze.

When the hymn ended, the men began converting the benches into tables for the noon meal.

Lizanne touched Mattie's arm. "Do you want to help serve the meal or would you rather sit and rest?"

"I'll help. I'm feeling fine." If Mattie sat down and relaxed, she ran the risk of more people asking her if she was okay. She needed to stay busy to avoid the curious congregation members and also to avoid Leroy.

"Okay." Lizanne turned toward their mother.

Mattie stood and smoothed her hands down her dress while waiting to file out of the barn.

"Mattie." Leroy's voice was close to her ear, sending an involuntary shiver zinging up her spine.

Mattie bit her lip and turned toward him standing beside her. *So much for avoiding him.*

"I need to talk to you alone." He frowned at her. "Please don't leave before I get a chance to see you."

The intensity in his eyes melted something deep inside of her, and she couldn't refuse him. "All right."

"*Danki.*" He nodded a greeting to her mother and sister before turning to help Hank and Al with the benches.

Lizanne squeezed Mattie's arm. "He sounded like he had something important to tell you."

Mattie pointed toward the barn doors. "Let's get to the kitchen so we can help serve the meal."

As Mattie followed Lizanne and *Mamm* out of the barn, Tillie caught up to her. Mattie suspected Tillie was helping Leroy, but instead of that upsetting Mattie, knowing Tillie cared almost made her smile.

CHAPTER 18

Anxiety pressed down on Leroy's shoulders and twisted the already tight muscles in his back. He tried his best to contribute to the conversations droning on around him during lunch, but his thoughts were stuck on Mattie.

He had glanced over at her during the service, and she looked beautiful, even though she was clad in black to mourn Jacob's loss. He'd caught her watching him more than once during the service, and his thoughts spun with curiosity. She seemed to miss him as much as he missed her, which made frustration swell inside of him. So why wouldn't she just come home?

He cupped a hand to his mouth to shield a yawn. He'd worked on her gift until late last night, and he'd written her another letter. The basket was tucked away in his buggy. Now he just had to get her alone so they could speak in private. He would wait until the women were finished eating and then ask her to go for a walk with him. Hopefully, she would agree.

When the women came around to fill their coffee cups, Mattie had given him a pleasant look but quickly continued on her way without speaking to him. He had to find a way to get her to talk to him again.

"You okay?"

Leroy lifted a pretzel to his mouth.

"Hello?" Hank nudged Leroy's arm with his elbow.

"What?" He turned toward his friend. "Sorry. I didn't think you were talking to me."

"You're in your own little world there." Hank raised a dark eyebrow. "Everything okay?"

"Yeah. Sure. Everything is fine."

"You're a terrible liar," Hank muttered before turning to their friend Titus. "So how is the dairy business these days?"

"Oh, it's the same. A lot of milk." Titus chuckled, and everyone around them joined in.

Leroy couldn't wait until lunch was over so he could finally speak to his wife alone.

. . .

Leroy leaned against the split rail fence and waved as friends walked by on their way to their buggies. Lunch was over, and the members of the congregation were slowly heading to the line of buggies patiently waiting to make the trek home. His focus was trained on the kitchen door as he waited for Mattie to walk outside.

Hank and Tillie approached from the knot of people walking to the buggies, and Leroy waved to them.

"Are you heading home?" Hank asked.

"Soon," Leroy said.

Hank raised his eyebrows.

Tillie smiled. "She was helping wipe down the table in the kitchen and someone pulled her into a conversation."

She's avoiding me. Leroy's back stiffened with frustration.

She took a step toward him. "She'll be out here soon, and you'll have a chance to talk to her. Don't worry. You'll have the opportunity to give her the basket and the letter. Trust me."

He nodded, but doubt coiled through his gut. *"Danki."*

Hank looked back and forth between Tillie and Leroy. "Am I missing something?"

She sighed and rolled her eyes. "I'll tell you in the buggy." She took Hank's hand in hers and gave it a tug. "Let's go." She looked at Leroy. "We'll see you later, okay?"

"Ya." He said good-bye and then turned his attention back to the house. He leaned back against the fence and crossed his arms over his chest. He refused to leave before having the opportunity to talk to Mattie and give her the basket and letter. He'd wait all afternoon if he had to.

Several minutes passed before Mattie stepped out of the back door. She scanned the driveway and pasture until her eyes found him. He stood up straight and rested his shaky hand on the fence rail behind him as she started down the path toward the rock driveway.

"I'm sorry it took so long." She came to stand in front of him. "Eva pulled me into a conversation. I kept trying to get away, but then she would ask me another question."

"It's okay. I'm not in a hurry to go home."

"Gut." She touched the ribbons on her prayer covering as she looked up at him.

A beat passed as they stared at each other.

"Would you like to go for a walk?"

Mattie shrugged. "Sure."

They fell into step as they followed the fence line leading toward the pasture. He racked his brain for something to say. He had mentally practiced what he intended to say to her, but the words had dissolved as soon as he looked into her eyes.

"You look *gut*," he finally said, and she snickered. He cocked an eyebrow. "That's funny?"

She looked up at him, and her eyes sparkled in the bright afternoon sunlight. "You have no idea how many people asked me if I'm okay today. Everyone wanted to make sure I was doing all right. And they all had to express their condolences. I know they mean well, but I actually wondered if I could hide in *mei dat*'s buggy until the service was over."

"Really?" He was grateful she was actually talking to him. "You wanted to hide from everyone?"

"*Ya*, I did. I didn't want to be the center of attention today. I just wanted to be another member of the congregation." She tilted her head. "Haven't you ever felt that way?"

"*Ya*. After *mei mamm* passed away I wanted to be alone with my thoughts. I was thankful for the outpouring of support, but I wanted to escape it at the same time."

"Exactly." She stopped and leaned forward on the split rail fence, facing the horses frolicking in the lush green pasture. "I never know what to say when they ask me how I am. I'm having a difficult time putting my emotions into words. Besides, I don't think people want to hear the truth. They just want to hear that I'm doing fine."

"I want to hear the truth." He leaned his forearms on the top railing of the fence and glanced up at the clear azure sky.

She looked up at him, her pink lips pressed together. "You already know how I feel. I put everything in the letter." She paused for a beat. "You read my letter, right?"

He frowned. "Of course I did."

Her eyes seemed to search his for something. "How are you doing?"

The question knocked him off balance for a moment. He never expected her to ask how he was.

He gazed out toward the horses as he considered his response. "I miss you." He met her gaze, and she bit her lower lip as her eyes glistened. "*Ach*, please don't cry."

She cleared her throat and averted her eyes by looking at the horses again. "I meant what I said in the letter. I can't be the *fraa* you need or should have."

"How can you say that? We know each other better than anyone else does. It only makes sense for us to be together since we already care about each other."

"I'm not capable of giving you the love you deserve." Her voice was soft as a tear streamed down her cheek. "I lost Isaiah and I married you too quickly. I didn't give myself a chance to process that loss. Then I lost Jacob, and it just tore my soul to shreds. Some days I can't find the strength to get out of bed. You don't need to be burdened with all my issues."

He stood up straight and faced her. "That's where you're wrong. I don't want to move on without you. I want to help you heal. I want to fix your broken heart. Let me help you."

She scrubbed her hand down her cheek. "No. I can't put you through any more heartache. I've hurt you enough."

"Come home with me, and we'll work through all this together." He held his hand out to her as hope swelled in his soul. *Please say yes, Mattie. Please come with me. Just give me one more chance.*

She shook her head, and his hope shattered. "I can't. I'm sorry."

Leroy sighed. It was time to relent. He'd pushed her far enough for one day. "Would you please walk me to my buggy? I have something for you."

"Okay." She wiped her eyes with the back of her hands and walked in silence beside him toward the driveway.

When they reached his horse and buggy, he retrieved the basket and handed it to her. "I hope to see you again soon. But if I don't, I hope you have a *gut* week."

As she took the basket from him, their fingers brushed, and electricity sizzled. Her mouth gaped for a fraction of a second. Had the electricity zapped her too?

"Danki." Mattie gave him a weak smile before he climbed into the buggy.

Leroy waved as he guided the horse to the road, and he prayed his letter would help change her mind about their future.

. . .

When she arrived at her parents' house, Mattie carried the picnic basket into her parents' room and sat down at the sewing table before opening it. The familiar aroma of leather washed over her as she pulled out a small leather coin purse shaped in a heart with the initials *MJF* embroidered on it. She lifted the coin purse and gasped as she turned it over again and again in her hands. The purse was beautiful with intricate detail. Her heart swelled with admiration as she examined it closely and imagined Leroy creating it for her. Leroy had been busy!

At the bottom of the basket she found an envelope with her name on it, and her pulse quickened. She opened the envelope and read the letter.

Dear Mattie,

I was disappointed your *dat* came alone to deliver the basket and your letter to me. When I saw Mose out the window of the harness shop, I thought maybe you had come to talk to me again. Still, I'm thankful you responded to my letter, even though you didn't send me the answer I had hoped to receive.

I disagree with you when you say I'm better off without you. I can't imagine my life without you.

Tonight I've been thinking about our childhood. Do you remember the time when you were ten and I was eleven and that *bu* Mahlon kept teasing you on the playground? He had you in tears, and I finally got in his face and told him to knock it off. You thanked me, and I said you could always count on me because I would always be at your side. I meant it then, and I still mean it now.

Let my shoulder be the one you cry on. Let me be the one who comforts you when you're feeling *bedau-*

erlich and alone. That's what husbands are supposed
to do.

As I said, I'll always be by your side ready to help you.

Love,

Leroy

P.S. Enclosed you'll find a heart-shaped coin purse I
created for you. I hope you like it. I included your initials on the front of the purse. The heart represents my
heart, which you've always had. I hope the coin purse
brings a smile to your face and reminds you of how
much you mean to me.

Tears stung Mattie's eyes and then flowed down her
hot cheeks as she read the letter three times. She wiped
her eyes and sniffed before she opened the coin purse
and ran her fingers along the smooth leather. The purse
was perfect and beautiful. The sentiment stole her breath
and squeezed her chest.

His handsome face filled her mind, and she suddenly remembered how their fingers had brushed when
she took the basket from his hands. She'd thought she'd
felt a spark, but then she convinced herself she had imagined it. Could there be a true spark between her and
Leroy? No, that just wasn't possible.

More tears spilled down her cheeks, smudging the
ink and dampening the letter as she held it in her trembling hands.

"Mattie? Oh, Mattie!" *Mamm* rushed into the room
and pulled a chair up beside her. She set a small book
on the table and pulled Mattie into her arms for a warm

hug. Then she rubbed her back as Mattie rested her cheek on her shoulder.

"Look at what Leroy made for me." She handed the coin purse to her mother.

"It's so *schee*." Mamm turned it over in her hands. "And he put your initials on it. It's lovely."

"I know." Mattie folded up the letter and put it back into the envelope. "I'm so confused. I'm certain he's better off without me, but my heart hurts when I see him and read his letters." She wiped away more tears as she looked up at her mother. "When am I going to feel normal again? When will all this pain go away?"

"*Ach*, Mattie. It will take time, but bearing your loss will get easier and the pain will lessen."

"How long until it does?"

"I don't know, but I have something I think will help you through this." *Mamm* picked up the small book and handed it to her. "This book helped me through some really difficult times, and I thought maybe it would help you too."

The little cover was worn and featured a picture of a rose and the title *God's Love for You*. She flipped through and found pages decorated with beautiful drawings of nature scenes and flowers, accompanied with Scripture verses. Many of the verses had been underlined.

She looked up at *Mamm*. "Did you mark these verses?"

Mamm had a faraway look in her eyes. "*Ya*, I did. It helped me when I lost *mei bruder*. There were times when all I could do was cry. I missed him so much, but I also felt so sorry for my parents. Sometimes I heard *mei mamm* crying. She would go out to the *schtupp* late at night, and I think she believed no one could hear her. But I always heard her because my room was just down the hallway. I bought this book at a bookstore in town, and I would stay up at night and read it, and sometimes I'd cry too."

"I'm so sorry." Mattie ran her fingers over the cover of the book while imagining her mother curled up in bed with it. "And did this book help you with your grief?"

"*Ya.*" *Mamm* gave her shoulder a gentle squeeze. "When Elias died, I thought my world was ending. I believed I could never recover from the depths of my grief. By reading the scriptures in this book, I realized I could go on. I will always miss *mei bruder*, but I also keep his memory alive in my heart. I married your *dat*, and then we had Lizanne about eighteen months later." She touched the cover of the book. "I thought it might give you some comfort too."

"*Danki.*" Mattie hugged the book to her chest. "I will cherish it."

"I know you will. And promise me you won't give up on Leroy just yet. "

"I promise." Guilt weighed heavily on Mattie's heart. She cared about Leroy, but she just couldn't believe their marriage would last.

"*Gut.*" *Mamm* squeezed her hand. "It's been an emotional day for you, and you look tired. Maybe you should take a nap?"

Mattie yawned, and she covered her mouth. "I think that's a *gut* idea."

"Go get some rest. I'll call you when supper is ready."

"*Danki, Mamm.*" Mattie gave her a quick hug and then carried both the letter and book to the sofa.

She curled up on the sofa and opened the devotional, reading by the light of the warm sunlight streaming in through the nearby window.

She flipped through the book and stopped when she found a verse *Mamm* had underlined three times and then drawn a heart beside it. The Scripture verse was Psalm 46, verse 1. "God is our refuge and strength, an ever-present help in trouble."

Tears sprung up in Mattie's eyes and then streamed down her cheeks. Oh, that verse spoke right to her soul. She repeated it until she had committed it to memory. It was as if *Mamm* had picked that verse out just for her and *Mamm* could feel Mattie's grief.

Hugging the book to her chest, she sank back onto the sofa pillows. She opened Leroy's letter and read it again as more tears threatened her eyes. She couldn't answer his letter today when her grief and confusion were so raw. She needed time to digest what he'd said and analyze how she envisioned their future.

Mattie set the book and letter on the end table next to the sofa and then closed her eyes. *Mamm* was right. She needed to sleep, and a nap might just be the balm her soul needed today.

CHAPTER 19

Mattie sat at the sewing table and stared at Leroy's letter. She'd spent the week helping her mother with chores and working on her lap quilt, all without her daily nap for the first time since she lost Jacob.

At night she read and reread Leroy's letter as responses rolled around in her head. It was now Thursday afternoon, and she still hadn't responded to him. Although he deserved a response, she didn't know what to say.

Mattie swallowed a sigh. She had to take her mind off of the letter. She glanced down at her quilt. She needed to lose her thoughts in her quilting project. Mattie folded up the letter, stuffed it into the envelope, and set it aside.

She worked on the quilt for a few hours, stopping only to get a glass of water. She glanced at the clock. It was almost suppertime, and she had promised her mother she would cook tonight since her mother had gone to work with her father to help with the accounting books.

By the time her parents arrived home, Mattie had the table set and chicken and dumplings, rolls, and green beans were warming in the oven. She was grateful she hadn't burned the meal, especially since it was the first meal she'd prepared by herself since she'd come to live with her parents.

Mamm set her purse on the counter. "That smells *appeditlich*."

"It does," *Dat* agreed before kissing Mattie's cheek. "*Danki* for cooking so your *mamm* could help me today."

"*Gern gschehne*." She carried the basket of rolls and bowl of green beans to the table. "Everything is ready."

"*Wunderbaar*." *Mamm* washed up at the sink and then helped Mattie bring the rest of the food to the table.

They all took their seats, and after a silent prayer they began filling their plates.

"How did your day go at the store?" Mattie buttered a roll.

"It was *gut*." *Mamm* smiled at *Dat*. "I was able to balance the books, which is always a very *gut* thing, right?"

Dat chuckled as he cut up a piece of chicken. "*Ya*, that is always a *gut* thing. How was your day?" he asked Mattie.

"It was okay. I cleaned the bathroom, and I did some sewing." She took a bite of her roll.

"So you never stepped outside," *Dat* asked, and Mattie shook her head. "That's a shame. It's a *schee* day. It's difficult to believe September is almost over. The summer flew by quickly. I think we're going to have a beautiful fall."

"How is your lap quilt coming along?" *Mamm* asked.

"I'm making progress." She was grateful her mother and grandmother had taken the time to teach her how to quilt and sew. She cut up a dumpling and took a bite. It wasn't bad. Maybe she could cook again. Maybe she wasn't completely inept.

"Have you written a letter back to Leroy yet?" *Mamm* asked.

She stopped chewing and stilled as her parents focused their gazes on her. She swallowed and then took a sip from her glass of water. "No, I haven't."

Mamm frowned. "Are you going to respond to him?"

Mattie nodded.

"When?" *Mamm* set her fork on her plate.

"I don't know. I haven't gathered my thoughts yet."

"Mattie," *Mamm* began slowly, "he's been waiting for a response since Sunday. Don't you think he's anxious?"

"*Ya*, I'm sure he is."

"You should write him a letter tonight and take it to him tomorrow," *Mamm* said. "It's not right to make him wait so long."

Mattie frowned as guilt slithered through her. *Mamm* was right. She did owe him a response.

"I'll write him a letter tonight, but I don't want to deliver it to him." She looked at her father. "Would you please take the basket and letter to the harness shop for me tomorrow?"

Dat's smile faded. "I think you should take it to him, *mei liewe*. You need to face him."

"Okay. I'll write him a letter after I finish the dishes."

"I'll wash the dishes," *Mamm* insisted. "You write the letter."

As Mattie took another bite of dumpling, she hoped she could string together a few coherent thoughts and write a letter to Leroy.

. . .

Leroy said good night to Hank, locked up the harness shop, shoved his keys into his pocket, and started up the path toward his house. His shoulders were sore from the hours spent hunched over the worktable. He'd poured himself into his work this week as a way to block the disappointment and hurt that radiated through him every time he thought of Mattie and his unanswered letter.

Every day he checked his front and back porches, his mailbox, and his voice mail messages in hopes of finding a message from Mattie. But each day he found his porches, mailbox, and his voice mail devoid of her response. He would take any response, any acknowledgment of the emotions he had infused into the letter he'd written to her. Perhaps the letter meant nothing to her, and she had truly written him out of her life.

His steps were bogged down with the weight of his despair as he approached his back porch. The rumble of a car engine drew his attention to the rock driveway as a van came to a stop by the barn.

Leroy hurried over to the van as Mattie stepped out of the front passenger seat holding the basket. His heartbeat sped up. Mattie had come to see him. Had she finally decided to come home to him?

"Hi." He breathed the word as she stepped over to him.

"Hi." She handed him the basket. "I wanted to bring you this."

"*Danki.*" He took the basket.

"*Danki* for the *schee* coin purse. I love it. It's perfect."

"*Gern gschehne.*" He jammed a thumb toward the

house. "Do you want to come inside? I could make you something to eat."

She shook her head. "I need to get back home, but I can talk for a minute."

"Oh." He pointed toward the path that led to the harness shop. "Would you like to go for a walk?"

"Okay."

He set the basket on the porch steps and then gestured toward the path. They walked in silence as they made their way toward the shop.

"How's the harness shop doing?"

"It's going well. It's been busy." He rubbed his shoulder. "I've been busy trying to keep the shelves stocked."

"That's *gut*."

"How have you been?"

"I'm sleeping a little better, and I'm working on a sewing project." Her eyes brightened. "I made supper for my parents last night, and I didn't burn it."

"That's *gut*. You're making progress."

"I guess, but I still feel numb." She cleared her throat as she stopped in front of the harness shop and stared at the front window. "Is Tillie taking care of your household chores?"

"No." He rubbed his sore shoulder again. "I'm doing them."

"Oh." She glanced over at him and then quickly looked back at the store. He longed to read her thoughts.

"Why don't you just come home to me?" If only he could suppress the hint of desperation in his voice. "I can tell you want to. What's keeping you away from me?"

She sniffed. "I can't. I'm not ready."

"You're not ready yet, but that means you will come home to me eventually?" A spark of hope ignited deep in his soul.

She faced him, her eyes twinkling with unshed tears. "I can't promise you that." She pointed toward the waiting van. "It's getting late. I should go. Take care of yourself." She walked quickly down the path and climbed into the van.

Leroy waved as the van backed out of the driveway. Once the van was gone, he carried the basket into the kitchen.

He sat down at the table, pulled out the letter, and began to read.

Dear Leroy,

First of all, I want to thank you for the lovely coin purse. The stitching is perfect, and I love how you included my initials. I knew you were a talented leatherworker, but I am in awe of the detail and precision in this coin purse. Thank you so much for giving it to me. I will use it and treasure it always.

I also clearly remember when you stood up to Mahlon for me. You left part of the story out, though. You got into trouble for handling the bullying instead of telling Teacher Marilyn. I felt so guilty you had to stay after class and help clean the classroom for me, but you never complained. In fact, you said you didn't regret putting Mahlon in his place.

You've always been there for me. I've been able to count on you since I was six years old. You mean so much to me. This is why I have to be completely honest with you. Please read the remainder of my letter slowly and take my words to heart.

Sunday afternoon *mei mamm* gave me a beautiful devotional, and I've spent the week reading it and re-reading your letter while trying to decide how to respond to you. I'm sorry I've taken so long. I didn't mean to delay my response, but I just needed some time to think things over.

I've come to the conclusion that you and I should remain *freinden*. We should continue to live separately. I care deeply for you, but I'm not ready for a real marriage. I can't give you the level of intimacy you deserve. I should have given myself time to grieve for Isaiah. My heart just isn't ready, and I don't know when it will be ready.

I'm so sorry. I hope you can forgive me.

> Always,
> Mattie

Leroy's blood boiled with white-hot fury as he read the letter a second time. When he finished reading it, he slammed the letter down on the table, yanked his shop keys out of his pocket, and hurled them across the room with such force they dented the sheetrock before falling into a noisy heap on the floor.

He stared at the damaged wall while taking deep breaths in an effort to slow his racing pulse.

Leroy shoved his hands through his thick hair and tried to think of something to do that would make Mattie believe in their marriage.

He needed more help.

After retrieving his keys from the floor, he pushed them back into his pocket and hustled out the back door and down the path toward Hank's house. He climbed the back porch steps and knocked.

Hank opened the screen door wide. "What's going on?"

"May I talk to you and Tillie?" He stepped into the mudroom.

"Come in." Hank gestured for Leroy to follow him into the kitchen.

The aroma of meat loaf filled Leroy's senses and caused his stomach to grumble as he stepped into the kitchen.

Tillie looked up from the table. "Hi, Leroy. Have a seat. Let me get you a plate." She stood and started for the cabinet. "I'm sorry I didn't think to invite you earlier."

"*Danki*, but I didn't come to eat. I need your help." He squeezed a hand to the back of his stiff neck and then shrugged. "I'm at the end of the rope, and I don't know what to do."

"What is it?" She turned to face him.

He summarized what Mattie's latest letter said, and Tillie and Hank frowned as they listened. "I'm on the verge of losing her. It seems like she's really confused, so I need to help her realize she's making a mistake. I want to do something big and make a grand gesture. Maybe that would get her attention."

Tillie snapped her fingers. "What if you took her on a picnic? You can take an entire meal over. Maybe do something like lunch meat, rolls, chips, and a dessert?

I can go to the market for you on Monday and pick everything up and pack it for you."

A glimmer of optimism took root in his heart, and some of the frustration in his jaw relaxed. "That would work. I'll give you money." He looked toward the counter and spotted an empty vase. "Would you get flowers too?"

"That's a great idea." Hank moved to stand beside his wife and looped an arm around her shoulders. "You like it when I bring you flowers."

"*Ya*, I do." She looked up at him with mock annoyance. "Come to think of it, it's been awhile since I've gotten any flowers, Henry Ebersol."

Hank sighed. "You're right, dear. I'll have to pick some wildflowers for you."

"*Danki.*" Tillie gave Hank a warm smile.

Envy coursed through Leroy. If only Mattie would look at him with the same devotion in her eyes.

Suddenly determination replaced his envy. He would try again. No, he would keep trying, until Mattie finally came home to him.

CHAPTER 20

Mattie's knees and back ached as the sun beat down on her head and shoulders. She brushed her forearm across her sweaty forehead as she walked toward her parents' cottage carrying the basket full of snap beans, cucumbers, tomatoes, and squash she'd gathered from her mother and sister's garden. She'd also spent more than an hour weeding.

Just before she reached the bottom steps, something glinted in her peripheral vision. She turned toward the driveway and gasped at the sight of Leroy leaning against his buggy with a basket in one hand, a vase of flowers in his other hand, and a quilt draped over his arm.

Blinking with confusion, she stared at him. "What are you doing here?"

"Hi." He held up the basket. "Do you have time for a picnic?"

She tilted her head as he walked toward her. "A picnic on a Monday afternoon?"

"That's right." He gave her a knee-weakening smile. "I have the food and a quilt." He held out the vase. "You might want to put these inside, though."

She set the basket of vegetables on the back porch steps and then took the vase in her hands. Her heart thudded in her chest as she inhaled the sweet scent of white daisies, pink roses, and baby's breath. "These are my favorite flowers." She looked up at him with bewilderment.

"I know. That's why I got them." He raised an eyebrow. "So about that picnic . . . ?"

She looked down at her soiled apron and cringed. "I'm a mess. I was just working in the garden."

"You look fine. You don't need to change." He gestured toward the house. "Just put the flowers inside. We can go sit over by the garden if you'd like."

"Okay. I'll be right back." She rushed into the house and set the vase of flowers and the basket of vegetables on the kitchen table.

"Oh my goodness! Those flowers are so *schee*," *Mamm* commented. "Did Leroy bring you those?"

"*Ya*," Mattie said as she picked out a clean apron and dress from her pile of clothes by the sofa. "He's here. He wants me to go on a picnic with him."

"A picnic?" *Mamm* grinned. "That is so romantic. Go and have fun."

"I'll be back." She hustled into the bathroom and changed before checking her hair in the mirror. Then she dashed out the front door and met Leroy on the porch. "I'm ready."

"Great." He held out his hand to her.

She hesitated for a moment before taking his hand and letting him lead her back toward the garden, where he spread out the quilt on a patch of grass and then sat down. He patted the spot next to him, and she lowered herself down beside him.

He opened the basket and pulled out a bag of rolls, roast beef, turkey, American cheese, two bottles of water, a bag of chips, and a zipper storage bag filled with brownies.

She studied the food with awe. "This is perfect."

"I'm glad you like it. May I make you a sandwich?"

"*Ya. Danki.*"

He made her a sandwich and then built one for himself. They sat in amiable silence as they ate their food. Mattie's thoughts spun with a mixture of admiration and bewilderment. She told him in her latest letter that they couldn't be together as anything more than friends, and yet here he was giving her a generous picnic lunch on a lovely autumn afternoon. His thoughtfulness and dedication warmed her battered heart.

She finally broke the silence. "Is the store busy today?"

He swallowed. "It is."

"Shouldn't you be there?"

"Everyone is entitled to a lunch break, right? I chose to take a longer lunch break with my *schee fraa*."

A smile overtook Mattie's lips.

"How has your day been?" He crisscrossed his long legs as he faced her.

"*Gut.* I swept the cottage, weeded the garden, and picked the vegetables I had in that basket."

"And you're sleeping better?"

"*Ya.* How did you know?"

"Your face isn't as pale, and the dark circles under your eyes have faded." His expression became hesitant. "You look *gut.* I'm *froh* to see that."

"*Danki.*" She needed to change the subject before he

begged her to come home with him. "How are Hank and Tillie?"

"They're fine." He leaned back on one of his hands and looked up at the sky. "This weather is heavenly. I love the fall."

"I do too."

They made idle talk about the weather as they finished their sandwiches and then each ate a brownie. Soon the conversation turned to friends in the community.

"Well, I'd better get back to work." He stood and held out his hand to help her to her feet.

She packed up the remaining food in the basket while he folded up the quilt and draped it over his arm. They walked over to his horse and buggy together. When they reached the buggy, she held the basket out to him, and he shook his head.

"You keep it. There's a letter in the bottom for you."

"Oh." She stared up at him, taking in his handsome face and gorgeous dark eyes. "*Danki* for the picnic."

"*Gern gschehne.*" He touched her shoulder. "I miss you, Mattie. Come home to me soon."

Before she could respond, he climbed into the buggy and waved before guiding the horse toward the road. After his buggy disappeared, she headed into the house and found her mother in the kitchen.

"How was the picnic?" *Mamm* sidled up to her.

"It was *wunderbaar.*" She told her mother about the meal. "Why would he take so much time away from work to bring me lunch?"

"I think you know the answer to that question." *Mamm* peered into the basket. "Is there a letter too?"

"*Ya*, it's on the bottom." She pulled out the envelope and then sat down on a chair.

Mamm moved to the counter, as if to give Mattie privacy while she opened the letter and read it.

Dear Mattie,

I get the impression you believe I'm going to give up, but I'm not. If I have to keep sending you meals and desserts for the next three years or more, then I will.

You seem to think that a nearly lifelong friendship is not a solid basis for a marriage, but I believe it is. My grandparents were *freinden* first, and then they were married and had six *kinner*. Why can't we have a family together? Why won't you even try to make it work with me?

In your letter you said I've always been there for you, and you've been able to count on me since you were six years old. You said you appreciated my friendship, and I mean so much to you. Then you said you care deeply for me. If all that is the truth, then why do you want to live separately from me? Isn't a *gut* marriage based on mutual respect and trust? Don't we already have those things?

I don't understand you. If you cherish me the way I cherish you, then why are you insisting on staying away from me?

You said you married me too quickly and didn't give yourself enough time to mourn Isaiah. I've never rushed you, and I won't rush you.

Well, I think I've said enough for this letter. I'm in

this for the long haul, and I hope you wake up one day
and decide that you are too.

Love,

Leroy

Mattie sniffed and looked up to where her mother
stood at the counter.

"*Ach, mei liewe.*"

Mattie sniffed again and then folded the letter and
put it back into the envelope. "There's food left in the
basket. Would you like to have a sandwich for lunch?
I'll sit with you while you eat."

"That sounds *gut.*" *Mamm* took a plate from the cabinet and placed it on the table. She sat down across from
Mattie and made a sandwich.

"He seems determined to win your heart."

Mattie sighed. "I know."

Her mother ate in silence for a few moments, and
Mattie's mind filled with images of Leroy and their
friendship. Suddenly she remembered the kiss they'd
shared the night of the shop's grand opening, and a
sizzle of heat thrummed through her. How she longed
to relive that kiss. But was she ready for all the intimacy
a real marriage required? Anxiety replaced the heat
that had rushed through her body.

After her mother finished eating, Mattie cleaned up
the kitchen and then she and her mother headed to the
bedroom to sew. Later in the afternoon, Mattie took a
break from quilting and wrote a letter to Leroy. Then she
sealed it in an envelope before dropping it into the basket.

Soon it was time to start cooking supper. *Mamm* told

her Lizanne and Al were coming, which was unusual for a Monday night. But Mattie didn't ask why. They were always welcome.

She helped her mother prepare the meal, which was ready just in time when her father, Lizanne, and Al all arrived. After greeting each other, they sat down to eat.

"So you've been busy quilting," *Mamm* said to Lizanne as Al and *Dat* began talking business.

"*Ya.*" Lizanne cut up her roast. "I'm making two king-size wedding ring quilts. They're due in a couple of weeks. Business has picked up, and I'm doing custom orders."

"That's *wunderbaar.*" Mattie spooned peas onto her plate.

"How's your lap quilt coming along?" Lizanne asked. "*Mamm* told me about it."

"It's going well." Mattie looked over at *Mamm* at the end of the table, and *Mamm* smiled serenely. So *Mamm* had been talking to Lizanne about her.

"What brings you over for supper on a Monday night?" Mattie asked her sister.

Lizanne's gaze turned to Al and then back to Mattie. She placed her fork on the plate and sat up straighter.

"Al and I have something we want to tell you." She looked back at her husband, who was discussing furniture prices with *Dat.* "Al? May I interrupt for a moment?"

"Sure." He nodded toward Lizanne. "We'll have to continue this later. Duty calls."

Dat chuckled. "It's no problem."

Lizanne smiled. "*Danki, Dat.* Al and I have something to share. We want to tell you all first before we tell Al's family."

Mattie stilled and her shoulders stiffened.

"We're expecting." Lizanne bit her lower lip. "I'm due in April."

Mamm gasped and *Dat* clapped as Mattie sat frozen in place. While she was happy for her sister and brother-in-law, envy and grief swirled in her belly like a cyclone.

Lizanne turned to Mattie and squeezed her hand. "I'm so sorry. I didn't want you to hear it from someone else. I didn't know how to tell you. I never meant to hurt you." Her eyes shimmered with tears. "Please don't be upset with me."

"Stop it." Mattie pulled her into her arms and hugged her close. "Don't be sorry. I'm so *froh* for you. You'll be a *wunderbaar mamm*, and I'm thrilled to be an *aenti*." She buried her face in her sister's shoulder and held her breath in an attempt to stop herself from crying.

. . .

"That raspberry pie was amazing." Lizanne carried the plates to the counter. "Were those raspberries from Leroy's garden?"

Mattie gripped the glass she'd been washing so hard she was surprised it didn't shatter in her hand.

"*Ya*, they were," *Mamm* said. "Leroy gave me some raspberries at the beginning of the summer. I made a couple of pies and froze them."

Lizanne turned to Mattie. "Have you heard from Leroy?"

Mattie glanced over at her sister's innocent expression.

This visit must have been planned between her mother and sister. Did that mean her mother had already known Lizanne was pregnant? Had she only pretended to be surprised at the news? Mattie gritted her teeth as she studied her older sister.

Lizanne's eyebrows drew together. "Why are you glaring at me?"

"Was this dinner a ploy to get me to talk about Leroy?" Mattie pointed at their mother. "Did *Mamm* ask you to come here to try to talk some sense into me?"

Lizanne gaped and then turned to *Mamm*, who frowned as she set her dish towel on the counter.

"Don't snap at your *schweschder* like that." *Mamm* leaned her hand on the counter. "Lizanne said she wanted to come over for supper, I assume to tell us her news, so I invited her and Al to come tonight. Your *schweschder* asked about Leroy because she cares about you."

Guilt grabbed Mattie by the shoulders and shook her. Lizanne had always been nothing but supportive of Mattie. She helped Mattie with her chores when they were children. She kept Mattie's deepest secrets, stayed awake with Mattie at night and listened to her talk about the boys she had crushes on at school, and dried Mattie's tears when Isaiah and Jacob died. Her sister didn't deserve to bear the brunt of her frustration or her envy.

"I'm sorry." Mattie slouched her shoulders. "I didn't mean to yell at you."

"It's fine. I shouldn't have stuck my nose in your private business."

"Leroy brought her those flowers today, and he brought her a lovely picnic lunch they shared too." *Mamm* pointed to the vase on the counter. She seemed to ignore Lizanne's comment about being nosy. "He brought her a whole meal." Then she counted off the contents of the basket on her fingers.

"That is so romantic." Lizanne hugged her hands to her chest as she smelled the flowers. "Are you going to respond to him?"

Mattie returned to washing the glasses. "I'm going to take the basket over to his *haus* later. Do you want to come with me?"

Lizanne grinned. "I'd love to."

. . .

"I'm really sorry for snapping at you earlier," Mattie told Lizanne as she guided her horse down the street toward Leroy's house. "I didn't mean to take all my issues out on you."

The sky above them was cloaked in darkness.

Lizanne squeezed her hand. "Stop apologizing. That's the third time you've said you're sorry. I'm not angry with you." She paused. "I was worried you'd be upset by my news."

"Upset with you?" Mattie gave her a sideways glance. "You're *mei schweschder*, my only sibling. I'm thrilled for you and Al."

Lizanne raised her eyebrows. "You didn't need to hear that I'm expecting now. It's the worst timing ever."

"That's not true. Your life shouldn't stop because mine has." She guided the horse to turn right and then headed onto Gibbons Road toward Leroy's house.

"Your life hasn't stopped." Lizanne touched her arm as she spoke softly. "Your life has changed drastically, but you're still here, and you have people who love you very much, including *Mamm, Dat,* Al, and me. And you still have Leroy."

Yes, I know, and everyone keeps reminding me.

Mattie squeezed her eyes shut for a quick moment. Then she sat up straighter. "How long have you known about your *boppli*?"

Lizanne sighed. "A couple of weeks."

"A couple of weeks?" Mattie shot her another sideways glance. "Why didn't you tell us?"

"I felt so bad about it." Lizanne frowned. "I saw you wearing black at church and I couldn't bring myself to tell you. The last thing I wanted to do was make your grief worse."

"Please don't feel that way. I could never resent you or your baby. This is a tremendous blessing. Don't shut me out because you're worried you might hurt me. I want to be a part of this."

"*Danki.* I want to include you, and I'll do my best to be sensitive."

"That's a deal." Mattie's stomach fluttered as she guided the horse toward Leroy's house. "Would you take the basket up to his porch?"

"Are you kidding me? No way. You have to do it."

"Please, Lizzie. I'll be eternally grateful."

Lizanne crossed her arms over her chest. "Why are

you afraid to face him? He's your husband. What's the problem?"

There it was—the question that got to the root of all the issues.

Mattie sighed as she halted the horse on the street near Leroy's house. A single lantern glowed in the kitchen. She silently prayed he hadn't heard the horse and buggy.

Lizanne studied her. "You're avoiding the question."

"I'm tired of hurting him." Mattie up threw her hands in surrender. "I don't want to see his sad face when I hand him the basket and then tell him I'm going home to my parents' *haus*."

"So then stop hurting him and stay here tonight so you have time to talk things out. I'll take the horse and buggy back to *Mamm* and *Dat*'s *haus* for you."

"It's not that simple."

"But it should be." Lizanne leaned over toward her. "You've been hurting since Isaiah died and it only got worse when you lost Jacob. Aren't you tired of feeling lonely and falling asleep at night with tears in your eyes? Stop blaming yourself for not stopping Isaiah from going to the bank that morning. And stop punishing yourself for Jacob's death when it wasn't your fault." She touched Mattie's shoulder. "Let Leroy love you. You deserve happiness just as much as I do, Mattie."

Mattie gasped at her sister's words as fresh tears stung her eyes. The buggy was closing in on her, and she had to get out of it. She lifted the basket from the buggy floor and pushed open the door.

"I'll be right back," she muttered before padding up the driveway.

When she reached the back porch, she stopped and stared at the two-story house. Memories of her brief time spent there as Leroy's wife rushed through her mind, and she pushed them away. Her sister was wrong. Mattie didn't deserve happiness. She didn't deserve Leroy's love when she wasn't capable of giving him the same love in return.

She quietly set the basket on the porch and then hurried down the driveway to the buggy.

"That was awfully quick," Lizanne quipped as Mattie guided the horse back toward their parents' house. "I guess you really didn't see him."

Mattie needed to redirect the conversation. She couldn't handle another lecture. "Have you and Al talked about names?"

"Oh." Lizanne seemed surprised by the question. "We have, actually. I was thinking of Malinda for a *mae-del*." She turned toward Mattie. "What do you think of that name?"

"I love it. What about a *bu*?"

"Well, Al would like to name him after his *daadi*, which would be nice. His name was Robert."

As Lizanne talked about names, Mattie's shoulders relaxed, but her sister's words about her happiness continued to swirl through her mind and haunt her thoughts.

How would Leroy react when he found the basket? He could send her another basket of gifts with a letter, or he could finally let her go. But how would she feel if he didn't contact her again?

CHAPTER 21

Leroy stepped out onto the porch and stopped short when he saw the basket near the steps. He picked it up and carried it to the kitchen counter. His hands trembled as he pulled out the letter and read it.

Dear Leroy,

Danki for the *schee* flowers, the lovely picnic, and the generous meal. The flowers have brought a lot of happiness and sunshine into the kitchen, and *mei mamm* enjoyed the lunch meat and rolls too.

I thought about your questions in your letter, and I really don't have any answers to give you. If we were meant to be a family then Jacob would have lived. Without Jacob, we're not a family. We're just two *freinden* who mistakenly decided to get married too soon.

Please forgive me for hurting you, but I owe you my honesty. I just don't see how this marriage can work if I can't give you back the love you've offered me.

Danki again for the gifts. When I look at the flowers, I think of you and smile.

Sincerely,
Mattie

Leroy stared at the letter, reading it two more times, and then disappointment lanced through his gut. He hadn't expected her response to be so short or so repetitive since they'd shared the romantic picnic yesterday. He thought they'd bonded during the picnic, and he had hoped his questions would have pushed her to examine her feelings for him and make a decision.

He sat down on a kitchen chair as his thoughts turned to Jacob. How different would their life have been if the baby had lived? Maybe he would have been the catalyst for Mattie to finally consider their marriage authentic, but Jacob was gone, and now Leroy had to find another way to show her the potential their friendship truly could have.

Leroy folded up the letter and put it back into the envelope. Then he crossed the kitchen and opened the refrigerator. He pulled out the loaf of banana bread and coffee cake he'd baked for her last night.

As Leroy set the baked goods in the basket, he pressed his lips together and wondered what his mother would say if she saw all the baking he'd done in the past couple of weeks for Mattie. A calm settled over him as he contemplated his mother. She'd always loved Mattie. Of course she would have approved of their marriage.

He blew out a deep sigh. If only his *mamm* were here to guide him through this confusing time. *Mamm* would have given him advice to help him win Mattie's heart.

"I miss you, *Mamm*," Leroy whispered as he gathered up his notepad, a pen, and an envelope.

Then he sat down at the table and began to write another letter to Mattie.

. . .

Mattie peered out the kitchen window Wednesday morning. Her pulse quickened and she hugged her arms over her middle as a horse and buggy came to a stop in the driveway and Leroy hopped out.

She admired his tall, muscular stature and attractive face as he walked up to the porch. She had a sudden urge to hug him.

Whoa. Where had that come from?

Pushing the thought away, she stepped out onto the porch. "Leroy. *Gude mariye.*"

"Mattie." He repeated the greeting before holding out the basket and a vase of red and yellow tulips. "These are for you."

"*Danki.*" She inhaled the sweet scent of the flowers. "They are *schee.*" She looked up at him. "Would you like to come in?"

He shook his head. "I need to get to work."

She studied his eyes, finding pain and sadness there. A pang of guilt slammed through her. Her letter must have hit him hard. If only she could make things work between them.

"Have a *gut* day," he said before sauntering back toward his buggy. After climbing in, he guided the horse to the road.

"What did he bring you today?"

Mattie jumped with a start as her mother appeared behind her. "I didn't know you were standing there. He brought me more flowers and the basket." She inhaled the sweet scent of the tulips once again as she carried them into the house. She placed the vase next to the flowers she'd received on Monday.

"They are *schee.*" *Mamm* sniffed the flowers.

Mattie opened the basket and lifted out a loaf of banana bread and a coffee cake. "Look at these. He should have been a baker."

Mamm clicked her tongue. "Those are perfect. Let me make some tea, and we'll have a piece of each." She filled the kettle and put it on the stove.

Mattie sank onto a kitchen chair and opened the letter.

Dear Mattie,

I'm *froh* you enjoyed the picnic and like the flowers. I wanted to do something special for you. I was disappointed your letter was so short after I poured my heart and soul into the last letter I sent you. Actually, I've been pouring myself into all of my letters, but they don't seem to be helping you realize how determined I am to make things right between us.

As I put the banana bread and *kaffi kuche* in the basket, I found myself thinking of *mei mamm*. I miss her. *Mei mamm* admired you and your family. She always appreciated how thoughtful and kind your parents were to her, especially after *mei dat* left us. I would have loved for her to be here now to help us through this difficult time.

Mei mamm always gave great advice, especially when we were cooking and baking together. I'm sure she'd have gotten a kick out of the baking I've done for you lately. She appreciated that I was always more interested in learning how to cook than Joel was. To be honest, I just enjoyed spending time with her, and learning how to cook was a bonus.

Joel once asked *mei mamm* if she thought he should get married someday. She didn't understand why Joel asked the question until he explained he was afraid he would wind up like *mei mamm*—alone and sad after *Dat* left us. *Mamm* told Joel not to judge all marriages on her and *Dat*'s. She said *Dat* made a mistake when he left us, but it was *Dat*'s mistake.

She explained love and marriage were a blessing, and we should all strive to find the right person to spend our life with. Joel asked if she made a mistake when she married *Dat*, and *Mamm* said no. She believed her sons were a blessing, and she had no regrets. I was grateful to hear she didn't resent her life, but I will always regret her sadness and loneliness after *Dat* left.

When I was a *bu*, I never thought I would understand *mei mamm*'s sadness, but I do now. I mean it when I say I miss you and I pray every night you will come home to me.

As I write this, I find myself wondering what *Mamm* would say if I had the opportunity to ask for her advice on our situation. She once told me she could see you and me married and raising a family together someday. Isn't it ironic that *mei mamm* believed in us, but you don't?

In your letter you said we're not a family without Jacob. I disagree. Wouldn't you agree Hank and Tillie are a family? Some couples are blessed with *kinner* and some aren't. They don't need *kinner* to be a family.

Well, I need to get to work. Today we have to do inventory, so I will most likely deliver this to you Wednesday morning.

I hope someday you will decide I'm worth fighting for.

Love,
Leroy

"Here's your tea." *Mamm* set the mug next to Mattie's hand.

Mattie looked up at her mother. She'd been studying the letter so intently and for so long she hadn't even heard the kettle whistle.

"*Danki.*" She gripped the letter in her hand.

"What did he say?"

"I don't understand why he's holding on to me so tightly. He said his *mamm* would have approved of us. He also said he understands his *mamm*'s sadness and loneliness now that I've left him." She folded up the letter and stuffed it into the envelope. "He's hurting, and I need to release him."

"No, don't say that." *Mamm* reached across the table and squeezed Mattie's hands in hers. "You don't mean it."

"I actually do. When I agreed to marry him, I thought I could make it work, but I can't. My heart isn't ready for the love he needs and deserves." She blew out a deep, tremulous sigh. "I've made up my mind. I need to just cut myself off from him."

"Don't do anything in haste. Give yourself a day to think about it." *Mamm* pointed toward the doorway. "After we have our snack, you should go work on your

quilt and think about it some more. If you need someone else to talk to, go and see Lizzie. Don't make a decision you might regret terribly later on."

Mamm cut a piece of banana bread and a piece of coffee cake and put it on a plate before handing it to Mattie.
"Here. He made this for you. Enjoy it and then go work
on the quilt and think about how much he means to you."

Mattie complied, but her mind was already made it
up. It was time to let Leroy go and move on with her life.
She had to stop hurting him. Prolonging the inevitable
with these letters and gifts was only making it worse.

. . .

Leroy stepped out of his barn after caring for the animals and walked toward his house Friday night. He
glanced up at the gray clouds clogging the sky and inhaled the strong scent of rain.

Thunder rumbled in the distance. Memories of sitting
on the back porch and watching the storms approach
with his *mamm* and brother filled his mind. His mother
had permeated his thoughts during the past few days.
He again longed for her wise advice, but he held on to
the hope that Mattie would come to her senses.

As he unlocked the back door, the sound of a horse
and buggy drew his attention to his driveway. His pulse
skittered, and hope swelled in his gut. Maybe Mattie had
come to her senses sooner than he'd expected. He descended the stairs, hurrying to the buggy as a light mist
of rain kissed his face and another clap of thunder roared,
sounding closer this time.

When Lizanne and Al climbed from the buggy, Leroy's hope dissolved.

"Hi." Al smiled. *"Wie geht's?"*

"It's *gut* to see you." Leroy forced a smile on his face as Lizanne hefted the basket from the buggy floor. "How are you?"

"I'm fine, *danki*." She held the basket out to him. "We had supper with my parents tonight, and Mattie asked us to deliver this to you."

"Oh, *danki*." He took the basket and then gestured toward the house with his free hand. "Do you want to come in since the rain is starting?"

Just then a bolt of lightning streaked across the sky, followed by a loud boom of thunder. Lizanne jumped with a start and then laughed a little.

"No, *danki*." Lizanne glanced toward Al. "We'd better get home."

"Oh, okay. I appreciate you stopping by to drop this off."

"Gern gschehne." Al waved before climbing into the buggy. "See you soon."

"Ya. Drive home safely." Leroy started toward the porch.

"Wait!" Lizanne rushed after him, meeting him at the bottom steps. "I have to say something."

He spun to face her. "What?"

She frowned and pointed to the basket. "You're not going to like her letter, but I need you to promise me something."

"What?" His shoulders tightened with foreboding.

"Mei schweschder is confused." She took a deep breath.

"She's convinced she somehow deserves all the pain she's endured, and she believes she's supposed to go through life alone now."

Rain soaked through his shirt, causing him to shiver as he listened to her. "What do you want me to promise you?"

"Promise me that when you read her letter, you'll keep an open mind and listen to what she has to say. But you also need to not allow her to alienate you. You have to be strong and keep trying." She hugged her wrap closer to her body. "I've been trying to tell Mattie she deserves as much happiness as I have with Al, but she won't listen. She thinks she had her shot at happiness and lost it. She doesn't think she can find it again, but I know she can."

Her eyes narrowed as she pointed at him. "You're the key to her happiness, and once she realizes that, you two will have a wonderful life together. It will be the brand-new start she both needs and is entitled to have."

Lightning blazed again, followed by a *boom* that shook the ground beneath their feet.

"Lizzie!" Al called from the buggy. "Let's go. You're getting soaked, and the storm is getting worse."

"Go," Leroy told her.

"Promise me." Her gaze held his.

"Fine. I promise. Now, go on before the storm gets worse. Be safe going home."

"Danki." She rushed through the rain to the buggy.

"Lizzie!" He called as she climbed into the buggy.

She turned toward him, her eyebrows raised.

"Danki!" he yelled over another clap of thunder.

"Gern gschehne!" she responded before Al guided the horse and buggy back toward the road.

Leroy hurried into the house, flipped on a lantern, and placed the wet basket on the kitchen table. As he wiped down the basket with a rag, Lizanne's words rang through his mind. The letter had to be bad if she had to make him promise not to give up.

Worry and dread coiled in the already tight muscles in his spine and neck as he opened the basket and retrieved the empty baking pan from the coffee cake. He peered in and found an envelope with his name written in her neat handwriting.

He held up the envelope and studied it while taking a deep breath. Lightning lit up the kitchen for an instant, followed by a loud roar of thunder.

"It's now or never," he muttered as he sank onto a chair and opened the letter.

Dear Leroy,

Danki for the flowers and also for the *appeditlich* banana bread and *kaffi kuche*. We all enjoyed them.

I appreciate all you're doing to try to save our marriage, but it's time to admit we're fighting a losing battle.

With this letter, I'm releasing you to live your own life without me. Please stop pursuing me and trying to convince me to come home to you.

You're wasting your emotions on me, and I'm not worth your time.

I will cherish your friendship the rest of my life.

Always,

Mattie

"No!" Leroy slammed his hand down on the table and then shoved his chair back with such force that it fell onto the floor with a clatter.

Fury swamped him as he marched to the counter and pulled out a book of matches. After lighting one, he held the letter over the sink as it burned, reducing Mattie's rejection to ashes. The acrid scent of the burning paper filled his lungs and wafted throughout the kitchen as thunder continued to rumble and shake the house.

He gripped the sink with his hands, and keeping his arms straight and elbows locked, he leaned his head down as anguish drowned him. His strength and his hope were crushed.

He couldn't fight this any longer, but he still believed to the depth of the marrow in his bones that he and Mattie were meant to grow old together. And Hank and Tillie couldn't fix this for him. What he needed was divine intervention.

"God, please help me. I need Mattie in my life, and I believe she needs me too. Please make her understand our marriage is worth saving and that we can be a family no matter what life throws our way. Make her understand I can comfort her during her grief and show her happiness again. Please guide me to the words and actions that will touch her heart and bring her back to me. Please, God. Please help me be the man Mattie needs. In Jesus' holy name, amen."

CHAPTER 22

Gude mariye!" Tillie stepped into Leroy's kitchen. "I hope you haven't eaten yet. I made a new breakfast casserole, and I thought you might want a piece." She stilled and her eyes widened. "Leroy. You look terrible."

He looked up from the table and held his mug of coffee up in a sardonic toast. "*Danki.*" He pointed to the percolator on the stove. "There's *kaffi*. Help yourself."

Hank emerged from behind her and approached the table. "The circles under your eyes are so dark you look like you haven't slept in a week."

"I didn't sleep much last night." Leroy leaned back in his chair and stretched before yawning.

"Why?" She set the casserole on the table. "*Was iss letz?*"

"I got a letter from Mattie. It's over." He lifted the mug to his mouth and took a long drink.

"What do you mean by 'it's over'?" Hank pulled out the chair across from Leroy and sat. "Explain it."

As Tillie cut and distributed pieces of the casserole, Leroy shared his conversation with Lizanne last night and then gave a brief summary of the letter he found in the basket.

"She wants me to walk way, but I don't know how." He looked down at the large piece of breakfast casserole.

Despite the delicious aroma of egg, cheese, and bacon wafting up from the steaming food, his appetite dissolved at the thought of losing Mattie forever.

"Maybe it's time for you to take a step back again and give her more space. Do what she *thinks* she wants." Hank forked a piece of casserole into his mouth.

"That's a *gut* idea." Tillie pointed to her plate with her fork. "If you step away from her, she'll have time to mull over everything you've shared with her and whether she's made the right decision. Don't send the basket to her. Just back off."

Leroy smiled slowly as he looked back and forth between his friends. "That's a great idea."

"Eat." She pointed to his casserole. "You need your strength. A tour company called yesterday and asked if they can bring their tourists over to see the shop. We're going to be busy."

Leroy cocked an eyebrow. "Is that why you brought me breakfast? You're trying to butter me up before a tourist invasion?"

She chuckled. "*Ya*, that's it. You caught me."

Hank frowned. "I should've known better. I thought you made the casserole because you loved me."

"That too." She touched his cheek.

As Tillie gazed at Hank, Leroy silently prayed the new plan would work.

. . .

"I'm *froh* you joined us for church today," Joel said as Leroy sat across from him at his kitchen table. "I'm just surprised you didn't want to go to church in your district."

"I needed a change of scenery. And it was nice to worship with you. It's been a long time since we were in the same church district." Leroy took the cup of coffee Dora handed him. *"Danki."*

"A change of scenery?" She set a platter of oatmeal raisin cookies in the center of the table and then sat down beside Joel. "What do you mean?"

Leroy frowned. He should be honest with his brother and sister-in-law since they could apparently see right through his facade.

"Are things still rocky between you and Mattie?" Joel asked.

"Ya." Leroy grabbed a cookie from the platter. "She's still living with her parents. I've tried to convince her to come home, but it's not working." Then he explained what had been happening and summarized the contents of her last letter, careful to leave out details that were too personal.

"Oh, the basket, flowers, and picnic were so romantic." Dora gave him a faint smile.

"Danki, but they didn't work. She still won't come home to me and give our marriage a fighting chance. But I'm going to keep my promise to Lizanne, and Hank and Tillie suggested I give Mattie some space. Tillie said maybe then Mattie will mull over what I've been saying in my letters. Maybe Tillie's right and Mattie will reread them all and think again about everything I said." He bit into his cookie.

"That sounds *gut*." Joel picked up a cookie and shook

it at Leroy as he arched an eyebrow and a teasing grin formed on his lips. "So you're using Dora and me to stay away from your *fraa*?"

Leroy shook his head. "No, I really wanted to come and visit you."

"I'm joking." His brother's grin faded. "I do think it's a *gut* idea. Give Mattie a chance to think about everything." He took a bite of his cookie.

"I have such a tough time taking a step back." Leroy shook his head and blew out a frustrated sigh. "I'm such a coward."

"No, you're not," Dora said.

"*Ya*, I am," he insisted. "A real man would probably go to her and not take no for an answer. He would insist she come home and behave like a real *fraa*. But that's not who I am. I don't want to force her to do anything against her will." He rubbed his chin. "I don't want her to come home against her will. If she did, then I would spend the rest of my life wondering if she's miserable with me no matter what front she put up." He paused, taking another bite of the cookie. "I guess Mattie is right. It's not a real marriage."

"No. Mattie is not right, and you're not a coward. Besides, no woman wants to be treated like that." Dora tapped the table with her finger. "Giving her space is the best plan at this point."

"I don't know." He propped his elbow on the table and rested his chin on his palm. "If the letters didn't touch her heart when she first read them, then I don't see how anything will change now."

Dora folded her hands. "Did I ever tell you about my

boyfriend Andy?" She glanced over at Joel. "I dated him before I met you."

"*Ya*, you told me about him." Joel rubbed her arm.

Leroy shook his head. "I don't think so."

"I dated Andy for two years."

"What happened?" Leroy asked.

"He died unexpectedly." She lifted a cookie and placed it on her plate. "It was sudden."

She picked up a napkin and began to absently fold it as she spoke. "I saw him the night he got sick. I had dinner with his family. Andy said he wasn't feeling well, and I tried to convince him to go to the emergency room. He insisted he just needed to rest. His *mamm* told me not to worry and to go home. She had promised me she would check on him during the night. She fell asleep, and she didn't wake up until the next morning. When she checked on him, he was gone. He had passed away sometime during the night. We found out through an autopsy that he'd had appendicitis. We were all devastated."

Leroy cringed. "I'm so sorry."

"*Danki*." Dora looked up at him. "It was a very tough time for me. I kept wondering if I should have called an ambulance and forced him to go to the hospital, or convinced his *bruder* to help me get him into a buggy and taken him there myself."

She looked down at the table. "In the end, I worked through my guilt and accepted there was nothing I could have done to change God's plan for Andy or for me." She gazed at Joel. "And then I met you and everything worked out the way it should."

Joel gave her a warm smile.

She looked over at Leroy once again. "I don't mean to disrespect Andy's memory. I'll always miss Andy, and my heart still breaks for his family. I'm just saying I know how Mattie feels. She needs time to work through her grief. She lost her husband and her son in a matter of a few months and never really gave herself enough time to grieve. That's incomprehensible."

Leroy's stomach tightened with guilt. "So you're saying I never should have married her, and I shouldn't try to force her to love me?"

"No, no, no. I didn't mean that at all." She paused for a beat. "I'm sorry. I'm not expressing myself well today. You're not doing anything wrong. In fact, you're doing everything right."

"I'm sorry, but you've lost me." Leroy took another cookie and bit into it.

"Okay. Let me try this again. I think you're right to give Mattie some space, but maybe for longer than you've been thinking. Stay away from her for a couple of weeks—maybe even a month—and give her a chance to miss you."

Joel touched Dora's shoulder. "That's a *gut* idea."

Leroy pressed his lips together. "I don't think she's going to miss me if she's telling me to stay way."

"That's where you're wrong." She lifted her cookie and swirled it through the air. "Mattie has been leaning on you whether she realizes it or not. She's become dependent on you. You've been there to dry her tears and hold her hand ever since Isaiah died. She's waiting for your next letter and your next gift. She may have pushed you away, but I'm certain she expects you to keep coming after her. Didn't you tell her you'd wait for years if you had to?"

Leroy nodded. "*Ya*, I did say that in one of my letters."

"Let her think you've given up on her. Let her come to you." She bit into the cookie.

"What if she doesn't come to me?" Leroy's throat dried.

"She will," Joel said. "Dora is right. She's going to realize how lonely she is, and she'll come back to you. I'm certain of it."

"Okay." Renewed determination washed over Leroy. "I'll do it, but if I don't hear from her after one month then I will send her one last letter." He blew out a deep breath. "I just hope and pray it works."

"It will," Joel said. "Have faith."

. . .

The cool October air drifted in through the open window as Mattie glanced out of it for the fourth time. She'd spent all morning sitting in the family room with her parents, reading from her mother's devotional while hoping and praying Leroy would come to visit her. It was now after noon and no one had come to visit even though it was an off-Sunday without a church service.

She hadn't heard from him since she'd sent the basket and letter over to his house with Lizanne and Al more than a month ago. It felt more like a year than a month. She missed Leroy so much that an ache of longing had taken root in her chest. Had he forgotten about her? No, that couldn't be possible. Could it?

"Are you okay?" *Mamm* asked from the sofa on the other side of the room.

"*Ya.*" Mattie lifted the book and pretended to read some more.

Although her eyes moved over the page, her thoughts were still stuck on Leroy. She'd been surprised he hadn't attended church during the past month either. When she asked Tillie about him, Tillie explained Leroy had decided to attend church in his brother's district. Most members of the community visited other districts every once in a while, but attending a different district more than once a month was unusual. Was Leroy avoiding her? She immediately pushed that notion out of her mind. Why would Leroy avoid her?

Because you broke his heart by rejecting him.

Mattie swallowed a sigh. She was still so confused. She wanted to push Leroy away and pull him close at the same time. What was wrong with her?

Every morning she checked the front and back porch for the basket, but the porches remained empty, devoid of any sign of Leroy. She missed the basket and longed for his letters, but she had no right to expect him to write her and send her gifts when she instructed him not to. It was all or nothing, as it should be.

Mattie's chores and sewing had kept her busy, and every night she read her devotional before going to sleep. But despite her efforts to remain distracted, her thoughts continued to find Leroy. She missed him to the very depth of her soul. Why did she miss him if their marriage was destined for failure?

A knock sounded on the back door, and she sprang

from the chair. She set the devotional on the end table, rushed to the door, and stopped a moment to smooth her hands down her purple dress.

"Tillie," Mattie said with surprise when she opened the door. "Hank. It's so *gut* to see you." She craned her neck to peek behind them, but the porch was empty. She made a sweeping gesture as she pushed the door open wide. "Please come in."

"*Danki.*" Tillie held up the basket. "I brought you something."

"Oh." Mattie's heart thumped against her rib cage. "*Danki* for bringing it to me."

"Tillie and Hank." *Mamm* stepped into the kitchen. "I'm so *froh* you're here. Have a seat. Let me put on some *kaffi.*" She turned toward the family room. "Mose! We have company."

"*Danki.*" Hank sat down at the table. "We thought it would be nice to come and see you. We haven't visited in a while, and we wanted to check on Mattie."

"We've been concerned about you," Tillie said to Mattie as she set the basket on the counter.

Mattie touched the skirt of her dress as she studied the basket. Curiosity and anxiety filled her. She couldn't wait to open the basket, but she was also afraid of what she might find inside. Was there a letter inside, and if so, what did it say?

"Mattie, would you please pull out that cheesecake I made last week?" *Mamm* asked. "I'll grab the *kaffi* mugs."

"*Ya*, of course." Mattie moved to the refrigerator and then carried the cheesecake to the table. "I'll get the sugar bowl and spoons."

"Hello there." *Dat* crossed the kitchen and shook Hank's hand. "So *gut* to see you, Hank. How are you doing, Tillie?"

"We're fine, *danki*." Hank smiled as *Dat* sat at the end of the table beside him. "How's the furniture store?"

"It's *gut*. Busy. We're doing a lot of custom orders. I keep saying I'm going to retire, but I still show up to work just about every day. How's the harness shop?"

"It's great. Busloads of tourists have been visiting the harness shop at least once a week for the past month. They're all eager to see an authentic Amish harness shop. We've sold out of wallets, leashes, key chains, and door hangers consistently, so we're trying to increase our production. Now we're trying to restock before the next busload comes on Wednesday. Leroy and I are taking turns running the front and making more stock."

Mattie froze, holding the sugar bowl in the air, when Hank said Leroy's name.

"That's *wunderbaar*." *Dat* patted Hank's shoulder. "I'm so *froh* for you and Leroy. I know this has always been your dream, and it's working out well."

Mattie set the sugar bowl in front of Tillie.

"How are you?" Tillie's pretty face seemed to be full of concern. "You look much better. Your color has come back, and you look rested."

"*Danki*. I'm all right." Mattie handed Tillie a spoon. "How about you?"

"Fine." Tillie studied her as if she had something to say.

Mattie paused, but when Tillie didn't continue, she turned toward the counter, where her mother had lined up the mugs. "Should I get the cake server and plates?"

"*Ya*," *Mamm* said. "That would be perfect."

Soon the coffee was ready, and Mattie filled the mugs while her mother cut the cheesecake. As they ate, Hank and *Dat* continued to talk business while Tillie, *Mamm*, and Mattie discussed sewing projects and news from nearby church districts.

When they finished their coffee and cake, the men moved to the family room to continue their conversation while the women washed the dishes.

"Mattie, would you please show me that lap quilt you mentioned earlier?" Tillie dropped the spoons into the utensil drawer. "I'd love to see it."

"Oh. *Ya*, of course."

"Great."

Mattie detected something in Tillie's pretty brown eyes. Once again, she had the feeling Tillie wanted to tell her something. Perhaps it was about Leroy. Her heartbeat tripped and then caught itself when she contemplated him.

"You two go on." *Mamm* waved them off. "I can finish up here."

"Are you sure?" Mattie asked.

"I think I can handle a few dishes." *Mamm* gave her a sardonic smile. "If you weren't living here, I would have to do them myself, right?"

"Right."

Tillie laughed as they walked toward the bedroom. "I love your parents. They are so funny."

"*Danki*." Mattie sat down at the sewing table and Tillie

pulled up a chair beside her. "This is the lap quilt." She handed it to Tillie. "I'm almost done. I just have a few more stitches to do."

"*Ach*, Mattie." Tillie ran her hand over the stitching. "This is so *schee*."

"*Danki*." She leaned forward toward Tillie. "How is he?"

Tillie looked up Mattie and tilted her head. "Who? Leroy?"

Mattie nodded and held her breath, anxiously awaiting a response.

"It's been a rough month." Tillie frowned. "He's crushed. He's devastated." She looked back down at the quilt, touching it as she spoke. "He rarely talks, except to discuss the shop, and he never smiles." She peered up at Mattie again. "He misses you."

Mattie's eyes filled with tears. "I feel so terrible. I never should have tied him down. I ruined his life by marrying him."

Tillie clicked her tongue. "That's where you're wrong. He's always loved you, and you were so *gut* together."

"No, we weren't. I married him too soon." Mattie rested her arm on the sewing table and ran her fingertips over the tomato-shaped pin holder. "If I hadn't married Leroy, then he could've found someone who would love him completely. He's entitled to the opportunity to have a family with the right woman. I can't be that woman for him. My heart has been broken too many times, and it can't be fixed. I'm not able to be a *mamm* or a *fraa* to anyone else."

"That's not true." Tillie touched Mattie's arm. "I

understand how you feel, but you're not broken. You can still function. You can still be a *gut fraa*. You don't have to have a *boppli* to be husband and *fraa*. Believe me, I know all about that."

Mattie's gaze snapped to Tillie's. "What do you mean?"

Tillie leaned back against the chair. "Hank and I have been married almost four years now. We've tried over and over to have a *boppli*." Her dark eyes sparkled with tears. "I've been pregnant five times, and each time I lost the *boppli*."

"*Ach*, I had no idea." Mattie took her hand and squeezed it. "I'm so sorry."

"*Danki*." Tillie ran her finger over the edge of the sewing table as she spoke. "The first couple of times it happened, I felt useless. I was certain Hank regretted marrying me, and I felt as though I wasn't truly a woman, if that makes sense. I guess you could say I felt as though I was less of a woman or that there was a part of me missing." She sniffed and looked down at the quilt again. "I went to stay with my parents for a week, certain Hank would be better off without me."

Mattie blinked. "I had no idea."

"We kept it quiet." Tillie looked up and wiped away an errant tear. "Hank came to see me and begged me to come home. He said he'd love me no matter what. He said our marriage wasn't just about having *kinner*. Hank also said we're a family no matter what, and he would always love me."

Mattie swallowed a gasp. The words from one of Leroy's letters said something similar.

Tillie chuckled, oblivious to Mattie's thoughts. "He

said that now he didn't have to share me with anyone." Her smiled faded. "Of course we want *kinner*, and I continue to pray it will happen for us someday. But if it doesn't, we'll be okay. Hank and I love each other, and we have nieces and nephews to love too."

Mattie blinked as regret stole her words.

Tillie squeezed her hand. "You're in pain right now, but the pain will lessen eventually. You'll never forget Jacob, and you'll always keep him in your heart." She paused. "Every one of my miscarriages was a loss. Even though those babies weren't named, I carried them, and they were part of me. I understand how much you hurt."

"*Danki*," Mattie whispered.

"Believe me when I tell you Leroy is pining for you. He needs you, and you need him too."

Mattie wiped away her tears.

"Tillie?" Hank leaned into the doorway. "Are you ready to head home? I need to take care of the animals before it gets too late."

"*Ya.*" She stood. "It was *gut* seeing you."

Mattie stood and pulled Tillie into her arms for a hug. "*Danki* for coming by."

"*Gern gschehne*," Tillie whispered. "Call me if you need to talk."

CHAPTER 23

Mattie's thoughts spun as confusion and anxiety coiled through her. After saying good-bye to Tillie and Hank, she opened the basket and pulled out a carrot cake, complete with cream cheese frosting.

Mamm gasped as she stood beside her. "Oh, that smells heavenly."

"*Ya*, it sure does." Mattie removed the letter from the bottom of the basket and then turned to her mother. "I'm going to go in the family room and read his letter."

"Okay." *Mamm* touched her arm. "Let me know if you need me."

"*Danki*." She stepped into the family room, flopped onto the sofa, and opened the letter.

Dear Mattie,

I decided to give you some space, hoping you would take the time to reread my letters and think about our relationship. I was hoping a month away from me would give you time to miss me.

To be honest, I've waited all month to hear from you. And since I haven't heard from you, I will take that as your answer. You obviously meant it when you said you were going to set me free. Well, I'm sending you this letter to set you free as well. But first, I have a few things I want to say to you.

I'm sorry for proposing to you and making you feel obligated to marry me. When I proposed, I thought I was doing it for you and Jacob, but I've realized I really did it for me.

I've always loved you. I suppose I thought someday you'd realize you loved me too. I was kidding myself, because you never shared the same feelings I've always had for you. It just took me too long to come to that conclusion.

When you met Isaiah, I was envious. I clearly remember the first time you looked at him. I was envious of how quickly you fell for him. I wanted to be the love of your life, but I see now it will never be possible for you to love me the way you loved him. I was naïve to believe that could ever be possible.

I'm sorry for trapping you, but now I'm setting you free. If the community believed in divorce, I would give you one so you could be completely free of me.

I've spent all month thinking about our short time together as husband and wife. I had believed that if I gave you your space, you would eventually fall in love with me and want to be *mei fraa*. That was why I told you that you could stay in the downstairs bedroom alone for as long as you needed, and that was why I told you to decorate the *haus* anyway you'd like. I wanted you to make our *haus* a home, but you never thought of it as your home.

Your aversion to our marriage was so obvious when you told the doctor's receptionist your last name was

Petersheim. I should have known then that I was setting myself up for heartache and failure. I had hoped
we could make it work, but we obviously can't.

I'm going to pack up your things Monday night.
Once I have everything together, I will ask Hank to
take them to you so you don't have to come back
here. I don't want to make things harder on you than
they already are. We can continue to live apart. I pray
someday we can be *freinden*. I will always miss your
friendship. You were the one person I always trusted
completely.

When I asked you to marry me, I only wanted you
to be *froh*. I was so worried I was going to wind up
lonely and sad like *mei mamm* that I didn't take a step
back to realize how all of this was hurting you.

Please know you'll always have a piece of my heart.

Love,
Leroy

Tears rolled down her hot cheeks as Mattie read the
letter over and over again.

When it was time for supper, she tucked the letter
into her devotional for safekeeping.

. . .

After her parents had gone to bed, Mattie reread the
letter while propped up on the sofa. Then she snuggled
down and switched off her lantern. She closed her eyes
as memories of Leroy played through her mind.

She recalled their time in school together. Leroy always picked Mattie to be on his team when they played softball. He defended her on the playground when bullies teased her for running too slowly. He picked her as his partner when they worked on math problems, and he walked her to and from school, sharing his umbrella in the rain and giving her his jacket when it was cold.

Leroy gave her a homemade valentine card every Valentine's Day, and he collected special rocks for her. Suddenly she remembered the shoe box full of old mementos Lizanne had brought to her. Lizanne had found the box when she was cleaning out Mattie's old room to start setting up her nursery. Mattie sat up, flipped on the lantern, popped up off the sofa, and picked up the shoe box.

Tears stung her eyes as she found several cards from Leroy—homemade birthday and valentine cards. All of them said "*To Mattie, Love, Leroy F.*" At the bottom of the box was a collection of the special rocks he'd given her.

Why hadn't she noticed back then that he loved her? Why had she been so blind for so many years?

Mattie wiped her eyes and put the cards back into the box before placing it on the floor next to her suitcase. Then she pulled out all the letters he'd written to her since she moved back to her parents' house. She sat on the sofa and read each of the letters, slowly taking in his words.

After reading them, she snuffed out the lantern, crawled under her covers, and closed her eyes. She wanted to go home to Leroy. She missed him. She needed him.

But how could she give Leroy her heart if Isaiah still owned part of it?

Mattie couldn't find the answer to these problems by herself. She squeezed her eyes shut and began to pray.

God, please help me. I feel Leroy pulling me to him, but I don't know how to give him what he needs. Please guide me, God. Please heal my broken heart and teach me how to love again. In Jesus' holy name, amen.

. . .

"Mattie? You're up early."

"*Gude mariye.*" Mattie glanced over at her mother standing in the family room doorway. "How are you?"

"I'm fine." *Mamm* studied her. "How long have you been up?"

"For about an hour." Mattie glanced down at the lap quilt. "I snuck in and got the quilt while you were still sleeping. I wanted to finish this for Leroy."

Mamm stepped in and sat down beside her on the sofa. "It's for Leroy, then. I thought maybe it was all along. He'll love it."

"I hope so." She ran her fingers over the quilt. "I didn't sleep well last night. I reread all his letters, and then I kept waking up and thinking about everything. I finally got up and started working on the quilt."

"Oh." *Mamm*'s eyes glinted. "Does this mean you're finally going to go home to him?"

"I don't know." Mattie frowned. "I'm still thinking about it. Today I'm going to do my chores and keep working on the quilt. I'm praying the answer will come to me while I'm working."

Mamm squeezed her hand. "That's a fantastic idea. You keep working, and I'll go make you breakfast."

"Danki." Mattie was so thankful for her patient and thoughtful parents.

. . .

After washing his dishes from supper, Leroy carried a large cardboard box into the family room. He knelt down in front of the bookshelf and began loading up Mattie's books.

He'd dismantled the crib in the nursery early that morning, but then realized he'd better keep all the furniture and baby equipment until Mattie told him what she wanted to do with it.

He glanced around the house and the ever-present silence seemed to roar in his ears. The house had been too silent since Mattie left. He missed her voice, her laugh, the sound of her footsteps, and the scent of her shampoo.

Sighing, he slipped the last two books into the box and then carried it to the kitchen, where he set it down against the wall. He grabbed two more boxes from the mudroom and then walked into the bedroom to pack up the clothes she'd left in the closet and dresser.

He picked up a small trinket box, a wooden frame containing a picture of a sunset, and the two candles that sat on her dresser and set them in the box. Then he cleaned out the clothes that remained in the dresser before moving to the closet. Soon the two boxes were full of her clothes and shoes, and he carried them to the kitchen.

After setting the boxes on the floor, he glanced up at the cross-stitch hanging on the wall. He recalled the day Mattie hung it there. His eyes took in the colorful butterfly and then silently read the words.

Happiness is like a butterfly:
The more you chase it, the more it will elude you,
but if you turn your attention to other things,
it will come and sit quietly on your shoulder.

The words rolled through his mind, and understanding coursed through him. He'd been chasing Mattie, his happiness, but now he had to turn his attention to other things while continuing to hope she'd come back to him someday.

"Will you ever find happiness, Mattie?" he whispered. "If so, will I ever be a part of your happiness?"

Leroy rubbed his temple where a headache throbbed as he padded back into the bedroom. When he stepped through the doorway, his eyes locked on her hope chest. He walked over to it, opened it, and pulled out a small flat box sitting on top of a few linens.

When he opened it, his fingers touched the blue onesie he bought before Jacob was born. He spotted a large envelope at the bottom of the hope chest and lifted it. When he opened it, he pulled out Jacob's birth certificate, death certificate, lock of hair, and footprints and handprints. Memories of his and Mattie's short time living together, waiting for Jacob's birth, flooded his mind, and his eyes stung.

"Why didn't I try harder?" he whispered. "I'm so sorry for letting you down, Mattie. I'm sorry for not being the husband you needed."

He put the items back into the envelope and tucked it into the bottom of the hope chest. Then he sat on the edge of the bed and glanced around the room. Soon Mattie's things would be gone, and his house would be back to the way it was before they were married—too big, too quiet, and too lonely.

He rested his hand on the back of his neck and recalled the basket. It had been more than twenty-four hours since Tillie and Hank delivered it, and he hadn't heard from Mattie. It was truly over. He was a husband without a wife.

He rubbed his eyes with the tips of his fingers. Now he had to figure out how to go on with his life without her, but he would never forget her.

Leroy's life and his heart would never be the same.

. . .

Mattie sat up straight on the sofa. She was drenched in sweat, and her hands were shaking. She lifted her hands to her face and found it wet. She'd been crying. No, she'd been sobbing.

She flipped on the lantern and looked at the clock on the end table by the sofa. It was four thirty in the morning. What had awakened her so early?

And then the dream came back to her, flooding her mind with its vivid visions. It had been a nightmare.

Mattie was dressed in black as she stood in Leroy's family room in front of a coffin. The coffin was open, and Leroy's body lay there. He was perfectly still, and when she touched his face, it was cold as ice.

Leroy was dead.

"Mattie." As Joel walked up to her and touched her arm, *his face crumpled. "Leroy died from the complications from pneumonia."* He shook his head as Mattie gasped. *"He'd been ill for days and refused to go to the doctor."*

"Why didn't he go?" She wiped tears from her face.

"He was all alone. You weren't there to take care of him, so he just died alone."

"It was my fault?" she asked, and Joel nodded. *"Oh. I left him, and he died all alone."*

Tears stung Mattie's eyes as the rest of the dream flashed through her mind. She had sobbed by Leroy's coffin as she greeted friends and relatives who shared their condolences. Her heart had been empty, and her soul was shattered.

Leroy, her best friend and her husband, was gone. And she was left all alone.

"No, no, no." She climbed from the sofa. "I can't lose him. I just can't."

Her sister's words suddenly filtered through her mind: *"Let Leroy love you. You deserve happiness just as much as I do, Mattie."*

Tears streamed down Mattie's face and soaked her nightgown as her thoughts turned to her conversation with Tillie. *"You're in pain right now, but the pain will lessen eventually. You'll never forget Jacob, and you'll always keep him in your prayers and your heart. Every one of my miscarriages was a loss . . . Believe me when I tell you Leroy is pining for you. He needs you, and you need him too."*

A wave of panic rushed through Mattie, and her breath came in short bursts. She couldn't run the risk of losing Leroy.

"I love him," she whispered, and she stilled.

Yes, she loved him. She loved his laugh, his sense of humor, his generosity, and his kind, thoughtful heart.

Mattie not only loved Leroy, but she was *in love* him with. She had relished that one kiss they'd shared. In fact, she craved more of those amazing, delicious kisses. She was ready to be his wife and live together every way a married couple should.

Now she had to convince him to take her back.

Mattie stood, pushed her feet into her slippers, picked up her lantern, and found the quilt on the end table where she'd left it before going to sleep. She had to finish the quilt for Leroy. She picked it up and set to work.

Two hours later, the quilt was finished. She ran her fingers over stitches, hoping the quilt would somehow be a fitting gift for him.

She remembered the picnic basket and rushed out to the kitchen to retrieve it. She carried it to the family room and opened the lid.

Her eyes took in Leroy's neat, familiar penmanship. *"2 Corinthians 1:7: And our hope for you is firm, because we know that just as you share in our sufferings, so also you share in our comfort."*

Tears pricked her eyes once again and she sniffed.
The scripture touched her soul, and she folded the quilt
and set it inside the basket.

*Yes, my hope in you is firm, God. Thank you for lead-
ing me to Leroy.*

Now she had to write a letter. And it had to be the
most perfect, heartfelt letter she'd ever written. She had
to make sure she told Leroy exactly how she felt so she
could somehow win back his heart.

Mattie pulled out paper and a pen and then set to
writing.

Dear Leroy,

I'm so sorry I've been blind since I was six years
old. I remember how you defended me against a bully,
walked me home with your umbrella in the rain, picked
me first for your softball team, gave me special valentine cards, and collected rocks for me. Why didn't I
realize then how special you were?

You are the kindest, most generous, most thoughtful man I have ever known. I just don't understand how
I have come to deserve you. You should have a more
thoughtful and generous woman than I am.

You've had me figured out from the beginning. You
knew I needed you before I did. Everyone asked me
how I was when Isaiah and Jacob died, but you were the
one who wasn't afraid to hear the true answer about
the depths of my grief. Everyone else just wanted me
to be all right. You sat with me and really listened. You
brought me meals.

You held me upright during Jacob's wake and funeral, and you held me while I sobbed after the funeral was over and everyone else had gone back to their own lives. And after I left you, you still came after me and offered me your precious heart.

I've thought long and hard about it, and no, I don't want to live separately. I wouldn't want a divorce even if our community allowed it.

Instead, I want to come home. I want to be with you. Could you ever find it in your heart to forgive me and give me a second chance?

I'm so thankful God led you to me. I told you in a previous letter about the devotional *mei mamm* gave me. The book helped her through her grief when her *bruder* died. I've been reading it every night, and one verse has really spoken to me. It is Psalm 46, verse 1: "God is our refuge and strength, an ever-present help in trouble." And the scripture you wrote on the basket lid also spoke to my heart.

I've realized God has been with me through all my grief and loss, and he also sent you to comfort me. You've been trying to comfort me all along, but I was too blind to see it. Now I see it, and I hope you will forgive me. I'm so very sorry for pushing you away and hurting you.

You are a blessing to me. And I love you, Leroy Fisher. I'm so sorry it's taken me so long to realize just how much I love you.

May I please come home?

> All my love,
> Martha Jane "Mattie" Fisher

P.S. I want to give you this quilt as a small token of my affection for you. You've given me so much and I could never repay you. But if you decide not to let me come home, please keep the quilt in your buggy. I hope it keeps you warm on cold winter nights.

Mattie set down her pen, folded the letter, sealed it in an envelope, and said a silent prayer, asking God to make the letter and quilt enough to convince Leroy she wanted to be his wife.

CHAPTER 24

A mixture of anxiety and excitement coursed through Mattie. Zac Crawford, her father's driver, had parked his van in Leroy's driveway, and now she watched as lights glowed in his kitchen and family room.

Leroy is still awake.

She'd waited until the evening to come over to see him so she could get him alone after the harness shop closed. She worried that if she came over too early he'd be distracted by work or a customer. Her hands trembled as she lifted the basket from the floor of the van.

"Thank you," she told Zac before climbing out of the van and closing the door.

Then she stood in the driveway and stared at the house. This was where she wanted to live. This was where she belonged. But was it too late to ask for Leroy's forgiveness? Worry and anxiety slithered up her spine.

"Mattie?" Zac called from the van. "Is everything okay?"

Mattie turned. "*Ya*, it is. Thank you."

"Do you want me to wait?" he offered, leaning toward the passenger side window.

"No, thank you. I'll be fine." Mattie waved. "Have a good night."

She stood in the driveway as the van backed down toward the road, and then she faced the porch again. She pulled in a deep breath, mustered up all the confidence she could find inside of herself, and then walked toward the porch. She climbed the steps and stared at the back door.

Mattie gnawed on her bottom lip and then knocked. She held her breath as footfalls sounded, and she envisioned Leroy walking through the kitchen toward the mudroom.

A lantern flipped on, and as Leroy pushed open the door, his eyes widened and his mouth formed a large O.

Her pulse quickened as she looked up at him. He was breathtakingly handsome. His deep brown eyes glimmered in the soft yellow light of the lantern, and his beard was full but carefully trimmed, accentuating his strong jaw. She stared at his lips, and her stomach did a flip-flop as she pondered that amazing kiss they'd share. Could she convince him to kiss her like that once again?

"Mattie?" He pushed the door open as he continued to search her face. "What are you doing here this late?"

"I want to talk to you, and I couldn't wait until morning." She pointed toward the door. "May I come in?"

"*Ya.*" He stepped back, allowing her to walk past him and into the kitchen.

Mattie glanced down at the boxes lining the kitchen wall. Packed in them were her books, clothes, and the beautiful cross-stitch her mother had given her. Disappointment replaced her excitement.

I'm too late. He's already packed up my things just as he said he would in his last letter.

When she looked up at him, he crossed his arms over his wide chest and leaned back against the wall.

"I was going to have Hank take those to you tomorrow." He gestured toward the doorway leading to the family room. "Your hope chest is still in the bedroom. I need him to help me carry that out."

"There's no hurry." She swallowed against her dry throat.

"Oh. Okay." He paused for a minute as he raised an eyebrow. "What do you want to talk about?"

"Oh, right." She suddenly remembered the basket in her hands. "I brought this for you."

He frowned. "You could have kept the basket."

"I'm not just returning it. There's actually a gift in it and a letter." She held it up, and he pushed off the wall. As he took the basket from her, their fingers brushed, and electricity sparked between them. She swallowed a gasp and hoped he'd sensed it too.

"Danki." He set the basket on the table and then looked over at her again. "So what did you want to talk about?"

"Please open it now." She pointed toward the basket. "Please."

He studied her for a beat and then opened the lid. His eyes widened as he pulled out the lap quilt.

"Mattie." He breathed out her name, and it sounded like a beautiful hymn to her ears. He ran his long fingers over the quilt and gasped. "Did you make this for me?"

"*Ya.*" She closed the distance between them and stood beside him. "Do you like it?" She inhaled his familiar scent, leather mixed with soap. Warmth buzzed through her like a honeybee. It was so good to be near him again!

"I love it. It's the most *schee* quilt I've ever seen. I don't know what to say." He looked down at her, and his eyes seemed to shimmer with confusion. "*Danki*, but you really didn't have to give me anything."

"There's a letter too." She pointed to the basket. "Please read it."

"Now?" he asked, his dark eyebrows raised.

"*Ya*. Please."

"Okay." He draped the quilt over the back of a kitchen chair and retrieved the envelope from the bottom of the basket. Then he opened the envelope, unfolded the letter, and began to read it.

Mattie folded her hands as if to say a prayer and held her breath while she waited for him to finish reading.

Leroy's dark eyes misted as he read. His face crumpled with a deep frown and he sniffed. When he finished, he folded the letter and stared down at her.

"Do you mean what you said in this letter?" His eyes seemed to search her face.

"*Ya*, I mean every word." Her voice scraped from her throat. "Is it too late for us?"

"No. It could never be too late. I meant it when I said I would wait years for you."

"But you packed up my things." Her voice shook as she pointed toward the boxes lining the wall behind her. "You were going to have Hank take them to me."

"I thought that was what you wanted." He placed the letter on the table. "I just wanted you to be *froh*."

"I can't lose you," she whispered as tears streamed down her face. "I love you. It just took me a little longer to figure it out. I want to be here with you. Please forgive me and give me another chance."

"Of course you can have another chance. I've loved you my whole life. Why would I stop loving you now?"

Reaching up, Mattie touched her hand to his face, savoring the feel of his whiskers. "I'm so sorry I hurt you. I want to start over. I want to build a life with you. I want to have a family with you, if we can. And if we can't have one, that's okay too. I just want to be here with you."

He closed his eyes and leaned into her touch. "I never thought I'd hear you say that. I feel like I'm dreaming."

"You're not dreaming. I'm here, and I'm not going to leave you again. I want to spend the rest of my life with you." She stood up on her tiptoes and brushed her lips across his.

Leroy let out a gasp as his eyes widened. Then his eyes softened. He wrapped his arms around her waist, and Mattie's breath hitched in her lungs. She looped her arms around his neck and pulled him in closer. He deepened the kiss, sending her stomach into a wild swirl. She closed her eyes and savored the feeling of his mouth against hers.

This is where I belong.

When he released her, she laced her fingers into his. "Is it okay if I stay tonight?"

He chuckled, and she enjoyed the deep, rich sound of his laughter. "Of course you can. This is your *haus*. You're *mei fraa*." He pointed toward the boxes. "We can unpack those tomorrow."

"Okay."

"Did you bring a horse and buggy?"

"No. *Mei dat*'s driver dropped me off." She glanced toward the doorway that led toward the bedroom. Her stomach fluttered with the wings of a thousand butterflies, and her knees wobbled as an idea took shape in her mind.

"What are you thinking?" His lips quirked.

"Lock the back door."

He tilted his head for a moment. "All right." He released her hand, went to lock the door, and then walked back to her.

She took his hand and tugged him toward the family room.

"Where are you taking me?"

"You'll see." She licked her lips as they crossed the family room and then stopped in front of the bedroom doorway. She looked up at him, and he gaped. "I'm ready."

"I don't understand."

"I'm ready to be your *fraa*." She reached up and touched his cheek again. "I love you, Leroy. I want to be with you and only you." She took his hand in hers and placed his palm flat on her chest over her heart. "You're here, where you should be. My heart belongs to you."

"Oh, Mattie." His eyes misted over once again. "I have to be dreaming now."

"You're not. This is really happening." She lifted his hand to her mouth and kissed it. "I'm sorry for taking you for granted for so long. You've always been there for me, but I didn't realize how much I cared about you until today. Isaiah and Jacob will always have a place in my heart, but I'm ready to give my heart to you. *Ich liebe dich,* Leroy."

"*Ich liebe dich,* Mattie." He trailed a finger down her cheek. "I always have."

Mattie grabbed his hand and pulled him into the bedroom, softly closing the door behind them.

. . .

"It's getting cooler." Mattie hugged her wrap closer to her body and then picked up her mug and cradled it in her hands. She breathed in the rich aroma of the hot chocolate and then smiled up at Leroy.

"*Ya,* it finally feels like winter is here." He leaned down and kissed her cheek before placing his mug on the table beside him. "I can't believe Christmas is next week."

"*Ya,* I know." She pushed on the porch floor with her toe, and the glider began to move them back and forth. "So now that it's cold, when are you going to make me some of your amazing homemade soup?" She leaned against his chest, and he looped his arm around her shoulders.

Leroy chuckled, and she relished the sound of the deep rumble radiating in his chest. "I've spoiled you too much with my baking. You should make me home-made soup."

Mattie looked up at him with feigned offense. "Is that so? I don't do enough around here?"

He touched the tip of her nose. "You're cute when you're annoyed with me."

She rolled her eyes before leaning against him once again. "Do you think we can start working on one of the spare rooms upstairs?"

"Sure. Which one, and what do you want to do with it?"

"I was thinking we should give the one I'm thinking about a fresh coat of paint on the walls." She gave him a coy smile and then set her mug on the table beside her. "You told me you'd paint it if I wanted you to. And we only have nine months to get it done, so we better get started now." She touched her abdomen, and he gasped and turned to face her.

"Are you saying what I think you're saying?"

She nodded, and he pulled her into his arms and kissed her.

"How long have you known?"

"I've had a feeling for a few days now, and I took two home tests this morning. Both of the tests were positive." She laced her fingers in his. "I have a doctor's appointment right after Christmas."

"I'm coming with you." He hugged her again. "I'm so *froh*. You have no idea how elated I am."

"*Ya*, I do know. I feel the same way." She touched his cheek and then rested her cheek on his shoulder. "I was worried it wouldn't happen for me again, but it did. I'm going to ask Dr. Sheppard to monitor me more closely this time." She looked up at him. "What names do you like?"

"You mentioned Veronica for a *maedel*."

"You don't have to agree to the names I said before—"

"It's okay," he insisted, interrupting her. "I think Veronica Fisher is a *schee* name."

"Okay. What about a *bu*?"

He paused for a beat. "Leroy Junior." He grinned.

She laughed at his adorable smile. "All right. Our *boppli*'s name will be Veronica or Leroy Junior." She pushed the glider with her toe again and sighed as she breathed in the crisp air mixed with Leroy's familiar scent.

"What was the sigh for?"

"I'm just so *froh*." She touched his thigh. "*Danki*."

"For what?"

"For loving me."

"No, *danki*, Mattie Fisher, for loving me."

As Leroy leaned down to kiss her, Mattie closed her eyes and silently thanked God for healing her heart and giving her a second chance at love.

EPILOGUE

Mattie wiped her eyes and then handed the tissues to Veronica, who took a handful and distributed them to her sisters.

"Why didn't you ever tell us about Isaiah and Jacob?" Rachel asked before sniffing.

"I just never knew how." Mattie shook her head, then picked up the blue onsie and pressed her fingers into its softness. "I'm sorry for hiding it from you all, for putting all these memories away in my hope chest and leaving them there all these years. But I just wasn't ready to tell you."

"It's okay." Emily took Mattie's hands in hers and squeezed them. "We understand. You went through so much." She paused, and then her eyes widened. "That was why *Dat* understood how I felt when Chris left me and went home to his family. He felt the same way when you left him, but I understand why you felt you had to leave. I'm so glad you came back, though."

Veronica sniffed and wiped her eyes with a tissue. "And now I understand why you said you could relate to me when I lost Seth. You went through the same thing. No, it was worse, because you were married and expecting a *boppli*. I can't even imagine how difficult that was for you."

"*Ya*," Rachel chimed in. "You had to feel so alone."

"I did until I realized how much your *dat* loved me, and also how much I loved him. Your *dat* was so patient and kind to me. It just took me a long time to realize how much I needed him. He was my strength and he taught me how to love again." She looked at her three daughters, taking in their beautiful faces. "I just pray you three have the same kind of love I've known with your father."

They all smiled and nodded.

"I love you, girls."

Mattie silently thanked God for the wonderful family she and Leroy had created with a sure foundation of love. Her hope chest had held not only memories full of pain all these years but memories full of love she would always cherish.

Today her heart was filled to the brim with hope.

ACKNOWLEDGMENTS

As always, I'm thankful for my loving family, including my mother, Lola Goebelbecker; my husband, Joe; and my sons, Zac and Matt. I'm blessed to have such an awesome and amazing family that puts up with me when I'm stressed out on a book deadline. Special thanks to Matt, aka Mr. Thesaurus, for helping me find synonyms. I couldn't ask for a more adorable wordsmith!

I'm more grateful than words can express to Janet Pecorella and my mother for proofreading for me. I truly appreciate the time you take out of your busy lives to help me polish my books. Special thanks to my mother, who endured my constant discussions about revisions and who also graciously read this book more than once to check for typos.

I'm also grateful to my special Amish friends, who patiently answer my endless stream of questions. Thank you also to Karla Hanns for her quilting expertise.

Thank you to my wonderful church family at Morning Star Lutheran in Matthews, North Carolina, for your encouragement, prayers, love, and friendship. You all mean so much to my family and me.

Thank you to Jamie Mendoza and the fabulous

members of my Bakery Bunch! I'm so grateful for your friendship and your excitement about my books. You all are amazing!

To my agent, Natasha Kern—I can't thank you enough for your guidance, advice, and friendship. You are a tremendous blessing in my life.

Thank you also to editor Julee Schwarzburg for her guidance with the story. I always learn quite a bit about writing and polishing when we work together. Thank you for pushing me to become a better writer. I hope we can work together again in the future!

I'm grateful to editor Jean Bloom, who helped me polish and refine the story. Jean, you are a master at connecting the dots and filling in the gaps. I'm so thankful that we can continue to work together!

I also would like to thank Kristen Golden for tirelessly working to promote my books. I'm grateful to each and every person at HarperCollins Christian Publishing who helped make this book a reality.

To my readers—thank you for choosing my novels. My books are a blessing in my life for many reasons, including the special friendships I've formed with my readers. Thank you for your e-mail messages, Facebook notes, and letters.

Thank you most of all to God—for giving me the inspiration and the words to glorify you. I'm grateful and humbled you've chosen this path for me.

Special thanks to Cathy and Dennis Zimmermann for their hospitality and research assistance in Lancaster County, Pennsylvania.

The author and publisher gratefully acknowledge the

following resource used to research information for this book:

C. Richard Beam, *Revised Pennsylvania German Dictionary* (Lancaster: Brookshire Publications, Inc., 1991).

DISCUSSION QUESTIONS

1. Mattie is devastated when her husband is murdered. Have you faced a difficult loss? What Bible verses helped you? Share this with the group.

2. Mattie pours herself into sewing and quilting as a way to deal with losing her husband and then her baby. Think of a time when you felt lost and alone. Where did you find your strength? What Bible verses would help?

3. Leroy believes he's helping Mattie and her baby when he proposes to her. He's devastated when Mattie leaves him, and he's determined to convince her to come home. Why do you think Leroy had a difficult time giving Mattie space and letting her find her way home?

4. Near the end of the book, Tillie feels compelled to talk to Mattie and share her own story of loss. Could you relate to Tillie and her experience?

5. Mattie is afraid of opening her heart to Leroy and she blames herself for both Isaiah's and Jacob's deaths. By the end of the book, she realizes she's ready to love again and she asks Leroy to forgive her and take

her back. What do you think caused her to change her point of view on love throughout the story?

6. At one point in the story, Mattie feels guilty for being envious of her sister's happy news. Have you ever been in a similar situation? If so, how did it turn out? Share this with the group.

7. Mattie feels God is giving her a second chance when she realizes she loves Leroy. Have you ever experienced a second chance? What was it?

8. Which character can you identify with the most? Which of the two main characters seemed to carry the most emotional stake in the story? Was it Mattie or Leroy?

9. What role did the basket play in Leroy and Mattie's relationship? Can you relate the basket to an object that was pivotal in a relationship you've experienced in your life?

10. What did you know about the Amish before reading this book? What did you learn?

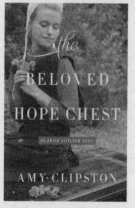

Enjoy new stories from

AMY CLIPSTON

in the Amish Marketplace series!

(available May 2020)

Available in print, e-book, and downloadable audio

ABOUT THE AUTHOR

Amy Clipston is the award-winning and bestselling author of the Kauffman Amish Bakery, Hearts of Lancaster Grand Hotel, Amish Heirloom, Amish Homestead, and Amish Marketplace series. Her novels have hit multiple bestseller lists including CBD, CBA, and ECPA. Amy holds a degree in communication from Virginia Wesleyan University and works full-time for the City of Charlotte, NC. Amy lives in North Carolina with her husband, two sons, and four spoiled rotten cats.

Visit her online at AmyClipston.com
Facebook: AmyClipstonBooks
Twitter: @AmyClipston
Instagram: @amy_clipston